T0267991

SILVER
BOUNTY

Books by Victoria McCombs

The Storyteller's Series
The Storyteller's Daughter
Woods of Silver and Light
The Winter Charlatan
Heir of Roses

The Royal Rose Chronicles
Oathbound
Silver Bounty

SILVER BOUNTY

The Royal Rose Chronicles

Book Two

VICTORIA McCOMBS

To Kinnick

Thanks for being the one to wake me up in the morning.

Without that, I wouldn't have had the time to write this book.

1

ARN

The gold buttons beneath my fingers felt oddly familiar, as if they'd tricked my mind into believing I was sixteen again and preparing to fight for the king of Julinbor. The once-vibrant blues were now faded, the buckle stripped of its shine, and the shoulders were tight—that part pleased me—but the look was the same.

Behold, a man of the law. Ignore the tattoo of a bleeding rose on my forearm. No relation to the pirates who sail under that flag.

I swung to face Emme and spread my arms as wide as the tight blue coat would allow. "There you have it. A proper navy man."

Emme absentmindedly traced a finger along the strip of octopus tentacle inked into her skin. I tried not to let my eyes linger on the way her arm's strength had clearly decreased as her disease continued wearing her thin. Even now her sea-green tunic appeared to hang off her shoulders rather than cling to them as it used to, and her bronze skin seemed paler. Life was fleeing her body.

She claimed we still had months together. I feared it was less than that. If we didn't get the healing tonic from the Elmber Nut soon, she'd fade away, and if we didn't fulfill her oathbinding, the ink would kill her. Two perilous means poised to end Emme's life, and yet she smiled fondly at me as if her mind knew nothing of worries.

"It's what you were wearing when I met you," she said.

"Almost." I tugged on the lapel with my right hand, finding it harder to place correctly now that I'd lost my other hand. The echo of my missing fingers was still there, and more often than not, I'd move to use them before remembering what I'd lost when we fought on the Island of Iilak. That list was lengthy. For now, I refocused my mind elsewhere as I shoved my stubbed wrist into my pocket. "That particular outfit got a fair amount of blood on it and had to be destroyed."

Her smile faltered. "Right. Well, you look the part."

Emme's attention stayed on my attire—the deep cream-colored cuffs, the knee breeches and stockings, unstained by sweat or sea, and the cerulean sash pulled taut across my waist. It was far more constraining than my open-chested tunic, and my trusted cutlass would be left behind, but for good reason.

Tonight I had a role to play.

She moved away from the table in the middle of the captain's quarters. "Can this sleeve come down further? Your pirate tattoos are showing." She fixed the cuff, then stood back with a hand pressed against the table for stability. "There," she announced. "I'm frightened of you already."

"You should be. I've never seen the king so determined to rid his lands of pirates. We are taking a risk by docking at Resyor." I closed the silver latch to the box that had held my naval outfit for so long. This box contained the only memento I had of those few years with the king's navy, that and the swarm of memories I tried to forget. I'd always planned to trade this outfit away, knowing how useful it could be for someone to masquerade as an honest sailor, never thinking I'd be the man masquerading.

Seeing myself in these clothes brought back memories in

snippets: Swearing in with Landon. Brutal training. Our first week at sea. That mysterious assignment that brought us close to Az Elo. The tightening of my throat as smoke filled it, and watching our burning ship go down.

I adjusted the lapel again.

"You'll be fine," Emme said. "King Unid's influence hasn't spread that far yet. One tale from Captain Jules on how a navy ship attacked him, and all you pirates are ruffled up." She took the box from me and slid it back under the bunk. She went to the porthole where salty waves sprayed mist that settled over her hollow cheeks.

"We might run into danger," I said. "It's a risk for the entire crew." I'd vowed to protect Emme from the darkness that stains the pirate life. To do that, she couldn't come on land when we docked. First, I had to convince her to stay behind. "I'd prefer you remain on ship. There's no telling what will come of this little con Ontario has constructed."

Her back straightened and she turned back slowly.

I reached for her hand. "Please, Emme. My ship is important to me, and I trust none other than you to protect it in my absence."

Her eyes narrowed at me. "Your ship?"

I grinned. "Fine. My ship and a little bit you. Please?"

"All right. I'll stay, just to let you feel like you're protecting me."

It took a moment to register the tones of relief hidden in her voice.

I should have left it at that. But I didn't. "You could stay on the ship forever if you'd like. You're as much part of this crew as any of us."

She didn't look at me as she answered quicker than I could take another breath. "No."

"Of course," I began, "it's understandable after Admiral Bones, and your brother . . ."

She jerked like I'd slapped her, and spun away. "We should go back on deck."

As she moved for the door, the words slipped out. "Do you like it here? The turn of the ship doesn't upset your stomach anymore?"

Her words were clipped. "Leave it be. I'm here until I find my brother, and that's all I can think of right now."

Her being here now should be enough, but it wasn't. It never would be enough. Tension thickened in the room until it was hard to breathe around it. It could have been my foolish desire to have her join my crew that blinded me to reality, but I swore every time I asked her to stay, she was closer to saying yes.

I went to her side. "I want to beg you to stay. I'm constantly thinking of how I can convince you to make a home here. Every time you smile when staring over the waves or bend your head up to look at a sky full of stars, I think you love the sea and would never wish to leave it. But then you look back to the land again and," I swallowed, "I'm terrified you're one storm away from abandoning me."

She slumped against the door, gazing at the room. "And I'm constantly thinking of how this is where he was."

I tried to see through her eyes and realized I was standing right where Emric had been when he agreed to join our crew. He'd done it for her.

As the ship swayed, furled maps rustled against shelves and footsteps padded across the deck above, sounding jaded through the aged wood. All else was still—far quieter than a ship ought to be. We'd lost too many men and remained haunted by their ghosts.

And Emric's ghost haunted Emme worst of all. "It's stained with his memory," she said quietly.

While the rest of us might mourn the lost men, this past month had been particularly cruel to Emme. First, she'd killed Admiral Bones to protect me, and she had to live with his blood on her hands. Now I not only worried both that his rumored son would rise up to find me, but that Emme would never forgive herself for pulling that trigger. Next, she'd watched her brother drown, but she wouldn't admit that he was really gone. That'd be a lot for anyone, even if they weren't dying early themselves.

Yet all I could think of was how to get her to remain with the ship.

Soon, she'd satisfy her unrest over Emric's death and flee my ship to leave me with another ghost to wander the deck. I was in a constant state of madness, wishing she'd accept that Emric was gone and wishing that she'd hold onto hope forever, if only to give her a reason to stay here with me.

Emme yanked open the door.

Ontario stood there. His black hair was twisted into a bun that let the dark-blue ink show through the shaved sides of his head. Like me, he was dressed up tonight—as the cunning pirate captain. A three-pointed hat hung on the hilt of his cutlass at his side, and he drummed his fingers against it while looking me up and down.

"Do I look fine?" I raised my eyebrow at him.

"Almost."

I registered his intent a moment too late. With a flick of his hand, Ontario took hold of my jacket and cut into it. When he let go, a flap hung open.

"Ontario!" Emme moved between us.

I inspected the jacket that now had limited use. "That wasn't necessary."

Ontario sheathed the dagger. "He needs to appear captured. I came prepared. I knew he would look too pretty."

Emme gave him a sideways glance. "I could have helped with that. Here." She ruffled her hand through my hair.

Ontario crossed his arms. "I think you could help more. He needs bruises. Hit him."

Emme wouldn't.

I backed up anyway.

Ontario grinned at the silence. "She won't do it. No one has reason to hit you but me."

How far we'd come from captain and loyal first mate.

Ontario had partaken in my deception when we'd made a deal with Admiral Bones, a deal that had led us to the Island of Iilak and the death of half our crew a month ago. It tortured both of us, but I stood alone in confessing to the lie. So I took the fall alone, and my role as captain was stripped and given to Emric, then later Ontario.

He refused to grant me back my position and seemed to know how much I was willing to put up with to get my ship back.

There were many slights I'd be able to pardon him for, but this was not one of them. The rift between us grew as wide as the sea until the brotherhood we once shared had turned into something far less amicable.

"One more thing." Ontario paused with a hand on the wooden frame and his head bent low. It was the posture of a man in repentance, but I knew better. "Now that I'm captain, it seems fitting that I have the captain's quarters. Emme can sleep with the rest of the crew."

"You can't be serious." I snapped. "Your name has no right being connected to my title. If half the crew hadn't fallen on the Island of Iilak, therefore destroying my credibility, the remaining men never would have seen you as a captain. You're only here because those men died."

It was a dry truth that tasted bitter on the tongue, and from the way his jaw clicked, it sounded no better to him. But that was the truth, wasn't it? If those men hadn't died, the crew would have forgiven my secret dealings with Admiral Bones.

No harm, no foul. But they died. And now, even knowing that Ontario was as involved as I was, the remaining men needed someone to blame, and the brunt of it all fell to my shoulders while Ontario walked away unscathed.

From the blaze in his eye, he wasn't as unscathed as I thought. His words were brittle as he spoke. "Why, because you're so much more revered than I am?" His lip curled with disgust. "Is that what you think? That I'm captain simply because they have no other option? That they secretly wish for you back? You're wrong, Arn. I've restored this ship. And I deserve these quarters."

I opened my mouth, but Emme stopped me. "It's alright. I'll move my things tonight."

I frowned but she shook her head at me. Ontario's fire dulled as he gave Emme a nod. "It's only fair, as we are risking our lives for you. But thank you." He spoke it casually, but the heaviness of his words couldn't be mistaken. The crew knew our task was to find and kill the king of Julinbor to free Emme's oathbinding, and they all knew death could find us instead. Yet they had agreed. I wasn't the only one willing to cross seas for her.

Ontario left before he could see the sour expression cross Emme's face.

I exhaled. "He's taking everything from me."

"You shouldn't fight." Emme's voice held hints of an edge. "It's been weeks, and you haven't made up yet."

"Weeks can't fix what he's stolen from me. I need years. Along with a heavy apology. And I want my ship back."

The faintest smile touched her lips. "Oh, is that all? Remind me to never take your ship from you."

"But you're better looking than he is. I'd only stay angry at you for six months."

The rocking of the ship changed as we approached the dock. Through the porthole came the golden hues of a setting sun over the glistening water, and the tip of land peeking from the side. Resyor was a foul town, similar to Kaffer Port in that it held people of questionable nature, but it was wealthier in status. While King Unid overlooked Kaffer Port, I suspected bribery kept Resyor from his laws.

Pirates were welcome there. Unwholesome magic-wielders, thieves in hiding, and businessmen, wealthy from illegal trading, were in abundance on these rich hills. The minerals in the land drew a large population that blended with the scoundrels to form an unsavory town. There was no telling what sort of character you'd meet creeping through the city.

As the king was entering that inevitable phase that all monarchs do of 'rid my lands of any foul folk,' this was an especially dangerous place to be landing now. If we had any other choice, we'd never come.

Emme watched the land. The sound of Ontario ordering the crew about filtered down to us. He'd be yelling our names soon, beckoning us like dogs.

I scowled, tying on an empty pistol holster to complete my attire. "I should not have to grovel for my ship back from a man no better than I. As his trusted companion for years, I never once did him wrong. And this is how—what are you doing? Stop that."

Emme pulled the sheet from the cot, opened a drawer, and tossed her few possessions on the sheet, wrapping them up inside. "He asked me to move, and I said I would. If you ever plan to reestablish a friendship one day, then this is what I need to do."

"Reestablish friendship? I plan to get my ship back, and I'm not doing that by you giving up the captain's quarters. Do you know how unpleasant the crew's quarters are?"

She rested on her knees and breathed out a sigh. "Yes, I know. But the crew is already doing so much for me."

She didn't see what giving him the quarters meant to me.

Being captain was more than being the one behind the wheel. It was my purpose. My honor came from becoming captain at such a young age—even after being sold to another crew. I maintained my ship. I educated my crew. Those things drove me each and every day, yet Ontario took that from me, even after watching how hard I fought for my men. He stripped away the best parts of me, and that was a wound deeper than any a blade could deliver.

Ontario's voice cut through the air as he called our names. *Just like dogs.*

"Come on." Emme pushed the bag to the floor. "Best not anger him further."

That sounded exactly like what I wanted, but I went with her from the room to where I'd have to watch Ontario command my beautiful ship while I checked the ropes for fraying.

My head poked above deck, and the familiar scents of sea mist and bay rum were replaced by wood polish.

I paused. Wood polish?

Emme pushed at me, and I clambered up. The crew was in a flurry, checking the lines and adjusting sails or yelling orders down to the men who rowed below. Ontario stood at the helm with his eyes fixated on the land.

Why did I smell wood polish?

My eyes swept over the deck. The shine on this ship was not from fetid water and an old mop. "Ontario," I shouted up to my old first mate. "How much silver did you spend on polish?"

He swept a hand over the ship with a proud smile. "Isn't she a beauty? And see these old sails? I've got a sailmaker at Resyor who will make new ones for us. They'll be pure white, made from the best wool there is." The whole ship could hear him announcing the finery he'd buy.

That fool. "What treasure did we plunder that you have the wealth to do such a thing? The stones we dug up last week won't trade for much, and sails cost a pretty coin."

We had a small wealth, which Ontario knew we needed saved for harder times. It was money stained by blood anyway, the blood of our men and the blood of Admiral Bones. Even if he'd traded some of those items, it wasn't enough to cover the cost of new sails.

"We will be the finest ship on the seas!" Clarice cheered, raising her fist in the air. Other crew members joined in. I gave Clarice a look. She was a navigator we'd picked up last week from Julinbor, but Ontario had failed to tell me how much he'd paid her to join us. Or the cook, who made tastier food than any aboard the *Royal Rose* had ever done. And we had a real ship physician now. As if we had money coming out of our ears.

Yet he hadn't batted an eye when I had asked him how we could afford such a thing. "I covered it," was all he'd ever say.

Clarice waved her tankard toward land, where streetlamps lit up the city. "Turn slightly north. Inworthton is nestled into that cove."

Ontario adjusted his wheel, while I frowned. "Inworthton? I thought we headed to the city, not to a tavern?"

"Have you checked all the lines? I need an inventory report if we need to purchase more." Ontario didn't give me a glance.

Emme looked over her shoulder to me from where she pulled at the riggings, and shook her head in warning.

I reached for the ropes, but couldn't help pressing. It was my blood that would be spilled if this plan failed. "What business do we have at Inworthton?"

"Meeting other soldiers, or anyone who can tell us where the king is."

"And, that is why we are to get to the city." I dropped the ropes and strode to the foot of the stairs leading to the quarterdeck. It still felt odd to pause below them instead of climbing. The helm called to me, the wheel begging me to retake it and claim back my ship. It took all my effort to remain on the main deck. "In hopes that other soldiers see me as your captive, and you barter for my life," I reminded him.

We'd made a plan, and I'd agreed to wear my old naval outfit to con any king's men we came across into trusting me enough to let information slip about the king's whereabouts. Rumor had it he didn't take his winters in the castle, and as winter was settling around us as fast as Emme's sickness was accelerating, we needed his location now.

"Honest men don't dine at Inworthton," I told him.

Wind picked at Ontario's open jacket as he guided us into the cove. Sharp rocks rose like a gate from the dark waves to welcome us into their fold. A fire burned in a large torch outside a stone-walled tavern, while numerous ships were docked outside.

"No, they rest in the holding cells of Arger while pirates dine above."

I stomped up the stairs. "Arger's cells? Are you mad? Do you know how expensive it is to ask that man to hold an item? Have you a talent for turning sand into silver that I don't know about? Because if you suddenly have all this treasure, now is a fine time to share it instead of a month ago when my neck was on the line."

Ontario pounded a fist against the wheel. "I do not"—his voice vibrated with anger—"answer to you. You aren't my captain anymore, and you will give me the respect of following my orders just as I did for you so many times."

We stood facing each other, the air as thick as a cup of grog. At last, with nostrils flared, I turned away. "Fine. Run this ship aground with pointless spending. The ruin of the *Royal Rose* will be on your shoulders."

"Thank you," Ontario mocked. "Now save your ire. You'll need it for when the Fates take Emme."

I froze in my descent. His words were like ice against the burning anger in my gut.

His voice drifted down to me. "You know I'm right, mate. We can play savior all we want, but she's struggling to trim the sails even now. Her body won't last long enough to find the king. Death has claimed her as his own."

My nails dug into the freshly polished railing.

"I can save her. And if it comes to it, I'll deliver the king's death blow myself."

2
ARN

Ontario passed a furled parchment to Bishop, who tucked it into the inside pocket of his jacket. After Ontario had paid Jenner to join the crew—a delightful cook with a heavy limp in his left leg and an even heavier northern accent—Bishop had been extra dutiful to preserve his place aboard the *Royal Rose*. He stayed up late building traps for fish, documenting inventory, or whatever other little task he thought would appease Ontario.

Ontario then handed a hefty pouch over that rattled as Bishop stowed it away. "Get all the supplies needed, and meet back here tonight. As soon as Arn gets information, we'll set sail. It'll be a long night of travel."

"Not a problem, Captain. I'll take care of this." Bishop patted his pocket, while Ontario clapped him on the shoulder.

"There's a good man. Take Timmons and Collins with you. They'll be handy in bartering."

The bilge of the *Royal Rose* knocked against the stone wharf. Emme picked up the ropes to throw them to land, but Bo came behind her and settled his hand on her shoulder. Without a word, she passed them over so he could successfully take care of them. Bo was right. The ropes would have landed in the water had she tried to make the throw.

Clarice grunted as she slid the gangplank down to meet the evenly laid stones and marched across. She tied the rope around a short post and hollered up, "Come on down, boys! The land is great."

Emme and I exchanged glances before I took a step toward the plank. Tess, a young lass who insisted on wearing a feathered hat every day, stayed behind with her. Tess was too young to hold up if a fight broke out in the tavern—a reason she argued against fiercely. The real reason Ontario asked her to remain here had more to do with her overactive mouth that would spill our secrets faster than the bartender could pour rum, but she agreed to stay before we were forced to remind her of that.

She wasn't the only one looking longingly after the men parading across the wharf. Emme had the same expression.

Someday, I promised in my head. *Someday you'll be healed and be free to go wherever you'd like.* Tonight would be the first step to that.

Ontario placed a firm hand on my chest as the other men left the *Royal Rose*. It took them no more than a minute. There were thirteen of us in total, the same amount we had before losing the others to the Island of Iilak.

Once the crew passed, Ontario said, "I have reason to believe Captain Melborn is here. He captured five of the king's men. Elite officers, if my knowledge is correct."

"Is Melborn mad? King Unid already detests us. He'll bring trouble upon us all."

"Trouble is already here, mate. Melborn thinks he can offer to return the prisoners in exchange for a full pardon from the king for his less-than-honorable deeds."

I barked a laugh. "He is mad. No king in his right mind would grant Melborn pardon. He's fouler than the whole lot of us."

Ontario stroked his black stubble. "Maybe. But that's why

I docked here. The men are being held in Arger's cells below the tavern. While you're in there, you can get information from them."

His full plan came together in my mind. I couldn't imagine how much it cost Melborn to keep five men in those cells, just as I couldn't imagine how much this intel had cost Ontario. There were secrets hidden there that I itched to uncover.

Ontario scanned the city as we spoke, and it felt as it would have before. Two friends discussing strategies, preparing to go into town at night and raise a drink together. Yet his dark eyes veiled his true thoughts from me, and I couldn't read beyond his hostility.

A pirate's life was never certain, but I'd never imagined losing my bond with Ontario.

"Can you do it?"

I nodded. "Aye. I'll get the information. We'll sail straight for the king and save Emme before the week is up." With luck, I'd have the information before the night was half over. Already, the sky was shaded in orange, and broken shadows began to creep over the town.

He didn't confirm my remark about saving Emme, though I wanted him to. Even though he'd make it clear that he thought Emme was doomed, I wanted to hear someone else say that we would succeed. Just one person who believed Emme wouldn't die.

Instead, he pulled handcuffs from his pocket and clipped one end to my wrist, holding the other to tug me along. "Keep your head low and try to look defeated. It shouldn't be too hard for you."

I kept quiet as Ontario dragged me down the plank and across the sloping track leading toward Arger's cells.

The last of our crew was trailing into Inworthton with the rest of the night crowd, letting their hoots be heard tumbling down the hill and over the open sea. Through the windows,

I watched as they rolled up their sleeves and placed elbows against the bar, blending in with the other guests. Plumes of smoke rose from the chimney, and our nostrils got their first scent that wasn't seeped in salt in weeks. My mouth watered at the steaming roast sitting on copper plates, and I had to turn my eyes away. The place I was going would be much more abysmal that this.

Ontario stopped short of the lacquered teal door to turn me south, where a narrow path led through a cluster of trees, their branches hanging low and masked in darkness as if marking a tunnel to another realm.

Ontario pulled harder than necessary on the handcuffs, and my feet stumbled over uneven stones. He kept a hand on his cutlass and scanned the thick overgrowth. "Keep up." The fading evening light showed me his face, but it was expressionless.

He tugged again.

"Stop yanking me." I sent a sharp look his way as he ignored my request. "What if the men aren't in the cells?"

"They will be."

"We're losing precious time if they aren't."

"I said they will be." His voice was as rough as his grip on me. "Before we return, I'd appreciate if you reported to me first. I'd like to know the king's location right away."

"Why? This crew makes decisions together," I said.

"That's rich coming from you."

"You said you wanted to be a different kind of captain," I reminded him.

He kept his tone even enough to not startle the still night, but his voice vibrated with his frustration. "You aren't treating me like I'm captain at all." He breathed to steady himself. "I am your captain, and you will submit to my orders."

Submit to my orders. Never once when I was in charge did

I speak to my crew in such a manner. My anger burned, but a slip could ruin our cover, so I gave a curt nod.

We could have continued to the cells with this heavy air between us, if Ontario hadn't muttered, "I'm a better captain than you were anyway. At least I'll keep my crew alive."

The air was snatched from my chest. I buried my feet in the rocks. "What did you just say?"

"You heard me," he said.

The dare was clear in his eyes. He knew what I wanted. I could do it too. He'd dropped my arms, and I could take a swing at him right now.

I didn't. Like it or not, I couldn't hit my captain.

He chuckled, almost disappointed. "Emme has turned you soft."

"Tell me, mate," I spat the last word. "What have I done against you to earn your hatred?"

Wind snatched dry leaves to rattle them against hollow tree trunks as splintered moonbeams cast their pale light across the branches, creating shadows like the legs of a spider that crawled over our skin. Ontario stood still for a while, until he coiled his hands around the chain of my cuffs and carried on.

"Did you ever think I could be captain of my own vessel someday?" he asked. "Or did you think I'd be your first forever?" His tone had leveled, and that sucked some of the tension away.

"I didn't know you wanted to be a captain."

From behind, I watched his head shake. "Because you never cared. That's all changed. I took the respect you wouldn't grant me."

He dragged me further down the path.

"You never gave me any indication that you were unhappy."

"I shouldn't have had to. You were my closest friend." Frustration echoed in his voice, and it was like a knife carving through my heart.

But his actions had been almost childish. And I had certainly handled my demotion as civilly as I could. My oversight of this side of his character could cost me my ship. If the man wanted more from me all those years—he should have just asked. As far as being captain, he could get his own blasted ship.

His mouth drew into a tight line. "There's more to me than you know." We didn't go much farther before he stopped. "We're here."

Here? This was hardly a hill. I was expecting an impenetrable prison.

Tiny lightning bugs, captured in bottles, hung beside a worn-out door, clad in bronze hinges and lacquered black. The flickering creatures acted as tiny torches in the night, framing the threshold in a green glow. Weeds scrabbled against the walls, which were no more than a few planks of timber piled against the side of the hill, and a putrid scent of moss seeped into our lungs.

Writing was scribbled into a sign over the doorway:

Arger's holding cells. A safe place for your items. No questions asked.

Ontario pounded against the door.

I let out a low whistle. "These are the infamous cells that hold treasured goods? Doesn't it cost a fortune to use them?" One strike of a match, and this door would burn to the ground, freeing whatever was inside.

The pirate in me was already forming a plan for our next thieving escapade, starting with breaking into this place. Just then, the knob turned and the door creaked open.

A fire might burn down the door, but now I understood the strength of this place. The walls inside were pure stone, unblemished by cracks. Weapons of all assortments hung on hooks. But the first dilemma one would have with trying to break in was the figure who stood before us.

Ontario and I stepped back. He was enormous.

Ontario looked Arger up and down. "Quite the large one, aren't you?"

"And you look like I could snap you with my hands."

I knew better than to laugh. I shifted in the handcuffs, and it wasn't entirely for show. Arger's body filled the doorway. His muscles appeared to be made from the same stone that built this place. A thick beard covered most of his face, leaving only dark eyes to peer at us.

Ontario tugged me closer, and I thrashed against his hold. "I have a man I'd like kept here for a few hours, if you don't mind."

"Another of our king's capable men, I see. Fifth one captured this week. I'm feeling very safe."

"The king's got nothing on rogues like pirates," Ontario said.

I didn't let my own optimism show, but at least we had confirmation that other officers were being held inside. Ontario dug a pouch from his pocket and flicked it to Arger. "This should cover it."

Arger rolled the coins out to count them in his palm. When he was satisfied, he tucked them away and nodded. "I'll take him."

Ontario undid the handcuffs and stepped away. As his eyes met mine, a hint of nerves flittered within. Mine probably carried more than a hint. I kept as far away from Arger as I could as he shut the door in Ontario's face and grinned at me.

Tension thickened in the crowded room, as I discovered the faults in our plans. One, *yes there are multiple,* was that if this went south, I had no way to escape. The cuffs were removed from my wrist, but if Arger decided to, he could keep me here forever and I'd have no way back. My focus had been on getting me into the cell, while underestimating the size of my jailkeeper. But now that the door was shut and bolted, the parts of me that used to be a slave were ripped from the deep hole inside where they liked to hide, and they took over my entire body. I'd taken the other men in the cells into consideration, but I'd neglected to weight the jailkeeper in my calculations.

But the second problem was arguably the bigger one. Now that I was here, Ontario could choose to not return for me.

He could leave me here, claim a fight broke out and I was slain, and I'd be trapped. He didn't care about removing Emme's oathbinding like I did. Now that the door was shut, the idea was likely crossing his mind, if it hadn't been there from the start.

I stood still, but was panicking inside. As if sensing it, Arger stepped back and spread his arms wide with a challenge lurking in his expression, like he wanted to see me try to escape. I thought about it. Greatly. In the end, it wasn't my faith that Ontario would return that kept me, but my faith that Emme would die if she didn't remove this oathbinding. I had to know where the king was, and I believed there were men in these cells that had that information.

When I didn't move, Arger sighed heavily like an animal that caught its prey and could no longer play with it. He pointed over my shoulder, and I turned to look. The room was built for simple living, with a cot and a chair and a makeshift kitchen to the side, where a window from above let in a strand of pale light. Beyond that, a tunnel led deep into the ground.

"Onward, rat. I've got a pretty cell just for you."

3

EMME

Arn and Ontario disappeared against the night, and I tuned out the rhythmic lap of shallow waves to focus on the other sounds of the city. If Arn shouted out, I wanted to hear it.

The scratchy ropes dug against my skin as I dragged them to the quarterdeck to sit with a higher view of our surroundings. White stones, like tiny moons resting on the ground, littered Julinbor's coast while the sea glistened like glass to reflect stars that slowly came out. Kaffer Port rested miles away from here, but I looked that way anyway and wondered what Bart would be doing tonight. He must have hired a second hand in my place, and the home that once sheltered me now belonged to another.

I returned my focus to the ropes and picked through them with the needle, repairing the frayed edges so they could be used again. Ontario planned to purchase additional ropes to last through the winter, but with some tender care, these ends could be tightened up, and we'd have more than enough rope to get through the coming cold months. The last thing we needed was the lines swelling with the frozen temperatures and leaving us helpless on the icy seas.

I couldn't afford anything to slow us down.

"Can I help?" Tess came up the few planks of stairs,

pausing to take the helm in hand and pretend to steer. A smile spread over her freckled face. In the short weeks that she'd been here, those freckles had multiplied as the sun soaked into her skin, and her black hat was already faded.

"You could check the fish traps to see if we've got anything to make a proper meal tomorrow."

Her nose wrinkled. "I'd rather be out there with them." She leaned against the wheel as she sighed. "That's where the real excitement is happening."

"This is where you're safe." I glanced up from the ropes. "How old are you, Tess?"

Her head hardly reached above the wheel, and her frame was still narrow, signs that she hadn't reached adolescence yet. "Fifteen," she replied, but didn't meet my eyes. I'd guess more around twelve.

Ontario swore he hadn't stolen any of the crew to get them aboard, and none of them acted forced to be here. The *Royal Rose* hadn't had prisoners since Arn took it over years ago. This girl must have abandoned her family to join our crew.

My heart twisted at the thought of her mother, somewhere out there worrying for her daughter's safety.

The ropes sat heavy on my lap as I set them down. "And this is what you want? A life aboard an odorous ship, chasing down merchants to rob and eating dried meat and fish for most of your meals?"

Tess moved to the edge of the helm. "You know what's out there?" She gestured toward the city. "People who do the same thing, day after day. But here," she turned to the midnight blue of the sea to fill her lungs with the salty air, "this is adventure. It's a promise of excitement and glory."

I wanted to see the magnificence as she did. But those dark waters told me a different story. They told of my mother, drowned in their embrace. They told of the black ship, hunting me down, driving our minds mad, and killing my brother.

They spoke of sunken family, bitter mermaids, dangerous creatures, and my lost crew.

Any beauty of the ocean was masked by the dangers it brought.

Perhaps the most dangerous thing about the seas was how easy it was to adore them. I saw it in Tess now. The seas made people fall in love with their glittering waves, the freedom of being surrounded by endless blue, the feeling of wind in their hair as they sat in the crow's nest. The waters entice everyone to love them, and who can resist? Until one day the thing you love the most turns feral, and it's all you can do to keep breathing as it threatens to drown you.

I clutched my tunic closer. If I buried my nose into the collar, I could still smell a hint of my brother buried in the fibers of what was once his shirt. A reminder of just how much the sea had taken from me. A warning to never fall in love with it again.

"Be careful," I warned Tess. "Keep studying the lessons Arn is teaching you. He told me you had a talent for numbers. That could provide a promising job on land. You never want to be trapped here."

She stared past me with a thoughtful expression, and for a moment I thought I might have spoken some sense into her. But her eyes flared. "She's coming toward us."

I whipped around. A crooked woman hobbled down the causeway. Her hair flailed in the wind, as wild as a storm, and even from here I could see her brilliant blue eyes.

"Is she a witch?" Tess breathed.

I pushed the tangle of ropes off my lap and hurried down the stairs as quickly as my weak legs would allow. "Don't say anything rash," I warned Tess as I fought to keep my balance. "If she is a witch, she isn't to be angered."

The woman moved with unexpected speed that surpassed mine, and she walked across the gangplank before I could pull it up. Her cane made a tapping noise as she looked up at us. I couldn't tear my gaze from hers, where the blue bored into me. She needed no weapon; I had no doubt those eyes could pierce.

"Can I help you?" I asked, shifting back as she inched closer. My hand checked for my blade.

Her tone was melodious as a song belonging to a much younger woman. "No need for that, dearie. I've come to tell your fortune." She took great effort to straighten her back. Wind carried her hair, making her appear far crazier than she already did.

I withdrew my hand from my hilt. "I'll pass. Only the Fates know the future, and I'd rather not know mine."

"I want to know." Tess scrambled forward and took hold of the woman's arm, leading her to a barrel to sit down.

I cast a look toward Inworthton. This woman appeared harmless, but if she proved dangerous, I might not be a match against her. Already my legs ached from standing for a few minutes, and I made my way to a barrel near Tess so I could keep a proper eye on things. Tess had settled on her knees before the woman, almost as if worshiping her, and begged for her future.

"We cannot pay you," I informed the woman.

"Your coppers are of no use to me." She cracked her knuckles, placed her hands on the sides of Tess's face, and closed her eyes.

We had fortune tellers in the town where I grew up, mostly ones who passed through with two-wheeled carts draped in charms, animal bones, and runes carved into stone. They'd sit in the market and weave scarves into their hair, luring young ones in with their odd collections and promises to tell them what the future held. Father warned us not to go, but it was Mother's adamancy that we steer clear which held Emric and me back. If Father and Mother both agreed that something was bad, then it must have been dangerous. Mother claimed that women such as this did more than predict the future, they controlled it through calculated readings.

"To control the future is a skill that I haven't managed," Mother had said.

"Not yet, my love," Father had replied. *"Though I have no doubt that one day you will."* The idea had pleased Mother, but not enough to let us go near the fortune tellers.

The woman before me didn't appear dangerous. She didn't move for the longest time.

After a moment, Tess closed her eyes as well, twitching her fingers in excitement.

A stronger breeze floated by, and the woman opened her eyes. "You have a promising future ahead of you. Filled with love, the ocean, and hints of unexpected magic. There's a sadness there, though. A longing for something more. If you don't learn to be content, you'll spend your entire life desiring what you don't have. And there's . . ." Her expression splintered. "What pain there is. Did you lose someone?"

Tess's lip stiffened. "Yes."

"You must let go. Holding on will only force you to wear that pain over and over every day."

I stood up at the frozen look on Tess's face. "Thank you, madam. Allow me to help you down the plank."

I held out my hand to help the woman. With a knowing smile, she placed her grip in mine, but as soon as she did, she gasped.

I quickly withdrew my hand, but those blue eyes had pressed shut. Tess and I exchanged looks as the woman began to groan in a low, eerie sound.

"Are you okay?" I reached for her, but her eyes flew open. She shrank back.

"A great darkness is there. She does not know. Do not make me the bearer of this fate." Her hollow words echoed, though we were not in an open room. She shivered and repeated her plea. "Do not make me the bearer of this."

Tess backed away, while I couldn't make my feet move. She spoke of me, I was certain. What had the Fates shown her through my touch?

They do not predict the future, they create it.

I had to know what she saw.

I waited until she'd quieted her wailing. Then her shaky hand grabbed mine, and she yanked me level with her. Though her hunched body had been trembling a moment before, it now stood perfectly still as she breathed over me. "Your path is a difficult one. Through either your life or your death, much blood with be spilled."

She let go of me suddenly, as if I were a sickness she might catch. I glanced at Tess to see if she heard. By her blanched face, she had.

"I'm not a killer," I said in a low voice to the old woman. "I won't kill anyone."

She clasped her cane between her bony fingers as her knitted shawl whipped around her in the chilly breeze. Her eyes were as glassy as the sea behind her. "The Fates make no mistake, child." She dug into her pocket and pulled out a golden pin, passing it to me. She kept her distance, withdrawing her hand as soon as the pin was in my palm.

I peered at it. It was no bigger than my pinky finger, colored amber, and shiny in the moonlight. Leaves decorated the sides, but they were withered and dead. They melded together in the middle, as if a fire had molded them into one. I brought the pin closer, then looked at her.

"Wolfsbane."

"Symbol of death." She eyed me. "The Fates speak in many tones to me, but none as loud as the one right now. They are like great storms in my head, warning me of you."

The words of the black ship's sailor came to mind. *You*

have a potential for such darkness, just like your mother. You are not safe to leave in this world.

The sailor had warned me then that I would become something terrible. Someone like my mother. It scared her enough that she'd been prepared to kill me.

This old woman was staring at me as if her gaze could unravel my soul. Tess held a hand over her heart and was murmuring some words under her breath.

"So are you going to save the world from whatever darkness I will bring?" I asked the old woman. My hand twitched for my cutlass.

She shook her head. "It is not for me to decide your fate. But keep that pin, so you never forget."

I didn't need this pin to remember the cold feeling her words brought. "I'm not a killer," I repeated, ignoring the images of Admiral Bones's body lying on the beach and the pistol in my hand.

"Maybe not." She looked at the flag on the mast to see the blood dripping from the rose. The blood had been my idea. "And yet, in one way or another, you will be a catalyst for death."

I didn't miss how Tess took a large step away from me.

"Fitting how you sail on the *rskvateer,*" she said, gesturing to our flag.

Tess's brows scrunched at the name, but I recognized the tongue of northern men. Much further north in Julinbor, though I knew a bit of the language.

Rskvateer. Grave ship.

Rumors traveled fast. Likely it was Landon, Arn's prior friend, whom we'd fought against on the Island of Iilak, who began these rumors. They stood on merit—half our crew now rested on the pale sands of the island—and such tales would cause others to shy away from us. Our trading at port, our attempts to get new crew members, it would all be difficult to do if attached to a name like *rskvateer*.

"The young should not be on a ship such as this," she said with a glance to Tess. The woman's bones cracked as she straightened. "The sun has set, dears, and old creatures like me ought to be in bed." She reached for Tess, who led her from the ship. I pressed against the taffrails to watch them leave, replaying her words in my head.

"I'm not a killer," I said once more to no one. "And this is no grave ship." The wolfsbane pin dug into my skin as I closed a fist around it. I shifted to throw it into the sea, but something made me pause, and I slid it into my pocket instead.

Though such a small object, the weight was noticeable.

Just a woman who's lost her mind, I thought. But in the next breath a second thought came. *Without me, Emric wouldn't have died,* and that was the first time I believed he was truly gone. That was a fate that was growing harder to deny.

4

EMRIC

It was warm here. That was the first thought I had. Humid, with hints of mango in the air.

I took time before opening my eyes to let my senses return. Perhaps that wasn't the best plan, because along with a numbness in my thighs, a deep pain throbbed in my belly.

I'd been stabbed, I reminded myself. The last remaining Nightlock Thief stabbed me as I'd guarded Emme from her. Then we'd plunged into the sea.

My eyes opened. I was in a home, but generous amounts of sunlight seeped through cracks in the wall. Perhaps less a *home* and more a hut held up by bamboo and slathered in mud. It leaned against a particularly strong bamboo shoot.

The calming sound of the ocean drifted in, and I strained to turn my head in search of it.

"You're awake." My mother sat on the dirt with her back against the opening of the hut, whittling a stick. A rope circled her waist, holding together what appeared to be the canvas of a sail, now fashioned into a yellowed dress for her to wear. Leather sandals decorated her feet.

"Are you real?" I asked. My voice rattled in my throat.

She stood. The sun came across the beach to flare behind her, making her look more like an angel than a human. But my mother had never been an angel. Twigs broke under her heel as she crossed to me, leaving her blade behind.

I bent my arms beneath me to prop myself up, but my stomach roared with pain. My vision darkened.

"Don't try to move," she said, placing a hand over my shoulder. Her palm was rougher than I remembered, and her skin several shades darker than before.

The edge of her braid tickled my cheek as she leaned over to stroke my brow.

"Where am I?" I asked her. The corners of my sight were completely black, and my hearing was fading. I blinked to refocus.

"Avalla."

The name meant nothing to me. It wasn't on any maps I'd studied, nor in any tales Mother told me as a boy. She offered nothing further.

"Am I dying?" I placed a hand over my stomach, where my tunic was torn, and found the rough edges of a bandage.

Arabella's smile was twisted. "No, Emric. That seems to be the curse of this island. It will trap you, but it won't let you die." I struggled to process her words, and she put a finger to her lips. "Shh. Sleep. You will get your answers."

Though I fought against it with all my strength, my body obeyed her commands, and I slipped from consciousness once more.

5

ARN

The oil lamp in Arger's hand cast long shadows across the wall as he shifted from side to side. The scent of root and soil engulfed us. Small grains of dirt flaked to the ground as I brushed my arm across it, and I marveled at the dedication someone had to hollowing this out.

"How long did it take you to dig this?" We'd gone deep enough that the air had turned noticeably warmer, and my body sweated beneath the navy uniform.

The tips of Arger's thick hair trickled along the cutout ceiling, but he never once ducked. If he spread his arms to each side, it'd be just enough to reach both walls, and I suspected that was his plan. If anyone tried to escape, they'd be forced to go through him.

"I didn't," he replied, and left it at that.

We came across the first cell, a circular dug-out room behind iron bars with a huge lock over them. Though dirt surrounded us, the cell was polished, and it gleamed in the flickering light. Of course, he'd want to keep these cells clean for the customers who came and paid a high price to hoard their things here. Beauty drove a high price.

As we passed the row of cells, Arger pointed out the items

with a jab of his finger. "Jewels. Spices. Artillery. More jewels. The head of some lieutenant. Jewels again."

My eyes grew wider as he kept on with the tour, monotonously showing off the items he stored. As we walked, I plotted ways to steal these items later, but my practical side recited why I was here. To deceive and gain information, not steal.

Though if the opportunity presented itself, one of those rubies would fit nicely into my pocket.

Up ahead came shuffling and a clink against the bars, as if hands were grasping the rails to peer through. Sure enough, with the next few steps, the lamp shed its glow over the last cell. Inside sat five men with their faces marked by bruises and scowls. One of them was covered in dirt. Another was so far buried in the corner that the shadows hid his features completely. At my appearance, he shrank further back.

The corner of Arger's lips drew up in a subtle grin as he inspected them.

"Let us out, sire, and you'll get double what Melborn is paying you." One of the officers had placed his face against the bars and yanked on them. A generous amount of blood stained his cream silk, and he appeared to be nursing a wound on his leg.

Arger chortled. "What do you take me for? A pauper who can be tempted by coin?" He took a key from his pocket and slid it into the lock, turning until it clicked. The moment the cell unlocked, the officer shoved his entire body against the bars, but Arger held his hand on them.

"Try that again; it might work this time." Arger grinned, amused. Wounded Leg glanced back to the other men, who shrugged. He tried shoving again, but the bars still didn't budge.

"Do you feel that, lad?" Arger held his arm out, and I ducked so the oil lamp didn't strike me. "I feel weaker already.

Go ahead, try once more," Arger encouraged the officer. "I'm sure you'll get the door to open this time." The officer growled as he shoved his body against the doors. When at last he fell to his knees, panting heavily, Arger let go of the bars. "If it's any consolation, I brought you a friend."

Arger opened the door. I tried to look upset as I stumbled inside, not letting him see this was where I wanted to be.

"I don't want a friend. I want freedom." Wounded Leg glared at Arger. The others had yet to speak, but they each glanced at the man covered in dirt several times with worry etched across their faces.

"Well we can't have everything." The massive man slipped the key back into his pocket and gave the bars a tug. "Yup, that's not going anywhere." He hung the lamp on a hook where it swayed. Then he gave us a sardonic nod. "Gentlemen."

He strode back up the tunnel, whistling a small tune.

"Our king will have your head," one of the officers sitting on the floor shouted. "He'll kill you. That should scare you."

Arger's footsteps continued up the tunnel, but his chuckle drifted down to us. "It's been a long time since I was afraid of anything. But if you see King Unid, tell him about Arger's cells. I'd be happy to store something for him."

The man cursed and leaned his head against the wall.

All of Arger's strength couldn't frighten me as much as my recognition of that voice. The blood froze in my body, and my breath turned sharp. My empty hilt scraped as I went for my weapon, cursing the Fates for my misfortune. It was five years ago that I'd trained with that man when we'd prepared for the king's navy, and it'd been just as long since I'd seen him after Landon and I had joined a company and were sent out on the king's orders.

Shortly after that, Landon and I burned down the king's ship and joined the pirates, killing our old crew.

And now he sat in this cell with me. If he recognized me,

he'd know something was amiss. I ought to be dead by his reckoning. His voice had a unique rasp, and I prayed I didn't bear observable indicators that he'd know me by.

The cells were heavy with disappointment and frustration, as the officers cursed intermittently under their breaths and kicked at the bars. I mimicked their posture, but buried my head into my chest to hide my features from Wren.

As soon as Arger was gone, the dirty man twisted and pulled something from beneath him. He jammed it between the iron and the dirt, scraping away at it. *He's trying to dig them out,* I realized.

For a while, the only sound remained the sharp draw of his tool against the dirt. I sorted through my thoughts, wondering how soon I might be caught.

It was Wren who spoke first, twirling some coin between his fingers. "So, what got you into these cells?"

I shifted my back against the door to block the light before looking up. I did all I could to disguise my voice, dropping it lower and adapting Emme's northern accent. "Attacked on the sea a month ago. Been with pirates since."

Wounded Leg leaned his back against the curved wall and dug his feet into the ground. "Long time. Which pirates?"

I hesitated, before curiosity got the better of me. "The *Royal Rose.* You heard of them?" The man buried in the shadows chuckled, and my eyes darted his way.

But it was one of the other two officers who answered, after the other four exchanged glances. He shook some dirt out of his shoe as he smirked. "I hear it's captained by a mere boy."

I absorbed the blow to my pride. "He was young."

"I wish we'd been taken by a boy captain instead of Melborn," Digger paused from his work. "Then we might have stood a chance."

I bit my lip against saying more.

"Where's the rest of your company?" Wren asked. His gaze didn't linger on me, and he showed no signs of recognition.

"Drowned. In the Redian Gulf."

Now they all looked at me, save for the one in the corner. "What orders put you there?"

Stars and seaweed. I'd been more focused on my pride than my story. The Redian Gulf was far off by the lands of Az Elo, where King Unid had sent my first company before Landon and I had turned.

"We were under strict orders not to speak of our mission. Even I didn't know the full details."

That much had been true, though I'd come by those details later. But those weren't important now. What mattered was getting the information I came for.

"Wonder if it has something to do with the orders of the 51st from four years ago," Wren said. I flinched at the mention of my former company. Digger made a noise in his throat. Wren stopped flipping his coin long enough to give me a solemn look. "They met a worse fate than you, mate. Each one of them now a pile of bones at the bottom of the sea, and from what we knew, King Unid never gave orders to return to that gulf." He resumed with his coin, but his voice lowered. "I lost some fellow trainees on that ship."

If he got too good of a look at me, he might realize his mistake.

"That is hard. I, too, know what it is to lose mates." I rubbed the back of my head, pretending to nurse some injury. I'd established a loose connection with these men. Now for any information.

"What of you?" I asked generally. "Do you think King Unid will come to rescue you?"

Wren snorted. "The king himself? I'd bet ten year's wages that he doesn't show up." The others voiced their agreement. "But someone might come to trade with Melborn."

"Or kill him, more likely," Wounded Leg said. His brows

were full and low, and as the light crossed his face, it didn't reach his dark eyes. "I hope someone kills him. Arger too."

"So King Unid stays in his castle while his lieutenants and officers suffer at the hands of pirates?" I pressed. Then, hoping my next question wasn't too forward, I nudged more. "Or does he take his winters somewhere else? The castle must get cold as the snow comes in."

Silence stretched through the cell, and I feared I'd asked too bluntly. They'd know I sought the king's location. They'd take my head before Ontario could get me out. I'd die and only be remembered as the boy captain.

Wren flipped his coin too far and bent to retrieve it. "Don't know. Don't care. He won't save us." He extended his foot, twisting it in and out of the light that broke through the cell bars.

One of the other men, the tallest of the batch, approached the bars. My breathing quickened. But he reached past me for the lock on the door. I stepped from his way, taking care to keep my face lowered and out of the light.

Tall Officer messed with the lock, using a found piece of twig to dig into the contraption. "We don't have to worry about those pirates for much longer."

The other three nodded knowingly.

I crossed my arms loosely and tried not to appear too interested. "What do you mean?"

Tall Officer paused long enough to look back at me. His copper eyes searched mine until I turned my face away. A few seconds later came the clicking of his twig once more poking through the lock. "The king's grown weary of rogue pirates. Says they're worse than witches. He's called in all his fleets to deal with them. Soon his shores will be freed of such scoundrels."

My body went numb. I'd known he was after pirates, but

not to that extent. His entire fleet . . . we didn't stand a chance. My determination to be rid of the king only grew.

"Perhaps the pirates and witches should team up," I joked. But as soon as I said it, I pondered the idea. Witches were notoriously fickle, and magic wasn't something I cared to dabble in too frequently, but I'd consider it to save my ship.

"Will the king himself come to fight the pirates?" I threw out one last attempt to uncover the king's location. I needed to come away from this with some glimmer of hope. I could see the disappointment on Emme's face already.

"Do you know where the king is?"

"No, but I know where his fleet it. You're going to love this."

Wounded Leg kicked against the bars. "He won't have to. When the fleet gets here, the pirates don't stand a chance."

The cell quieted, and once more all that could be heard was the scraping against dirt as Digger continued his work. The repetitive sound marked the time for us, as minutes dragged into hours. All the while, the man in the corner faced me, and I had no trouble picturing him staring at me. I tried to see his features in the dark, but it was impossible. Soon, I shifted my face away and sent a silent prayer that Ontario would come soon. These men were of no further use to me.

It was then that the man spoke for the first time. He eased himself forward as hints of broken light speckled his cheeks. "You know what? I think I've heard of the *Royal Rose* after all."

I yanked my head back to him.

"I hear that the captain wasn't wanted by his first crew and got sold in the night. His new crew is a band of misfits . . . what's left of them that is. They're too dull to manage, and half of them died recently."

My heart stopped. His voice wasn't distinct like Wren, but I recognized it all the same. This man had the capacity to ruin everything. And the fact that he'd sat near me for hours set my teeth on edge.

"What are you doing here?" I asked.

Landon's face came into view. His bones were more pronounced than usual, and the bags under his eyes darker than ever. But he smiled like he was having the time of his life. "Captured by a crew, stored here until they decide what to do with me. Same as you, I reckon."

"You fellows know each other?" Wren asked, curious.

Landon kept his features angled away from him. "We do. We used to play together as lads. It's been a long time, friend." He stretched to his feet and held his arms out. "Long time indeed."

He came to me, and I had no choice but to embrace him back. He smelled of trout and evergreen. He whispered in my ear, "When Ontario returns, you will take me with you. Or else I'll tell everyone who you are right now. They'll be more focused on killing the one who burned down a ship of their comrades than getting out of here." He stepped back.

"They could also kill you," I hissed under my breath.

His shoulders raised then dropped. "I've got nothing to live for."

The others gave us a look, but at that moment, Arger's footsteps reverberated in the tunnel. His large frame paused outside the cell. Tall Officer stepped back and placed the twig between his teeth, crossing his arms and looking to the floor.

I kept to the back with my face lowered as Arger grabbed the lamp and held it up. "You," he pointed at me. "It's your lucky day. Your ward has come back for you. Pity though—you won't get to try some of my carrot-and-pea soup." He placed the key into the lock and gave Wounded Leg an amused grin. "Care to try to escape again? I swear, I've lost some muscle since I was here last."

Wounded Leg just scowled and looked away.

"Shame. How about you? Dug a hole out yet?"

Digger flushed in the dim light.

Arger peeked his head around the door. "Not bad work. Another few months and you'll be free for sure. Are you coming?"

I couldn't get out of there fast enough, but at my back, Landon coughed, and I hesitated.

Leave him here, every bit of me cried. But he looked at me knowingly. "Remember who I am."

I took it as a promise to carry out his threat to tell the men here who I was, but the urgency in his tone sent his real message. Remember who I am. He was more than a boy I grew up with, and now those powerful relations could prove useful.

If it wasn't for Emme, I'd have turned away. Instead, the words dragged from my throat, "Arger, I'd like this man released too."

Arger barked a laugh. "Not my choice."

"My ward will pay you. I'm certain he'd want this prisoner."

At the mention of coin, Arger licked his lips. "Worth a mention. This lad's ward likely won't be back for him, and I've already been paid in full. Come on, you."

Landon's face was of pure victory as he sauntered out. I had the urge to push him back in.

"Much thanks," he said.

"Farewell, lads," Wren said after us. "I hope to meet again someday." Landon and I shared an uncomfortable look, and I resisted glancing back. If I ever saw those fellows again, we'd be on opposite sides of a fight. Their orders were to hunt down my kind and banish us all.

Would they stop at banishment? Or was King Unid set on killing us?

It was with that thought that I followed Arger to his room above, where Ontario stood in the doorway with a glum frown on his face. The handcuffs dangled from his hands. "Come along; we are setting sail tonight."

Landon appeared from behind Arger, and Ontario's frame went slack.

"Ontario! Good to see you, my friend. Care to purchase me?"

"I care to throttle you," he said. "What's the meaning of this?"

"You have money," I suggested. "Buy him."

Arger was looking between the three of us, and I feared he'd soon put together that I wasn't Ontario's prisoner. Luckily, Ontario clasped the handcuffs to my wrists and yanked me with believable force.

"Why would I want another rat aboard?"

"I'm not any rat," Landon said. "I'm a royal rat."

"Just do it," I hissed before Landon said too much.

"Fine," Ontario growled. He reached into his pocket to open a sack of coins and flick some to Arger. "That enough?"

"That'll do. That'll do nicely." Arger smiled broadly as Ontario dragged me out the door with Landon following.

My lungs celebrated the return of fresh, open air.

"Safe travels." Arger shouted. "And don't forget to tell your friends about Arger's cells."

Ontario lifted his hat and waved it without bothering to turn. "Did you get what we needed?" he asked. The moon had reached its peak in the sky, and it illuminated the scowl on Ontario's face.

"No. I got something worse."

6

EMRIC

A dull ache rolled through my abdomen, waking me from the deepest sleep. Arabella stood over me with a muddy salve in her hand and a tight expression on her face. She looked so much like Emme in that moment—with her long hair braided, whisps loose by her face, and teeth gnawing on her upper lip—that my clouded mind confused the two. Remembrance shocked me. I bolted up.

"Emme, she's in danger."

"Quiet." Arabella set the salve down on a strip of bark fastened into a shelf.

"Did you not hear me?" I asked more forcibly, planting my palms into the splintered bed to help me sit. "My sister is in danger. She's being hunted."

She placed a firm hand on my shoulder to keep me from rising further. "Who hunts her?"

I shook my head to clear it, but the action only summoned a headache.

"A girl. A ship. I don't know exactly." I struggled to recall what the girl had spoken of as she attacked us, but all that my memories cared to remember was the blinding pain of when she stabbed me.

"Does your sister sail as a pirate?"

I nodded, and Arabella brightened.

"I knew she had it in her. Does she captain her own ship already? How many foes does she have? What great treasure has she uncovered?"

"None. Emme cares for none of that."

Arabella's enthusiasm turned sullen. "What mighty pirate does she apprentice under? Do they know she is my daughter? She should have her own sail by now."

"Emme isn't quite like that. She has but one enemy, the black ship that haunted us." I placed a hand over my wound as I took a deep breath and rested against the rough wall. "I must get back to her. This girl, she spoke of penance for her sins with the Nightlock Thieves and claimed to see something in Emme's future that frightened her."

She stiffened.

"Nightlock Thieves?"

"Aye, from the tale you told us."

Arabella stood. "What business does she have with your sister?"

"Do you know the girl I speak of?"

"I do. My one regret is failing to kill her before she banished me to this cursed island."

"I might have done that," I remembered. "I believe that I killed her. A, er, a mermaid helped me." I regretted the words as soon as they were out of my mouth. There were details there that I was unready to share. My gaze flicked to the tumbling seas. Where was Coral now? Surely if I approached the water and dipped my toes in, she'd feel my presence and come to tell me that the girl was dead and Emme safe.

The sands touched empty waves. We were alone here.

Arabella didn't ask about the mermaid. "Let us hope you did. When I rejoin your sister on the seas, there will be no Nightlock Thief to bring us down."

Her confidence encouraged me. "Do you have a way off Avalla?"

She crossed the hut to gather a collection of enormous palm branches in her arms, and I realized, if she did have a way, she wouldn't still be here. "Not yet," she admitted. "But as soon as you are strong enough, you will help me finish building this raft, and we will sail back home." She nodded over her shoulder, where I noticed a raft I'd missed earlier. It consisted of bamboo tied together, and palm branches woven to create what could only be generously called sails. There was no rudder, no wheel, no cabin to sit in and enjoy the view. There were hardly walls, and we'd be fighting to keep afloat as soon as we set sail.

She turned before she could read the skepticism on my face.

"You still need rest," she ordered, trudging to her raft. "Sleep, my son. May you dream of the day you, your sister, and I rule the seas together."

7
EMME

Tess offered to clean the barnacles from the hull, a tedious and unpleasant task that tore at the fingers, yet she rushed to do it. I didn't fail to note it was the chore that put her the furthest away from me. She gave me a long look before dipping under the waves with her tools.

"It's nonsense." I whispered the words into the wind as if the breeze could take them away from me, strip me of the future the Fates planned. But the breeze settled, and I felt no different.

I braced myself against the rails, watching the city. My finger trailed against the nick in the wood, the place where Arn had almost kissed me months ago. I'd felt so alive that night—a girl in love with the captain, falling in love with the seas, and hopeful that she'd soon be rid of the disease in her body.

Not once thinking she'd become someone people could fear.

"Nonsense," I said again.

The ache in my legs moved up to my thighs. I'd been standing too long. That was my life now, keeping track of how long I'd been on my feet, when I could take my next nap, and minimizing the activities I engaged in so I wasn't wearing myself out. It was hardly a life at all.

I sat down, squeezing my hands together. It was almost

impossible at this point to keep them from shaking. My muscles were no longer solely mine to control. No wonder Arn didn't want me coming along with them. It took all my energy to hold a blade upward, and it shook as if caught in a storm.

As soon as the king is delivered, you'll return for the Elmber Nut, I reminded myself. *This sickness will not carry you to the grave. Please don't let this end with a grave.*

The oathbinding peeked through the sock on my foot. That was why we needed to kill the king, though I might oathbind myself again if only to get an easier assignment. But Serena's instructions had been clear, and she was too far away to find now. An owl hooted in the distance, and I trailed my eyes over the trees. A strip of overgrowth separated the tavern from the rest of the city, dividing the cove from the shops along the slope of the shore. While the city was lit by lanterns, the only light here came from the moon's reflection on the black waves, the fires in Inworthton, and two torches on the cusp of the wharf.

The old woman had disappeared from the glow of the flames and into the cover of the trees, headed back to the city. Perhaps to give another young girl a message of death.

From the tavern, our crew trickled down the slope. First, it was Clarice and Jenner with sacks in hand that I hoped was dinner for me and Tess. Then, it was Bo and the remainder of our new crew. Before they'd reached the dock, Tess was hauling herself back on deck and wringing the water out of her hair.

"Did you finish?" I asked.

"Yes," she said as she arranged her hat back on her head. But I doubted she had completed the task; it was more likely that she heard the voices of the crew and didn't want to miss the fun.

"Dinner," Clarice said, tossing us a bag. Tess grabbed it

and stretched it open. I was about to reach for my portion when Ontario called from the trees.

"Prepare to set sail, crew!"

Bishop, Timmons, and Collins emerged from the south path leading from the town at the same time Arn and Ontario wound through the thickets from Arger's cells. Bishop had gathered the supplies and delegated the other two to carry them as he whistled a tune down the stony path by the water's edge. His tune stopped short as his jaw fell open. From the looks of it, Ontario and Arn had gotten something too.

I gasped. "That can't be." I pressed against the rails and motioned to the main deck. "Bo, how much have you been drinking?"

The large man paused from letting down the sails. "Why? Am I doing something wrong?"

I couldn't take my eyes off the man walking behind Arn with a slight limp but a swagger in his movement. The straight cut of his jacket and the tight curl of his hair was too familiar. Beside him, Arn's face was stern, and Ontario looked positively furious. "Just tell me," I said to Bo. "Are you drunk or sober?"

Bo looked around the ship. "Right now, you're the only one who is swaying, and I'd say that's more to do with your sickness than any drink. I'm sober, I think."

"It's not my sickness this time," I clarified. I pointed a shaky finger across the port. My voice wavered. "Is that Landon?"

At the name of the pirate who'd led the crew that deceived us—killing half of our mates on the shores of the Island of Iilak, cutting off Arn's hand, and almost poisoning him to death . . . forcing me to give up my Elmber Nut to save Arn instead of myself—Bo dropped everything. He clambered up to the helm to stare. His large hands grabbed the rails, and he squinted into the mist of the night, looking like a wolf glaring over the fjord to see its enemy coming its way.

"By golly, I'd say so." While my voice was shaky, his was steady as a mast. "Where's my pistol?"

I placed a hand on his arm, both to still him and myself. "Not yet."

Bo's eyes narrowed slyly. "Yet? Is that permission to shoot him later?"

I hesitated. "Let's see how this goes. Keep your pistol on hand."

He patted his holster. "Will do. Just give the word."

Bishop, Timmons, and Collins had reached the pier before the others, and Bishop threw a casual glance at Ontario and Arn. His whistling stopped mid-note. Landon's smile grew wider, while Ontario's frown deepened.

"We'll talk on the ship, mate," Ontario told Bishop.

"He's not getting on the ship," the man countered, placing himself in the middle of the pier and taking up as much room as he could. Timmons's and Collins's eyes grew wide.

"We will talk *on the ship.* Go."

With a grunt, Bishop stormed down the pier, but the sharp line of his jaw was more pronounced. "Is Arn okay with this?" Bishop asked over his shoulder.

"Get on the ship!" Ontario roared. Arn smiled faintly at Bishop's question, but he didn't take his eyes off Landon beside him.

Clarice dropped the sacks of food and mounted her hands on her hips, while Tess squirmed beside her. Jenner paid us no mind as he took the food downstairs. Those three wouldn't know why we despised this man. They hadn't been there.

My stomach knotted as Landon came up the gangplank freely, and every instinct told me this wasn't fine. He was the reason this ship was without half its crew. He was the reason we didn't have jolly nights by the fire listening to Timmons play the flute.

A man such as he shouldn't be allowed near our ship, let

alone to stride across it, inspecting the crew with an amused eye. "You all look like beaten-down rags."

Ontario and Arn were the last to come aboard, and Ontario immediately barked out orders. "Bishop, organize the inventory so we are ready to go. Clarice, Timmons, and Collins, prepare to set sail. Tess, stay out of our way. Bo, you steer. And you," he wheeled on Arn. "What in the name of Sea King Valian is he doing here?"

"You must be letting me stay if we are setting sail," Landon asked as Clarice slipped by him to untie us. The ship began to drift out to sea.

"If I decide differently, I'll throw you into the water." Ontario's gaze could cut steel.

"We need him," Arn said through his teeth. I brushed past Bo to climb down the stairs, keeping a healthy distance away from Landon. When he saw me, he grinned.

"Emme, right? Where's your brother?"

"Gone," I said as plainly as I could despite the tightening in my chest. Arn cast me a look.

"Pity," Landon said with no emotion. "He's not the only one, right? You guys took quite the beating if I recall."

"Throw him into the sea," Ontario demanded.

Arn sighed, removed the cuffs from his wrists, and dropped them on the deck. "We can't."

"Throw them both over then," Ontario flung out an arm. He pushed past the two of them as if the conversation was over. "You can drown together."

Landon's brows raised. "You'd throw your own captain over?"

"He's not captain anymore," Ontario shot back. "I am."

Arn said nothing as Landon slowly turned to face him. Landon's jacket was torn at the hems and covered in cracked mud, his shoulder-length, dark hair tangled in knots, and his beard grown out. His frame was narrower than last time we saw him, and he was surrounded by a crew that openly hated him, yet he carried himself with cocky confidence.

"Not captain, eh?" Landon said. "This isn't the first crew to reject you."

Arn's eyes sparked. "And what happened to your crew, huh? Or were you in Arger's cells for the fun of it, looking like death?"

"Speaking of looking like death," Landon gestured at me. "What happened to her? The next storm is going to blow her away."

His words drove too close to home, gnawing at the parts of me that feared he was right. I looked at the helm where Bo was watching us, and he patted the pistol at his side with a suggestive raise of his brow. Though it tempted me to let Bo have a go at Landon, I shook my head. I had a better idea.

"Tie?" I held my hand out to Arn. Knowing what I meant, he pulled the band that kept his hair up out of his eyes and passed it to me, amusement on his face.

"And I wasn't the only one in Arger's cells," Landon said as I raked my hair on top of my head and tied it together.

I slid Emric's ring off my finger. "Ring," I said, handing it to Arn.

"Ring," he said back.

"You were there too," Landon went on, ignoring us. "And lucky for you to run into me. I always did have to help you out of trouble when we were children. You couldn't manage without me then, and you can't manage without me now."

I placed one foot in front of the other, balled up my fist, and decked Landon across the jaw.

His eyes widened as he stumbled backward, and I grabbed Arn's arm to rebalance myself. Three months ago that punch would have dislocated his jaw, but now it only left a red mark that I hoped would turn into a respectably sized bruise.

For Emric, I thought as I rubbed my knuckles. *And for everyone else.*

"Well, someone had to do that," Ontario said. "You're lucky it was Emme and not me." He turned to Arn. "Now why can't we throw him over?"

"Unfortunately, he'll be extremely helpful getting us where we need to be," Arn said.

Landon rubbed his jaw and inspected it as if for blood. He eyed me warily. "You seek King Unid?" he grumbled. "I can get him."

Ontario's eyes narrowed. "How?"

"I'm a special breed," Landon replied. Satisfied with the minimal injuries to his face, he shoved his hands into his pockets. "I'm the king's cousin. You acquire us invitations to the king's palace, and I'll lead you right to his chamber's doors. You want to kill him, right? You and me both. Arn knows as good as any that I'd like to see that man dead. I'll help it happen."

Ontario exchanged looks with Arn. He gave a loud sigh. "Blast. I really wanted to throw him over."

8

EMRIC

I thought of Emme as I worked, and whether she was safe. Arn would watch out for her in my absence, but I was increasingly aware with each passing day that her sickness could take her at any time. I needed to return to her.

Occasionally, I dipped my feet into the water to let Coral sense me, but if she did, she didn't show. In truth, the merpeople's powers were a mystery to me, but touching the water excited me with the thought of unraveling them all. How did their lungs work? Was Sea King Valian real? Was there power beneath the waves that humans didn't know of?

But for now, there were other mysteries that needed to be solved, and they were clothed in heat and sand and my mother's attitude.

"How does this island work?" I asked Arabella as she tied twine around a post. We'd be lucky if that held against wind, but I kept from saying so.

She wiped her brow before answering. "It is a prison. You can be sent here, but there is no path off."

"Whose prison?"

"The Fates," she answered with disdain.

"Then how will we leave?"

She waved a finger over the raft in silence.

I placed a hand against the healing wound on my stomach. "If there is no way off, then what good will a raft do?"

"The Fates will reward us for our strong will and free us. We only have to sail away."

Only. She'd been here for five years, so it couldn't be as simple as that.

My eyes turned to the water. The ocean stretched for as far as I could see in all directions, washed in sunlight and flashes of white, but no traces of land. Behind us raged the overgrown island with rampant trees and citrus fruits. Green one way, and blue the other. The green could feed us, keep us alive, but held us trapped. But the blue? That could save us. Or it might kill us.

The water surface shimmered like a million stars. It held such beauty for such a wild thing. "How do we know how far we have to sail to find other land?"

"There's no way for me to know that. But I'm not staying here." She worked with sure hands. "I'm getting back to the ocean, and back to my home."

I wondered if she meant those as the same thing, or different things.

I decided to humor her. "How long will it take to finish this?" The raft looked almost complete, though woefully unprepared for the turmoil of a ferocious sea. The boards weren't even, the sail weak, and we had mere branches for oars.

But Arabella looked over it with a satisfaction. "A few weeks at most. I want to be certain this time that it'll hold."

"This time?" I glanced up at her words. "This isn't the first time you've tried to leave the island. You said we'd be rewarded for trying to leave."

She shook her head just as a breeze carried her hair over her shoulder. Her skin was darker, her body leaner, but there was still muscle on her. Even here, where food must be scarce and difficult to come by, she'd kept up her strength. Preparing for her return to the sea.

"I've built thirteen rafts over the past years. And thirteen times I've had to swim back to shore on broken remains. The last time, I made it far enough out that it took two days to return to land, using a few planks to keep afloat."

I shuddered at the image of her desperation as she fought to return to us, her family, while we thought she was dead. I placed a hand over hers. She pulled back.

"Soon none of that will matter. Now keep working."

The sun may have dulled her hair, but it hadn't dulled her sharp tongue.

"It'll be good for Emme to see you," I said while picking up more bamboo to fasten to the sides. "We all thought you drowned."

"Still here," she said with no emotion. But a moment later she asked idly, "Your father . . . did he ever remarry?"

I turned to stone. All I heard were the birds in the trees and the waves at the shore, but both were outmatched by the beating in my own chest.

She didn't know.

"No," I said hesitantly.

She nodded once, as if assured of something. I continued, "Mother, father died four years ago."

Her head snapped up. She looked through me for a minute before resuming with her work.

"I'm sorry to hear that. Was it the Paslkapi?" Still no detectable emotion in her voice.

"Yes. And it was hard losing you both so close together." I wanted to see some emotion in her. "Harder still, learning that Emme carries the disease."

"Emme is sick?" Arabella stilled. Even the wind halted, as if the entire island held its breath to hear news of the ill daughter.

It wasn't news I cared to deliver. "We almost lost her," I went on. "She got one dose of the Elmber Nut before giving the rest to save another's life. If she doesn't return to the Island of Iilak—which we reached, by the way, using the secret passage you told me of—Emme will die."

I couldn't be certain, but I swore there was a slight tremor in Arabella's hand.

"We will save her," she announced. "Or she will save herself. I won't lose my daughter. The three of us are meant to rule the seas together."

It was an image that I'd long wanted as reality myself. Many days as a young lad were spent dreaming of the time when I'd sail with my mother and sister, take on the fearsome foes and discover lost treasures at the bottom of the sea. I'd practiced filling my lungs with air and slowly letting it out time and time again until ready to be dunked into a trough to see how long I could last. Arabella would count behind me then tell me how far I could have gotten in that much time. *"There, you would have reached an old ship. You found a chest in the helm master's quarters and a key underneath. But you hadn't the time to open it. Try again, and maybe this time you'll see what's in the chest."* I'd prepped my lungs then dunked again.

"We can't rule the seas if she's dead," I said bluntly. "Let's get this raft working, and we can save her together." Sweat ran over the collar of my shirt and dripped into my eyes, but Arabella couldn't be convinced to pull the raft under the shade. She kept it here so she could set it in the water occasionally to test it out.

I cupped some of the lapping water in my hands and splashed it over my face. As I did, I hoped the water would send a message to Coral.

I'm here, I told her. *You sent me here, remember? Where are you now?*

Arabella's voice interrupted me. "How much do you love your sister?"

I looked up at the oddity of the question. "With my everything," I answered honestly.

"Then you don't need the Elmber Nut to save her," Arabella said. "I know of another way to heal."

"How?" I asked. I searched my memories through the stories she'd fed us as children, looking for mentions of healing tonic. She'd never even mentioned the Elmber Nut. Most of her stories entailed killing, not saving. Her philosophy was if you've found a magic strong enough to save the dying, keep the magic and let them die. A magic powerful enough to hold a soul against the Fates desire is worth more than the soul.

It made sense in a self-serving world. I'd lose myself before I lost my sister.

"It's not a pleasant method," she continued.

"None of yours ever are."

She smiled like that pleased her. "She must wash her hands in the blood of someone who loves her more than anything."

I almost fell into the water. "That's . . ."

"Effective."

"I was going to say horrifying. She has to kill someone she loves?"

"No, she must wash her hands in their blood. Literally. If you love her more than you love anything or anyone else, then spill some of your blood into a bowl and let her run her hands through it. The love pulls out the sickness."

It wasn't pretty, but it was an answer. But doubt latched onto my heart like an anchor.

I stared over the water, letting my thoughts drift to Coral, who was going to lead me to a grand adventure beneath the seas. What if I loved her more than Emme? The love for a sister could only go so far.

"You look like death yourself, boy. Is that not the answer you seek?"

"It is," I said too quickly. "It'll work. I've always loved my sister."

Arabella didn't press. She nodded as if it was as good as done and returned to the raft.

But I remained rooted in the sand.

My father had been sick before Arabella left us. It wasn't terrible, at the time, but she had to have known where his illness would lead him.

I turned, almost afraid to ask. "You didn't save father."

Her lips tightened, but she didn't speak.

The heat inside me had nothing to do with the sun, now. "You knew he would die," my voice shook, "All it would have taken was a bit of your blood. Why didn't you save him?"

She tilted her head back and merely looked at me. The answer hit me with such a force that I stepped back.

"You loved the sea more than him. More than anything. Your blood wouldn't have worked."

She collected her hair back from her face and returned to her work. "I'm sorry about your father. I'd hoped he would survive."

For years I'd thought her strong. I'd claimed my mother was a warrior, a fighter who let nothing break her armor. But I'd failed to see when her armor morphed into indifference, and she'd stopped caring about anything at all. Perhaps she never had.

Now I saw the strength in Emme and how she opened herself up to the world. Her heart for others would take her further than Arabella's cutlass could ever do. Her love could have saved father.

I knelt in the sand across from her. "I finish this raft for Emme, not for you. You don't deserve a life off this island."

Arabella kept working. "As long as we get off this island, I don't care who you've done it for."

9

EMME

Ontario faced the ocean as Landon and Arn stood flanked on either side of him. He flexed his fingers. "How does a cousin of royalty come to be a pirate?"

"Distant cousin," Landon corrected. It wasn't hard to picture him as nobility. He carried the darker tan skin of Julinbor, along with the thick brows and lashes, and a wide jaw that was so coveted here. If he put on a brocade vest and pointed shoes, he'd fool anyone into believing he was a prince. I ought to have realized he wasn't from Lemondey with Arn, where their skin was pale and their hair stained by the sun.

Landon rested his back against the side of the ship as he told his tale. From across the deck, Tess listening eagerly. "My mother was romanticized by the idea of a life in a small cottage with a good man. She settled for my father. But she held onto her connections to the castle, often taking me on visits, which was how she convinced officers to allow lanky things like Arn and me a position in the navy." He glanced to Arn as if expecting appreciation of thanks. When he got none, he went on. "My mother still gets invitations to the castle, and I've no doubt she'll be invited to the Winter Night. It's the King and Queen's 40th anniversary this year, so it ought to be a big one."

"Good," Arn said. "Lots of people and exhausted guards who won't check invites properly."

Landon nodded. "Exactly."

I found a barrel of gunpowder to sit on as my legs failed to keep me balanced now that the *Royal Rose* had fallen into its rhythm over the gentle waves. Night had settled around us like a dark blanket coating the sky, and Bo lit the oil lantern to hang it near the helm. It swung back and forth with a creak that filled the silences between us.

I tried not to notice how Tess settled on a crate as far away from me as possible. I pinched the wolfsbane pin in my pocket and shifted my gaze from her.

"His knowledge of the castle will be useful," Arn was telling Ontario.

"I'm also an experienced sailor," Landon added. Arn gave his head a brief shake, and Landon quieted.

Bishop, Timmons, and Collins were cleaning fish on deck with set expressions to let us know of their displeasure at Landon's presence, while the rest of the crew who weren't familiar with Landon whispered between themselves and tried to glean information.

Ontario took his eyes from the sea to direct Bo to turn a few degrees east. He ran his hand over the shaved sides of his head. "That'd be one invitation. The castle will be layered with guards, so we aren't sneaking in. We'll need more invitations."

"I know exactly how to get those," Landon said.

Ontario looked at him. "What's in it for you?"

Landon shrugged while gliding his gaze over the *Royal Rose*. "I need a new crew. This one will do."

Bishop had been quiet so far, but now he slammed his foot down. "Absolutely not." He jabbed a finger in Landon's direction. "I'm not sailing with that murderer."

"It was a fair battle," Landon said, showing the first signs of unease. "I lost many as well."

"You played dirty." Bishop gripped his fillet knife so tight that the muscles in his forearm flexed. "It was savage, and you know it. There was no honor there."

The crew's whispers fell to tight-lipped stares as Timmons placed a hand on Bishop's arm. "I'm with Bishop," he said. "Landon can't join us."

Arn and Ontario looked to each other. It was nice to see them united on one front, even if Landon had to be the one to do that.

"We need him to get into the castle," Arn reminded us.

"We'll find a way," Ontario said. "Frankly, I don't care whose cousin he is. He could be mine. I'd still rather skin him and throw him to the fish. He doesn't sail with us."

"Do it," Landon said. "Throw me into the sea. You'll never get those invitations without me, and you'll never find your way around the castle without getting caught by guards."

Arn held up his hand and glared at Landon. "For once in your life, be quiet and let me handle this." The urgency in his tone was enough to make Landon stop. Arn took a breath before speaking in a lower voice to Ontario. "We may find another way, but it won't be an easy one. I need to get to the king fast."

Ontario glanced to me and lowered his voice, but not enough that I didn't catch his words. "Are you forgetting what that scoundrel did to us? I'd rather run him through with my cutlass a thousand times than let him live. I'd rather run myself through."

Arn was still a moment before the quiet words came. "It's for Emme." He shucked off his navy jacket to roll it in a ball and tuck it under his arm. Now he looked more like the pirate I was fond of. Almost. His shoulders sagged like they held an unbearable weight. He ran a hand through his loose hair with a heavy sigh. "I don't care for the man any more than you do. But I care for my girl. This is for her."

"What's in it for me?" Ontario wanted to know.

It was only because I knew Arn so well that I caught how his response snagged in his throat as if spoken with great reluctance. But I never would have predicted his next words. "Do this, and I'll never ask for my position back as captain. You get the respect you want, and Emme lives."

I pushed off the splintered rim of the barrel to reach for Arn. "Don't."

He didn't acknowledge me. "Do we have a deal?"

Ontario's eyes brightened, and I knew the battle was won. But instead of agreeing right away, he laced his fingers around the hilt of his cutlass and faced the crew. "A good captain seeks the council of his crew to gain their camaraderie," Ontario said. "You tried to teach me that. What do you say, mates? We've already lost so many. Do we let our pride drive us to forfeit the life of one more?"

I tried not to let my spirit dampen at the painfully long pause that followed as Bishop, Timmons, and Collins huddled together. After a few hesitant nods, they pulled apart. "Aye, he can stay for Emme's sake."

Arn exhaled. "Thank you."

"Don't thank anyone yet," Ontario said. In a quick motion, he pulled out his cutlass and buried the tip of the blade against Landon's neck. Landon went rigid and his eyes widened.

Arn jumped to intervene. "Don't kill him."

"Not your ship," Ontario said. "You don't make the calls. As for you"—a drop of blood ran down Landon's neck—"I've been around enough lying pirates to know one. You tell us why you want aboard our ship, then I'll think about letting you stay."

Landon's words were choppy. "I need a new crew."

"Lies." Ontario didn't put his cutlass away. I couldn't see his face, but Landon's was frightened enough that I had no trouble picturing the triumph on Ontario's.

"I think I'll start by hanging you upside down from the

crow's nest for three days," Ontario said. "If the hunger doesn't kill you, I'll move you to the edge of the ship, letting you hang close enough to the waves that you think you can breathe, but every time you suck in air, the water fills your nose, slowly drowning you as you frantically try to survive. All we'll hear are your desperate pleas until Sea King Valian takes mercy on you and ends your life." As Landon paled, Ontario shrugged. "Or you could tell us the truth. Why our ship?"

"Fine," Landon growled. "I seek the Caster."

Ontario's blade dropped. "Who?"

Landon took a gulp of air. "The Caster. They say she is only a child, forever bound to her youth as life itself bends to her will. She has a unique set of skills, but none so wonderful as her ability to create new identities."

Ontario shot a glance at Arn.

"She gives you a new name?" Arn asked.

"More. She takes away the old one. You could walk up to your own father and he wouldn't know you from the boy who delivers bread in the morning."

Arn blinked, while Ontario pressed. "What good is that to you?"

"Plenty," Landon said with a frown. "After losing the treasure to you and many of my own mates on that island, I've been branded an insolent fool who has no business running a ship. But with a new identity, that goes away."

"It's a lie you can't get caught in," Arn mused. "No one would know."

"Precisely. I get you to the king, and I get a new name."

After a pause, Ontario put his cutlass away. "Sounds simple enough." He didn't officially say that Landon could stay, but he might as well have. Landon visibly relaxed.

Ontario went to relieve Bo from his position at the helm, who let go of the wheel with great reluctance. It was hard not to picture Emric there, holding tight to the posts as Arn reminded him who was captain, until Emric threw back his head with a laugh and relented.

I tightened my fingers on the edges of my brother's tunic. "One invitation for me and one for Landon as my guide," I said. "How do we acquire additional ones?"

Landon looked me up and down. Despite how hard I tried to keep myself still, I'd never be able to control my hands from shaking. Landon studied the movement. "I'm not certain you should go at all."

"I have to. I can't ask someone else to do this for me."

"If you can walk from one end of the ship to the other without stumbling, then fine."

"That's not up to you," I said to cover the fact that I couldn't do that.

Landon unbuttoned his jacket and rolled up his sleeves, making himself look at home on the ship. He even yanked on the riggings. "While I'm curious why you need to get to the king so desperately . . ." He paused to glance at Arn, then Ontario. Neither offered an answer. "I think it'd be best if another went. Still, I have a way for us to get a few more invitations. The Sea Gala."

The sail cracked against the sharp wind that followed as Landon looked at us as if we ought to know what that meant. Finally, Arn sighed. "I'll bite. What gala?"

"Did you learn nothing from those men in Arger's cells?" Landon appeared pleased that Arn had to ask. "There is to be a gala outside Kvas to mark the coming of Winter Night. All we need is to attend, cozy up to nobility, and be offered invitations to Winter Night rightfully."

"And how long until Winter Night?"

"Ten days."

Arn shook his head. "That's too long." He glanced to me, but despite my hopeful smile, he repeated, "It's too long."

I spoke up. "I can make it." But I knew we were thinking the same thing. Even if I made it to Winter Night, that only fulfilled my oathbinding. I still needed to return to the Island of Iilak. At best it'd be an additional month for that, and that would be a harder journey to survive.

In that one moment, Arn looked like a lost boy on the seas, tossed by every wind and clueless on where to turn. It was the same feeling I had.

But I repeated my words with more confidence. "I'll make it."

"I'll go as fast as I can, mate," Ontario assured.

"You better, because if she dies, I'm fighting for my ship back."

Landon glanced between us. "I have so many questions."

"You'll get nothing from us," Arn said shortly.

"Fine. Where's the galley on this ship?" Landon asked, poking around the deck until finding the hatch. He swung it upward. "I'm famished." He descended the ladder leading belowdecks, where we heard him greet the other crew members as "a new mate."

Clarice and Tess were still above deck. I'd leave it to them to fill the others in on how we felt about Landon. I think we all breathed a little easier now that he was gone.

Arn came to me. "How are you?"

"I'm okay. How did things go in the cells?"

"Could have been better." He rested against the rails and said in a low voice, "I don't trust him."

"I don't think anyone does."

"He's lying to us. He plans to retake his old ship, just with a new identity." His eyes were stormy blue and focused on the hatch, and his hand fussed with his navy jacket restlessly.

"That's good," I said. "It means he will only be here a short time. Why do you not look happy about that?"

His eyes were fixed on mine. "Because I plan to take his ship too."

My breath caught in my throat. "It's practical," his words

came quickly. "This crew sees me as a liar, and Landon's crew is likely scrambling with the loss of their captain. They'll be prime for the taking." His attention turned to Ontario now, standing at the helm, focused on the dark waves ahead of us. "And someday, when I rebuild that crew to be strong enough, I will retake this one."

I had no right to feel abandoned, but a part of me had hoped that when I left the crew, Arn would come with me. Or I'd hoped that if I chose to stay, Arn would be here too. But I could never join the crew that'd killed ours. The *Dancer* would forever feel stained with their blood.

The words sucked the air out of my belly. "If that's what you want."

He glanced at me. "I'd never ask you to come with me."

Not asking me was worse than asking. It meant when he looked to the future, I wasn't there.

But it was fair, because I'd made myself clear. "I don't want to stay on a pirate ship," I said. "All I think of here is death."

He worried over his lip, and it was impossible not to feel like we were caught in something that had no resolution. We were trapped in this space that fit the both of us for now, but it was growing smaller, and one day one of us would tip out. He'd drive himself further out to sea, or I'd seal myself on land. And I feared we could never recreate a place where we'd both fit together again.

His words only cemented that. "I know. But I don't see myself on land." He went past me, but I kept staring at the sea that Arn loved so much. The waves rolled past to catch the light with rainbows of colors, but as hard as I tried to love them, all I saw were my brother and mother's bodies somewhere beneath them.

Being here felt like sailing on their graves.

"I can't love the thing that killed you," I whispered to them. *And I've no right to ask him to choose me.*

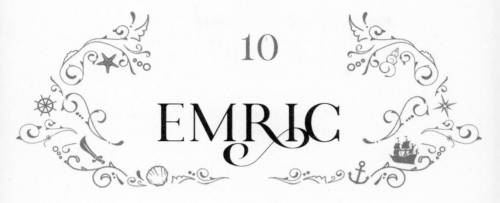

10

EMRIC

I rested my tired body in the shade of the hut, while watching the sea. It must have been torture for Arabella to sit here every day on this worn-out log, watching the dancing waves while stuck ashore. It'd only been a week and I was miserable.

That misery propelled me to work harder, and we'd made progress on the raft. It still wasn't ideal, but it was almost complete.

Arabella picked at the fire, feeding it more wood. Water boiled above it as we'd make clean water, then cook dinner.

"I can take the spear out and try to get more fish," I called out.

"No, save your strength. I don't want the sea to infect your wound."

"It'll taste the sea as soon as we take that raft out. If it's going to get infected, that'll happen either way."

She shot me a look. "I'll get us fish on my own." She stabbed her cutlass into the ground, picked up the spear, and made for the sea. She could hold her breath for much longer than I could, a fact I discovered while watching her fish. Many times I thought she'd be close to drowning, but she always came up again.

She could handle herself. I ought to know that by now.

I circled the hut, looking for other ways to be useful. Arabella didn't have much here, only whatever had been on her when she'd arrived years ago and the few things she'd created since then. Dry clay formed into a plate. Sticks whittled into utensils. A chain locket with two *e*'s carved into it.

Behind a cup of wild berries sat an object I didn't recognize, one that appeared to glow in the shadows of the hut like a silver fire holding onto its dying embers. I reached for it. The edges were rough, but it was small enough to fit into the palm of my hand. Once there, the brilliant colors dulled to reveal an ordinary white shell with hints of pink curling around its base.

It was pretty, and that's what made me examine it further. Mother didn't keep pretty things with no purpose.

I tried to picture her casually strolling the beach, discovering a shell and keeping it because of how beautiful it looked. No matter how hard I tried, the image didn't fit. It served a purpose, and I wanted to know what it was.

Perhaps this shell was a gift she couldn't bear to part with, caring enough to have grabbed it before her ship went down. She wasn't often one for sentiments. The only reason she had the locket with my initial on it was because it was always strung around her neck. If she started to sink, she wouldn't waste time grabbing anything that wasn't on her.

I turned the shell between my hands while settling into the cot.

I was still there when Arabella came back an hour later with three coastal fish in hand.

She settled at the mouth of the hut, pulled out a knife, and scraped the largest one from tail to head, peeling off the scales. They collected at her feet along with a pool of seawater.

"What is this?" I held the shell up.

"Put that back," she ordered.

"But what is it?"

"I said, put it back."

The intrigue grew. I ignored her demand. "Is it a special memento of sorts?"

The knife twisted between her fingers. "It's bold of you to defy your mother while she holds a blade in her hand."

My heart skipped a beat, but she grinned. Whether her grin was to show me she jested, or to declare delight at my fear, I could only guess.

I shifted back.

"It's pretty. Prettiest thing you've got in this pitiful excuse for a hut."

She glared.

Pain burned on my side as I stood, but it wasn't as unbearable as yesterday. I hardly felt it as I moved out of the shade to stand at her side. "Which is why I'm so curious about it. Tell me, does it carry the final words of those you've slayed?"

"I wish." I winced as she gutted the fish as she spoke. "But no, what this does is far more practical." She looked at me with hesitancy before relenting. "I speak the name of one I wish to communicate with into it, and it allows me a conversation with them."

The words were punctuated with the scrap of her knife as the full force of what she'd said hit me.

The shell weighed heavier in my hands now that I knew it's importance. It sent a sick feeling wrapping its way through my body. "Anybody you'd like? No matter where they are?"

"Correct. It cost me more than you can imagine, so put it back. And do it carefully."

Instead, I dropped it in the sand at her feet. Her blade froze as she stared frostily at me.

But there was fury in my own eyes as I enunciated each word clearly. "And yet, you never communicated with me."

She only tilted her head to the side and said in the most condescending voice, "Now, Emric."

"I thought you were dead. For five years I believed that my

mother had drowned at sea. And when I was on my own on Norwa, begging for scraps to eat and taking on the lowest of jobs just to get by because my father was in the ground and my mother was in the sea, you were here the entire time, and you could have spoken to me. You could have let us know you were alive."

I'd known she was cruel. Oftentimes, she was that way on purpose. But I'd never really been on the receiving end of her heartlessness. She didn't care that she could have spared us from pain.

"Me, Emme, Father. You abandoned us all."

"What would you have done, Emric?" she chided. "This shell can only be used once. One chance to communicate with someone. So I ask again, what would you have done? You couldn't save me."

Knowing she could only use it once did put a different spin on it. But five years later and it still sat here, while she'd built thirteen rafts. She couldn't be planning on communicating with anyone to come rescue her.

"Father would have done anything to save you. Instead, his heartbreak sped up his disease and drove him to his death."

She scaled the second fish. "He knew nothing of the sea. He was useless to me. When I use that shell, it'll be for good purpose."

It was as if I were seeing my mother for the first time, the way that so many others must have seen her. Arabella the Ruthless. More in love with the sea than her family.

The anger in me was as strong as my disappointment, and I turned away before she could say something further.

My feet punched into the sand, leaving frustrated footsteps as a trail.

"You can't let yourself stay mad for long," Arabella called after me. "The raft will be done tomorrow, and then we free ourselves."

11
ARN

Everywhere I turned, there was either Ontario or Landon, so I was left sifting through the cracks between them, trying to keep my head down. I'd found some solace in the crew's cabins, but any quiet the room offered was accompanied by the reminder that I was stuck in this cramped space instead of the finer captain's quarters. The cots were hard, and the planks above creaked with any movement. I had gladly given up the finery earlier for Emme, but now she was here with me.

She groaned as she woke from a nap. It was as close to complaining as she'd ever get.

I sat near the door with school books on my lap, studying the mess of Tess's writing as she had attempted pages of arithmetic that she claimed she'd never need to use. Tess was on her cot, reading a book, but the page hadn't turned in a while, and I suspected her of being asleep. I closed the school book as Emme stretched.

"Sleep any better than yesterday?" I asked.

She let her hair loose and ran her fingers through it. "I can't tell if this ache is from the bed or my disease."

"I'll steal the good blankets from Ontario's quarters for tonight."

"Please don't." But there was hesitation in her tone. I

determined to do it. Emme got down and knelt on the floor, returning to her work of picking through old ropes. It wasn't a complicated task, but with how bad her hands shook, it wasn't easy to watch.

"What will we do once you're healed?"

She stilled, until I doubted she'd even heard the question or had any intention of answering. Her grip adjusted on the ropes before she looked up at me. "I don't know. I'm trying not to get my hopes up."

"That's a horrible way to live."

"It's practical."

"It's morbid. Seriously, what would you want to do next? Do you plan to return to the sheep farm?"

She twisted her fingers around the thick rope. "The sheep farm feels like a dream at this point. Something that wasn't meant to be mine. But I still want it, as foolish as I feel for that."

Tess stirred on her cot, and I spoke more quietly. "That's not foolish at all. It was your home, it's a part of you, and you'd make an excellent sheep farmer. I'd buy wool from you every day."

The faintest smile touched her lips. "You'd be disappointed. We don't have wool to sell every single day. But thank you." As she ran her hands along the length of more rope, her eyes went to me. "I don't want a life without you," she said softly

"You won't, love. I'm as solid about us as the water beneath this ship."

She leaned toward me. "Would you give up being a pirate? Could you see yourself on a sheep farm?"

I couldn't, but I wasn't about to say that right after claiming to be as steady as the sea itself. "It's an . . . interesting picture. If any of the sheep get feisty, I might duel them. Perhaps spar with a tree or two. But there's something nice about the idea that excites me."

She didn't look convinced. "You'd let Ontario keep the *Royal Rose*?"

"No. I will most definitely be dragging that all the way to the farm with me. That ship is mine."

There was a gleam in her eye. "The ship that you stole from someone else?"

"It's been years. His claim has expired. It's mine, and I'm attached."

She smiled, and that was all I needed. She'd been too downcast recently, worrying herself over what would come that she hadn't smiled in ever so long. Even if this trip led to her death, I would do all I could to give her happiness before she went. It wasn't much, but I could grant her that. "Give me a few more years on the sea, then I'll leave them for you."

Her smile fell then, and she stared at her hands.

I came close and dropped my voice even lower. "We could be like we were before when you worked at The Banished Gentleman and I visited when my ship came to port."

Her reply was toneless. "My father did that with my mother—waiting for her to have time for him. I won't be like them."

My throat was dry, and my words felt like stones in my throat. "I promise I'll leave the seas for you someday. Are you asking me to leave now?"

A lock of her hair fell over her face, and she took her time to tuck it behind her ear. She smiled sadly. "I feel lost, Arn. I feel like I'm hardly here, and I don't know if I should be preparing for my death or what I'd want if I lived. But you?" She reached for my hand. Her fingers were like ice. "You have been my one constant. And yet I'm terrified that one day the choice will come and you won't pick a life with me."

"I'll always choose you."

"You aren't ready to choose me now. How do I know you'll choose me then?"

Her words were like a punch to my gut. "I promise you. I promise I'll be there for you."

She studied me for a while, and I kept my unwavering gaze on her. I hoped she found reassurance there, because I did know that I'd give up the seas one day for her. This girl was my future. It'd kill me if she didn't always know how much she meant to me. I tightened my hold on her hand. "I'd die for you, Emme. Stars, I'd oathbind myself to you to show you how much I care."

"You'd be a fool to do that," she said. But when she turned her face away, the frown had lessened. She went back to her stretching, until her fingers grazed her toes, and wincing as she used her other hand to massage her leg. It was the same ritual she went through each morning, claiming it ought to help slow the disease or keep her balance. Soon she'd switch to do the other leg, then practice standing on each foot as the ship rocked, but she was hardly able to do so without holding something for more than a few breaths.

If this was slowing the disease, I'd hate to see how fast it progressed without the exercises.

"Here." I moved behind her and collected her thick hair to tuck it over her shoulder and rub her back to soothe out the muscles. I couldn't do anything to help with the Paslkapi, but sailing was hard on everyone's body, dying or not. "The first year was hard on me too. I used to walk crooked, but it gets better over time." I kneaded into the ridges of her skin until the knots loosened, moving my way across her shoulders and to the base of her neck.

From the holes in the tunic came glimpses of the octopus tattoo, a grand thing that wrapped around her entire back, to her neck, and circled her arm. Serena had given her that tattoo, along with her others and the oathbinding. Every mark Emme wore on her skin was from the banished mermaid, but she was still untouched by scars as a pirate. But there were scars, unseen ones from losing her mother, then her father, and, more recently, her brother.

Her fingers went to her arm, where my favorite tattoo was. It showed the night we'd stood on deck, the first time it felt like she was a real part of this crew, and watched as the stars fell from the sky to touch the seas.

I'd felt a high that night, and I'd been chasing it ever since. The idea that she loved the seas and would sail them with me. We could visit all the islands, live off papayas and fish, find treasures unknown.

I worked my fingers down. She had seemed so alive that night, back when I'd mistaken her stumbling for sea legs, and I'd sworn she'd wanted this too. But then flashes of the next few weeks sliced through my mind.

Her fright as her mind was haunted.

The slaughter of our crew on the island.

Her brother's figure sinking in the sea.

The echo of the gun as she shot Admiral Bones.

It was no wonder that any love she had for sailing was stripped away as those memories burned themselves into her mind.

"Thank you," Emme whispered. "I feel better already."

"That's what I'm here for."

She threaded her arms through her coat as the sun rose further over the sea, pulling through the porthole and trapping itself in her hair. "Eleven more days," she said as she glanced outside. "Ten more days until Winter Night. I hope Landon is true to his word. He could easily ruin this all."

"If there is one thing we can bet on, it's Landon's desire to get to the castle too. We'll get there. The king is as good as dead."

As if summoned by the sound of his name, Landon came through the door at that moment to strip off his jacket and throw the damp thing on his cot. He'd worked the ship through the night, and the weariness of it hung in the darkness under his eyes. As he took his blanket to dry his hair, the casualness of him reminded me of when we used to sail together, as if the years hadn't changed a thing between us. Now he even brought extra apples with him, which he tossed to both Emme and me.

"That's right he is," he said boldly. "The reign of the crooked king will end."

Emme rubbed her thumb against the apple. "Tell me something, what do you two hold against King Unid?"

I shot a glance at Landon as he paused with the blanket over his hair. I'd made it five years with Emme blindly accepting my hatred for the king without raising the question. And while it might be a story Landon felt free to tell, I'd never reshared what happened.

But with how Landon paid extra care to roll his blanket and keep his eyes from Emme, I guessed he didn't talk openly about it either.

I made a decision. "I'll tell you, but you might be sorry you asked. It's a tale sadder than you can imagine."

She cocked her head. "My curiosity grows."

Now that I thought of it, I should have told her the story as soon as she found out we had to have the head of King Unid. It'd make our task easier to stomach knowing what sort of man he was. She'd only ever known him as the king who opened trade ports and ended the thirteen-year war.

But Landon and I knew him as more.

I settled with my back to the cot. "Before the end of the war, Landon and I finished our training and were assigned to the same company. We were sent on a mission to Az Elo to deliver cargo, at least that's all the captain told us."

"He was always a shady guy," Landon interjected.

"This cargo was meant to be the peace offering that united our countries and ended the war. We didn't mind the secrecy; we were just elated to be traveling to Az Elo. The adventure grew when one month in, we were attacked by pirates." That part was easy to call on as I shut my eyes, still hearing the first shot in the dark that echoed in our ears. The deck had turned from drinking games to a scramble to gather weapons and load pistols, peering through the fog hung over the deck. I'd trained before, but that night I got my first taste of real battle. I hated it.

"Who was the pirate?"

"Nathan Orvensen," Landon and I said together.

"You wouldn't recognize the name," I told Emme, "but I sparred with him during the battle before he gave himself up to save the lives of his crew." It was lucky his crew wasn't faring well, because another few moments and he would have run me through. "The deal was they were to go free. Instead, my captain took them all and strung their ship behind his like a prize, even though it slowed us down. He kept the pirates belowdecks like rats with scraps for food. Landon and I, of course, were fascinated by them and often volunteered to be their watch. And these pirates, they told us a story of a girl whom Nathen loved that was taken. They said they attacked us trying to rescue her."

"But we had no girl on board," Landon added. "None that we knew. So we ignored them."

Emme took a bite of her apple. I noticed Tess was awake and propped up on her elbows to listen as I went on.

"Then, on a night so stormy that the moon was hidden, Landon and I snuck into the captain's quarters to search for extra blankets. That's where he'd kept the mysterious cargo we were delivering to Az Elo, and we discovered what the cargo was."

I waited for Emme to piece it together. Her eyes widened. "The girl?"

I nodded. "She was in a box in his quarters and had been

the entire time. She looked wretched, and she begged us to free her."

Emme was horrified. "And, of course, you did."

Landon and I looked at each other, and we were transported back to that moment—the girl's hair matted against her tear-soaked cheeks and her cracking voice as she reached desperately for us through the slats. We were the first people she'd seen other than our captain in weeks, and the inside of the box was streaked with long marks where she'd tried to claw herself free.

We could have been her heroes.

I stared past Emme, then hung my head. "No," I said dully. "We left her there."

Emme gasped, and I realized she thought me to be a stand-up man who rescued every damsel in distress. I felt sick.

"She was the key to end a war," Landon was trying to explain. "We thought it was the right thing to do. She was the daughter of King Unid and was being offered to the king of Az Elo as a bride to bring peace to the seas."

We chose the end of the war over that girl. I'd never seen a lass weep as hard as she did as she cried out to us for freedom. Instead, Landon and I had left, closing the door behind us.

I couldn't look at Emme as I continued, "But we fed her often and delivered notes from Nathen. You can't imagine how badly I wanted to go back and free her, but we were to be the company who ended the war. We had a way to end the battles without another death, and I thought surely that was worth it." I closed my eyes against the memory, and Landon finished the tale for me.

"Our own captain found us sneaking in one day and chastised us for being fools. It turned out the king's deception went further than his daughter knew. He wasn't sending her to marry the king. She was a sacrifice."

Emme's eyes bulged. "*What*?"

Landon shook his head. "They do things differently in Az Elo. Not a friendly place."

"Why would King Unid do that?"

"That was the first thing out of my mouth too," I said. "And do you know what the captain answered? 'Sometimes during war, sacrifices are made.' Landon and I had been the only ones aboard who didn't know the mission, because the captain thought us too soft."

Landon's jaw clenched at that part. No one would think that about us now.

"That was when we decided to rescue the girl. But our captain wouldn't let her go. He said it wouldn't matter if she died here or on Az Elo, and he was suspicious of mutiny, so he took out his pistol and killed her."

It had been the most traumatic thing I'd witnessed up to that point, only to be outmatched by half my crew dying on the Island of Iilak. The blame I'd placed on myself was immeasurable. I glanced at Emme's face and hesitated before going on with the story.

Landon continued it instead, "The captain sent us to our cots with harsh reprimands." He shifted. "But we went right down to the pirates and freed them all. Then we killed the captain and company and burned down the ship. We sailed away on the pirate's vessel instead and joined their crew. Though," he added, "it was a mercy that Nathen let us live at all after we brought about the death of the one he loved."

For a moment our eyes met. "We both became pirates that day," I said.

That was my story: a king trying to end a war, a captain trying to obey his king, and me—desiring to do the right thing and only bringing destruction.

The wind picked up outside, whistling through the cracks in the boards, and my words were almost lost in it. "That is why I despise the king. He is a man who would kill his own daughter to win a war. I may be a pirate, but a man like that truly has no morals."

Emme was staring at her apple. "That'll make capturing him easier."

"You won't do it."

Her eyes snapped up. "What?"

"Ambush the king? It won't be you. When the time comes, it'll be me who takes him and delivers him to Serena."

"You don't have to do that for me," Emme said.

"I'm already corrupt, love. Let me be the darkness for you, while you remain my light."

She smiled, and everything I would do was worth it to receive a smile like that.

Tess rolled out of her cot. "If you two were such good friends, what happened?"

I uttered a short laugh. "This is another fun story. Would you like to explain, Landon?"

He looked up from the old dagger he'd been cleaning. Ontario must have lent it to him since it was a blade I'd once given Ontario to celebrate the first week on our own ship. "I don't think I will," he said blithely. "You seem bitter still."

"Landon betrayed Arn, and they don't like to talk about it," Emme said matter-of-factly.

"Betrayed?" Landon snorted. "Is that how the story goes? You never would have been half the captain you became without me pushing you to be your own man."

I stood. "I'll speak of it no more. Let the past die. I care only for the next few months."

"Fine," Landon agreed, but he looked around. "But who would have thought we'd end up sailing under the same flag again."

I'd rather endure Ontario's prickly silence than Landon's cocky tongue.

"Just for a month, mate. Let us not forget that."

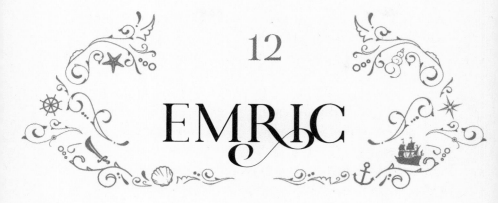

12

EMRIC

Arabella took only the shell, a dollop of salve wrapped in leaves, and the weapons in her belt as we loaded the raft. I had no belongings other than my cutlass and the bloodstained clothes on my back, but I packed some cooked fish and chips of coconut in her bag to fasten to the corner of the raft.

She nodded once. "Let's go."

She didn't look back. The morning sun shrouded the beach in orange that caught on the ends of her hair, matching the fire in her eyes as she marched to the raft. We'd finished yesterday then went to bed early to prepare for today, though I'd stayed awake with anticipation until the moon was high.

As soon as slivers of light had broken the night sky, Arabella was up. "Get up boy," she'd said. "Today we rid of this place."

We now pushed the raft as far into the water as we could before climbing aboard.

"Fair skies," I observed. "And calm waters."

An optimal day for taking a questionable raft out to sea. We'd kept an eye on the weather all yesterday as we worked. *Fair skies, calm waters. Maybe we have a chance.*

"Turn the sail slightly," she ordered a minute into sailing. "The wind is shifting."

I untied the sail and adjusted it according to her instructions.

It plumed out with the direct wind behind it, pulling us westward. Ideally toward land. Possibly toward nothing.

Mist from the sea flitted across my arms as I held the rudder. It was a sensation I'd missed—feeling the sea greet me. As if welcoming us home.

"Lead us well," I said to it. "Lead us to Emme."

We heaved our oars through the water, bringing us further into the vast, blue openness. Only when the island was the size of a small rock behind us did Arabella glance back. When she faced forward again, there was a smile on her face.

It was a foreign sight. Even more strange was her hearty laugh. "We've done it. I'm free."

"Not yet," I said. "We still have to find land."

"You ruin the fun."

I indicated up ahead, to where I'd been keeping an eye. "It's those that might ruin the fun."

Giant waves collected along the surface of the water. The raft swayed over the uneven rolls of the sea, and I planted my feet into the planks to keep steady. The swaying turned to rocking, then violent thrashing. I swallowed hard.

The skies had been fair. The seas calm. But now that we'd stepped out into them, they turned on us.

"She'll handle it." Arabella patted the raft. "She'll survive." But her brow creased.

Water hadn't leaked through yet, which was both a good sign and a wonder. The boards were holding, and the sail stayed put. But even the mightiest ships could be brought down by a brutal wave. And the further out we got, the larger they became.

We dropped to the deck and held tight as a wave raised us higher, just to drop us on the other side. Without relief, a second came, and the cycle repeated.

"See, she holds!" Arabella shouted, but I could hardly hear. What I could hear was tinged with uncertainty.

Water splashed up the side and soaked me as the wind whipped salty spray against my face with such force that it felt like cuts.

"The sea is angry with us," I yelled. "It means to kill us."

"Perhaps I'll throw you in to see if that satisfies them."

If I were anyone other than her son, she'd likely try it. I held tight as another wave, the tallest yet, swamped us.

I thought the raft would flip, but somehow we slanted to the other side and stayed upright. The oars shifted, and I shoved them under my feet to keep them from falling out. The mist against my arm no longer felt thrilling. Instead, it came as a warning, the first taste of the water before it enveloped me and I couldn't breathe. Waves reached into the raft from every side, making not drowning our only desire.

Wind howled in our ears, sending us onward to the next crest.

"This will bring us down," I shouted. My words were lost in the air, and my grip on the soaked boards was slipping.

The island knew we'd left. It was bringing us back.

The raft leaned again to the side. I thrusted my weight against it to keep us from rolling over. My force was no match against the might of the sea. It shoved back, sending us into the cold water.

I clamped my mouth tight against the chill. Arabella swam to the raft. I joined her to help flip it upright, but another wave toppled it again, splitting the hull.

My head broke the surface. "It won't work," I sputtered. "We need to rebuild."

"No!" Arabella screamed beside me. "I won't go back there. I will swim the other way if I must."

I kicked to keep afloat. "You'll die if you do that! We must go back!" Saltwater filled my mouth.

She clung to the raft with crooked fingers and wild eyes. Another wave came, lifting us with it and sending a blanket of water over our heads. When we resurfaced, Arabella still gripped the broken raft.

"Go back now," I ordered.

She glared at me, but the fight in her expression started dying.

"I won't lose you twice," I said as I kicked harder and calculated how much strength I had. I needed to start swimming back now if I planned to make it.

It took her five breaths, each more frustrated than the last, to relent. "Catch the other half and use it to swim back."

I swam to the broken raft before it drifted too far away and clutched it under my chest. We still plunged under the water and were chilled to the bone, but now each wave sent us closer to the island.

All our focus went into swimming back to the land we'd left behind. It was cruel of the sea to let us get so far out before rising against us. To give us hope then nearly drown us.

Each bob underwater, I sent out another call to Coral. Before, all I'd needed to do was place my hand in the waves— she'd hear me, and I could sense her. Something in my heart would feel her presence, her warmth somewhere far away, and she'd find me. It was a new sort of magic that thrilled me, but now the connection felt empty. Wherever she was, this island kept her from me.

The sun moved through the sky at a painstakingly slow speed. Each hour, each minute took an eternity. My legs ached, my lungs roared, and my spirits were as damp as my body. And still the island loomed forever away.

"Keep going," Arabella shouted. It was the first thing she'd said since we'd turned back. That was the only encouragement I expected from her.

We kicked as the gray storms faded into brilliant yellows of the day, and kept kicking as those colors threatened to blind us. My lips were chapped and my mouth dry, but I kept my legs moving. It was that or die, and I would not die here.

Just as the sky bled to orange again, we spotted the floor of the sea beneath us. A short while later it met our feet, and we dragged ourselves onto shore.

My hair stuck against my neck as I dropped onto the sand, letting the grains grind against my cold skin as I felt the safety of something that wouldn't move or turn upon me. It was a small comfort, for this was not the land I had hoped to touch. My legs were like heavy stones, unable to move even as the waves licked against my toes. I'd lost my boots somewhere in the ordeal.

Arabella untied her sack from the raft, still attached but drenched. "Curse the Sea King Valian," she hissed.

"We should thank him," I rolled to my back and stared up at the darkening sky. "We are fortunate to be alive."

But she offered no thanks. "The curse of the island, remember? It holds fast to its prisoners, but it won't kill them. We are stuck here a while longer." She threw her bag to the floor, spilling out some of the coconut and the shell. She stomped back to the hut, already working herself into a sour mood.

She'd be delightful company tonight.

I faced the waters once more, sending out a wish. After today, I wasn't sure the sea would grant my wishes, but it owed me one. "Please don't leave me alone for forever with my mother."

Coral was the only one I'd be fine to be stranded with forever. But she was too far away to hear me now.

My gaze pulled down to the shell. Perhaps not.

I peeked for Arabella, who had pushed through the thick overgrowth and must be in the hut by now. She wouldn't come back for her things until morning. I didn't take time to think. I scurried through the sand and collapsed next to the bag.

I scooped the shell into my hands. Arabella might not have had someone to call to save her, but I did.

"Coral," I spoke her name into the shell, ignoring the thought of what Arabella would do when she found out I'd used the one communication the shell allowed. But it would be worth it if it got us off this cursed island. "Coral, please hear me."

Nothing happened. No connection was made, no tingling in my hands, no warmth in my heart at the sense of Coral. The shell lay plainly in my palms, nothing more than a pretty ornament. My heart sank all the way to my feet, and I was just about to throw the useless shell into the ocean. But then it heated in my hand, and the sweetest voice I'd ever heard drifted through.

"I'm here."

13

EMME

Arn must have been quiet entering my blanketed partition because he woke me by waving a plate of mutton and hard cheese under my nose. I pried my eyelids open. The crew's cots were far stiffer than I was used to, and every muscle protested as I eased myself upward.

"Eat," Arn encouraged. "Build your strength. We are discussing plans on deck soon. By discussing, I mean Ontario is ordering us." He went to the door. He wore a loose tunic with stretched-out sleeves and frayed edges. It might have once been white but was now stained a yellow color and heavily wrinkled, since he no longer had a place to hang his clothes.

He cast a glance to Landon's cot. "Try not to wake him," Arn mouthed.

But Landon stirred anyway.

"Sleep well?" Arn's voice was indifferent.

"Well enough," Landon replied.

It was the same dance of words they did each morning like a ritual—never straying from the script. Arn would grunt once after that, then tip his head and walk away. Or it'd be Landon who woke first, and the ritual would be reversed.

But at least they were speaking to each other.

As soon as Arn left, Landon stretched in his cot and sat up. "He didn't bring *me* food," he complained.

"Jenner seems chummy with you," I said dryly. "He'd make you a fine breakfast if you asked." I arched my back and rolled my neck out a few times before starting my morning stretches. I swore I only reached half as far as I did yesterday. My hands barely passed my knees.

When I straightened, Landon was grinning. "You'd rather the crew hated me as much as your pirate does?"

I lowered my chin to my chest and flexed my feet. Even that action hurt. "No. I'd rather you showed remorse for what you did."

He went silent. I glanced up, but he was busy checking his belongings. His black beard grew in choppy patches that twisted over his upper lip, hiding part of his expression from me, but I was fairly certain the only time I'd see that lip quiver was when Ontario had pressed his blade against that man's throat.

Landon was as carefree as a man could be. Arn used to be that way. We all were, once.

As soon as I was content with my stretches, I picked at the food on the plate.

After a few minutes, Landon spoke up. "I lost friends on that island too. If I could go back, I'd play that differently."

"But you'd still play us."

He gave a puff of air through his nose. "I'm still a pirate."

His words echoed those Arn had once said to me in the cabin on deck months ago. *I'm a pirate.* It was a lousy excuse to act however they wanted. I pushed the food away and moved for the door. I could feel Landon's eyes on me.

"Was that Emric's tunic?"

I paused with a hand on the knob and a sharp sting in my chest. It wasn't often that someone spoke his name, and

I hated hearing it in the past tense. It made his death feel more absolute.

"Arn put me on laundry duty," Landon remarked. "Which is how I noticed you haven't worn another tunic in the five days that I've been here. You clean that one on your own."

I checked the shoulder for Emric's scent. It was long gone.

"And you keep sniffing it," Landon observed.

"Please don't speak of my brother." My voice was rough.

Landon ignored my request. "Arn tells me you don't believe he's really dead."

I whirled around. "You are on thin ice, Landon." I shut my eyes tight to refocus myself. I couldn't protect Emric, but it was important to me that Arn was safe. "Are you going to betray Arn again?"

He drew to his full height, which put him close to the splintered rafters. "I couldn't if I tried."

"That's not a lovely answer."

"It's the best one there is. I can't hurt Arn because he cares nothing about me, nor does he trust me. You can't hurt a man who doesn't care."

I studied the dark almond hues of his eyes as they fixated on me, unwavering. There was something misguided in his thinking, but I could hear sincerity in the rumble of his voice. However, he was a pirate and they lied as surely as the waves hit the sand—unavoidable and consistently.

I ducked into the narrow corridor leading to the ladder. Shards of gray seeped through cracks in the board and caught on the dust in the air that I wove through. Ontario's voice came from above as he ordered Timmons to check the storm glass again.

Landon's voice came to me. "He could hurt you, though."

I craned my head over my shoulder to see him in the doorway. "He won't."

"You don't want a life on a pirate ship? Arn won't leave it behind. No matter how sweet the kisses."

I boiled. But I still heard him as I climbed to the deck. "I know him like a brother. He will break your heart in the end. He loves the sea more than anything else."

I tried not to think about Arn's plan of taking over Landon's ship, knowing I didn't care to stay on board. It was hard to picture him leaving the seas for me. More likely, when the time came, I'd be walking away alone.

I stomped up the rings of the ladder.

But a small hope flared. The future was a fickle thing, and none was set in stone. Arn could lose his taste for the waters. Or I might find mine. Either way, I doubted I'd lose my attraction to him or his to me, and that could carry us through the storms.

I came aboard deck to an icy breeze.

The skies were stubborn today. A heavy mist shrouded the air with frigid droplets that reminded us winter approached. Soon it'd be here, the ice collecting along the rails and nipping at our heels when we slept. Today, the sun broke through the wispy clouds. It was as if the air had collectively decided not to harbor any of its warmth, leaving us with damp clothes and cold bodies. The taste of the bitter parts of winter with none of the beauty.

Back home, winter had always meant fires, warm cocoa, and good business as families bought wool for coats. It also meant that Mother would be in town more often as the seas were unfavorable to sail. Father was in his highest spirits then, and it was the season we felt most like a family.

Father would sit in the rocking chair and usher us outside. He'd move only enough to collect his brewing tea then perch himself by the lull of the fire once more. "Enjoy it until the seasons change. Because they always change," was his way of saying that all things come to an end.

I always thought him to be a bit of a hermit. Now I understood that the cold hurt his bones, and the freezing weather made him more stiff than usual.

Until the seasons change. Enjoy it, because I no longer can.

I wrapped my arms around myself and searched the deck for Arn. He was in the cabin, turning through books with Bishop. Bishop frowned at the pages, but Arn gestured at them in animation. When he glanced up, he caught my eye and grinned.

"He won't leave this." Landon had come up the ladder behind me.

"Please leave me be."

When I looked back, he'd gone to the riggings to busy himself. Tess scurried to his side, having decided that he had the most exciting stories as a pirate. When he left the crew after this mission, she'd undoubtedly ask to go with him.

"Storm won't be coming until tonight, I'd guess," Timmons said as he inspected the storm glass.

"We'll be at land by then," Ontario replied. The cold had turned his voice raspy, and he coughed before calling us near the helm.

Arn and Bishop came from the cabin to peer up at Ontario.

"One week until Winter Night. Five days until the Sea Gala. We need to be in Kvas that night, so I don't want to risk going to Lemondey to get the invitation from Landon's home. It's a too-narrow window of time."

"That's fine," Arn said.

"Scared you'll see your father?"

Arn brushed aside the prod. "I have a healthy fear of him and his belt. I'm never too old for him to whip me into shape."

Behind me, Landon leaned to whisper to Clarice. "His father would sooner bake him scones than whip him." Clarice didn't reply, but Arn overheard.

"You'd be scared of your father too."

"My father would whip us both," Landon admitted. "I tend to stay away from that man."

"We get it," Ontario said impatiently. "We all had fathers who weren't proud of us. Let's prove them wrong when we infiltrate the castle and single-handedly bring chaos to the monarchy."

Every father's dream for their child.

A chill swept up my arms at what my own father would think of this. I shook the thought away.

"We need supplies from somewhere though, so we stop at Gillen Port in two days," Ontario went on. "Then we move to the Sea Gala outside Kvas, where we gather as many invites as we can. These make it that much easier to get into the castle and find the king. Every invitation possible gives us one more person to bring to Winter Night, and one more chance to take out King Unid."

My father would hate this.

"What then?" Landon asked. "What do you do once you have his head?"

"Emme needs it," Tess blurted.

Landon's attention swung to me. "What does the sweet lass want with the king's head?"

Serena had warned us that others sought the head of the king. If I was to fulfill my oathbinding and get it to her, we needed to be quick, and Arn, Ontario, and I had decided that discretion was best. Arn and I had avoided letting Ontario in on our real plan. And by *discretion*, we'd meant not telling Tess. It appeared she'd heard anyway.

"You focus on getting to the Caster," was Arn's response. He propped the door to the cabin open with his foot and gestured for Bishop to go back inside.

"Does everyone understand what to do?" Ontario called over us.

Most nodded and drifted away, but Landon stayed. "I've

become quite curious. What does a band of thieves and sailors want in all this? I know Sea King Valian has offered a favor in reward for anyone who brings him the king's head. But I suspect half the seas are seeking him."

Arn's face froze. Bishop's eyes bulged. Even Tess stilled, and that child was always in motion. Only Ontario remained unfazed, besides the slight purse of his lips.

He knew. I checked to see if Arn noticed, but his eyes were elsewhere.

"That is why we are making haste," Ontario informed us. "And why you will speak of our plan to no one. We don't need others racing against us. Again." He gave Landon a knowing look. The last time we'd raced against a crew for a prize, we'd lost half our men. Ontario gestured for Timmons to take over the wheel so he could rest before we made land. "Remember," he warned Landon in passing, "if you're on our crew, you'll act like it. Speak of our mission to no one."

Landon waited until Ontario disappeared to give me another look. "What do you want from the Sea King?"

"Emme's dying," Tess said. "Somehow, this will save her."

Landon's jaw went slack.

"All that matters is that we get to the king quickly." I didn't like that now Landon knew as much as the crew. It made him seem like more a part of it instead of someone along for a ride.

I also didn't like knowing just how prized the king's head was. We had to get to Kvas quickly.

I headed belowdecks after Ontario.

The captain's quarters were small, yet Ontario had transformed them since I had moved out. He'd acquired a new blanket as thick as my arm and as red as blood to cover the large cot. An earthenware bowl burned incense of charcoal and juniper, so the cabin smelled less like the sea and more like a merchant's home. Envelopes were scattered over the table, where Ontario sat.

He stood at my presence. "What is it?"

"We need to get to Kvas quickly." I had to hold the knob of the door to keep myself steady. People with Paslkapi weren't made to sail—our bodies shook enough without having the literal ground moving as well. It was a wonder I stood at all.

"Don't worry, Emme. I'll get you there. I take care of my crew." He gave a half smile before turning to ruffle through the letters.

"Thank you. And, Ontario?" He glanced up. "Be cordial to Arn. If you aren't, I'll remind the crew that you headed the deal with Admiral Bones as much as Arn did, and urge them to reconsider your position as captain."

It was hard to make threats when I couldn't turn and march away, but I hoped my words packed the punch that my steps couldn't. I closed the door firmly between us.

14

ONTARIO

Would I get no respect?

Emme left the cabin to allow me a few hours of sleep before we met land. Her departure marked the first moment of silence I'd had in days, but the madness in my head never quieted. It roared.

In the open porthole, a carrier hawk ruffled its wings as it landed. A few weeks ago, I'd jumped each time it did that, but by now the bird was a welcome friend. It always came with gifts.

"Come, Talen. Show me what you have today." I held out my arm, and the bird landed on it. Its sharp claws braced themselves on my skin, gentle enough not to pierce, but I couldn't ignore the sharp glint of the nails.

When Talen was my father's bird, I'd seen him deliver messages just as frequently. I'd also seen those nails dig out throats.

Talen held its foot out for me, and I took the proffered note. "Let's see if that merchant can pay yet, ey?" I unfurled the parchment and scanned the writing. I clicked my tongue. "He wants six more months. What do you think Talen? Shall I give it to him?"

The slit of Talen's eyes seemed to reply. Still . . . "I'm not as cruel as my father was. What's six more months?"

But as I dipped my quill in ink, I hesitated.

"We will need outfits if we are to parade through Winter Night as nobility. And those sails cost more than I'd planned." I tapped the end of the feather quill on the desk a few times. "And I still need to purchase more sailors. Wages aren't cheap, you know. It's hard to acquire more loot while on this mission."

What was it my father used to say? *"You give them one splinter of mercy, and they steal a barrel more. You show them an armor of steel, and they bow before you."*

I refreshed the ink on my quill. "He must pay when it is owed. It's how my father's empire was built."

When the ink had dried, I folded the note and gave it back to Talen. "The next time I see you, it should be with a pouch of silver, beautiful one." I stroked his head. "You've done well."

With my permission, he took to the skies.

I scanned through the remaining letters on the table. Talen had been busy for me. The debt Arn owed was small compared to the hole others had buried themselves into, and desperate people were willing to do anything to remove the noose around their necks. Before acquiring my father's business, I'd never had someone beg me for anything, and it was wildly satisfying to hold that power. A lovely balance of respect came with having wealth. And none had such a wealth like Admiral Bones. If I played my cards right, his empire could grow.

Not his, I reminded myself. Mine.

An image flashed through my mind of Mother with a pot on her hip calling to Father though he rarely came. She'd shaken her head and said he was obsessed. Father hadn't minded the term, but my mother had failed to see that it wasn't obsession, it was dedication. That same dedication had won her hand many years prior, but she was like so many nobles' wives—drawn to the money and soon bored of the life. They'd seek attention elsewhere before too long. In my mother's case, it was before I was even born that she strayed. After a few years, she'd bored of me too.

The letter she sent me, granting me my inheritance, was the only thing I kept of hers. It was the only thing of value she'd given me.

Another envelope on the table caught my eye, one that I'd shoved away earlier. I picked it up and eased the edge open. This letter stood out from the others—both in that it was decorated much finer and that the contents were asking for payment from me instead of a payment I was owed. It seemed my father wasn't as blemish-free as he'd led me to believe. For years he'd let this debt fester, and now the king of Az Elo was calling on it.

I took out another piece of paper. "One more note to write," I said to myself. *It's what I should have done weeks ago.*

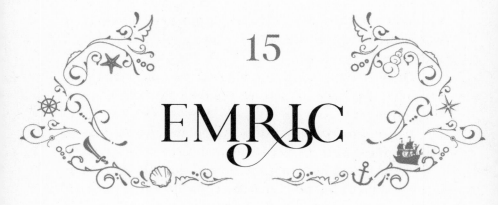

15

EMRIC

I heard her before I saw her. Arabella stomped through the trees with a growl loud enough to scare birds from their perches.

She came closer to the mouth of the hut, her bag in one hand and the shell in the other. My breathing stopped, but I wouldn't let her see how afraid I was of her. Instead, I looked back to the stick I was pointlessly whittling. I'd asked her for some time off before beginning the second raft, time for Coral to save us and keep us from slaving over another doomed ship.

She threw the bag at me, and it hit my ankles. She shoved the shell under my nose. "The magic is gone from here. What did you do?"

I slowly sat back on my heels. "I saved us."

"You doomed us!" She threw the shell into the sand and ran her hands through her hair, pulling at the ends. "You've doomed us!"

Her angry breathing came as loudly as my heartbeat, but I stepped out of the hut, planting my feet in the coarse sand, and faced her. "I called a mermaid to come save us. She'll be stronger than the waves."

The strength Coral had was beyond anything humans possessed. She'd come visit me on the *Royal Rose*, then the next day be all the way to Julinbor, and the next day find me again. While she had thick muscle and a way with the water, I was stuck on the ship bending to the will of the wind to carry me where I wanted to go. Coral would not be bound by such restraints. She'd make it through unstable waters.

That ought to please Arabella, but her body stilled. "What dealings do you have with the mermaids?" She looked at me sharply. "Are you in love with her?"

There was silence before I finally answered. "Yes."

"Then you are more of a fool than I believed." She snorted. "Love makes you do stupid things, Emric. Do you think I didn't want to call your father? I wanted to. But I didn't because there was nothing he could have done. And there's nothing your mermaid can do either. This island isn't easily reached."

"I had to try." I backed up from the warmth of the fire, though heat still stirred through me. My mother was many things. Ambitious. Strong. Brave. Self-dependent. And while those things made her a terrific sailor, it also made her a miserable person to be stranded with. "I had to do something other than build a raft that would break whenever the island called us back. So I used the shell that you were never going to."

"That shell was my hope." Her voice didn't break, but it might as well have. It sagged with desperation. "That was how I had the strength to build one raft after another when each one broke. That was how I found the motivation to keep going, because I knew that those rafts weren't my only hope. I still had the shell, and perhaps someday I'd have come up with how to use it. But you've gone and taken that away, so all we have left to rely on are the blasted rafts."

She faced the sea, her grown-out hair circling her shoulders like a scarf. I ought to feel pity for her, but I couldn't summon any.

"You are too stubborn to see that I just saved us. Coral will come."

"Ha! It's because you think you love her that you want to believe that. Unless she is stronger than the fiercest storm, she won't touch this island."

"She's strong. She'll make it."

"You better hope so." She shoved past me down the beach toward the morning waves that rippled over white sands. "I swear, if you weren't my son."

The threat faded as she pulled out of earshot and set her feet into the water before diving in, sinking under.

"She'll come," I promised the wind. "Coral will come."

16

ARN

If it weren't for the piercing cold, the bitter wind, and the wetness in my boots, this would be an enjoyable sail. As it was, the evening remained wretched at best.

Bishop was teaching Tess how to clean fish, and as I watched her run the blade along the fins, it slipped and nicked her hand. She tucked her hand between her thighs and tried to keep going on. She was determined, I'd give her that. But if we didn't find a niche for her soon, she'd be dead weight on board.

I looked above her to Ontario behind the wheel. He'd been awake for almost two days by my count. I couldn't tell if it was his drive to prove himself as captain or worry for what waited at Julinbor, but he held to the helm with no signs of moving. When he caught my eye, his fingers tightened on the wheel, and it felt like he was reminding me of his ownership.

I turned for the cabin below.

Emme sat inside, going through dozens of maps, chewing on her lip with the rolls of parchment surrounding her like a blanket against the cold. From her pink nose, they weren't doing their job.

She looked up as I came in. "This room has never been so clean," she observed. "I think you must clean when you're stressed."

I shut the door. "It's not clean now."

"Well no." She flushed. She brought the maps in closer, where they showed traces of the Seas of Lost Lands and the Moving Lands. Two tricky places to map, as either the lands would move or they would disappear entirely, leaving most to go around them instead of through. We'd managed through to save time in getting to the Island of Iilak and had left a girl named Pearl on its shores.

I doubted Emme was thinking of Pearl as she looked at those maps though. From how she rubbed Emric's ring on her finger, I guessed who she sought.

Sure enough, she pushed the maps to me. "Do you think only the lands move, or does the water beneath them as well?"

I picked up the maps. There were fifteen differing designs per location, and each guess was as possible as the last. "I'm not certain. Both?"

She furrowed her brow as if that wasn't the answer she wanted. "If Emric went down here, he could have been pulled to one of these lands."

"Or," I said, "He was pulled toward the High Seas to the Sea King Valian's lands."

Emme's head sprang up. "Do you think King Valian took care of him?"

I didn't think the Sea King was real, but I knelt beside her. "I thought you were coming around to believing he was lost." I took care not to say drowned. For some reason, that word tasted more bitter.

She removed his ring to roll it between her fingers before answering. "Sometimes I have. Then other times the hope that he's alive hits me so hard that I can't breathe. I can only picture him out there waiting for me to save him. I don't know how to let go of that." She licked her lips. "Frankly, I don't want to let go. It feels like he's still alive until I accept that he isn't, and giving up would be like killing him." She buried her head in her hands, muffling her voice. "I know it makes no sense."

I put my hand on her arm. "I think your brother is at peace."

Her cheeks dimpled with her clenched jaw. She fumbled with the papers more, drawing them close and tracing her finger along the lands. "Maybe. Or maybe he's stuck on an island."

I'd happily take her exploring along the Seas of Lost Lands. There could be treasure there to find, and it could take years to exhaust the search for Emric, but each day would drive her closer to madness in her obsession over finding him. I bit my tongue against saying so, instead wiping away the tear that fell down her cheek.

She sniffed and thrust the papers together in a messy pile. "The Seas of Lost Lands is just a theory."

From behind, Tess spoke. "I'll go to the Seas of Lost Lands. Sounds exciting."

I jumped. "How long have you been there? I didn't hear the door open."

Tess shrugged, twisting the hilt of a blade to run it along her belt, the black leather matching the bandages on her hand. "Not long. Bishop wanted to see if I could be of use here."

"Not until you can count," I replied. "Care to do some lessons?"

She bolted out, but now that she'd caught me off guard, I listened to her movements. Her feet carried her over the boards without a sound like she was but a slip of wind pulling through the air with no weight to keep her down. It could be because she was young, but most children I'd seen were more prone to crashing into things than gliding among them.

"Has she always been agile like that?"

Emme glanced up from the maps as she tied a ribbon around them. "Yes, she's frightened me more than once."

"That could be a handy skill," I mused. "I could use a spy."

"Don't." Emme tucked the maps in a cupboard. "I don't want her corrupted."

"She's on the *Royal Rose*. She's already corrupted." I reached down. "You missed one."

But the drawing on this map was different. It was a country, not islands, carved with sloping lines and marks for cliffs and mountains, more rock than soil. The western side of it abruptly ended where the landscape was unknown to me.

"What interest do you have in Az Elo?" I asked.

She took it from me. "I've grown curious after your story. Whatever came of that prince the girl was engaged to?"

"She was actually meant to be killed," I reminded her.

"So there was no prince?"

"There was. But he died shortly after. As far as I know, neither kingdom has moved to forge a relationship since then."

Her expression shifted into one of pity. "It's such a sad story." Her finger went to Emric's ring again, so I couldn't be certain which story she meant until she said, "One girl dead before her love could rescue her, and another boy gone."

"Such is the way of kings," I replied. "Death surrounds them."

At that moment a messenger hawk came through the porthole with far less stealth than Tess mustered, flapping its wide wings to settle on the table, its talons curling into the wood. My breath hitched until realizing it wasn't Admiral Bones's hawk—this creature was much smaller and not well trained if it came through the porthole instead of finding the captain. That, or it was instructed to be sneaky. It watched me with beady eyes, its brown feathers combed and slicked down and its claws sharp. A parchment was furled and tied to its leg, and it lifted its foot for me when I reached out a hand.

"Are you expecting letters?" I asked Emme as I messed with the ribbon. As soon as it was free, the hawk sprung to the porthole, tested its wings, and took off again.

"No. Maybe it's from your father?"

"Please no," I muttered. I opened it. The note was short and written in sloppy handwriting, either rushed or not well schooled, but the message was clear, and it wasn't for me. "This is interesting." I held it for Emme to read.

The Captain, we are ready.

"Is Ontario planning something?" She examined both sides of the note while I checked out the window to the deck, making certain none were watching.

Something had hit me about the wording. My body tensed. It'd been a while since I'd heard that name, so long that he might have thought I'd forgotten it. I hadn't. "Not Ontario." I pointed. "It says *The Captain*. That's the nickname Landon used to go by when we were kids. This message is for him."

He might be after more than his old ship. The last time he crossed us, we lost a lot of men. If I let that happen again, then I didn't deserve to retake my place as captain.

Emme glanced at me curiously. "What did you go by?"

"Hummingbird." At her chuckle, I took the note back. "I had different aspirations as an eight-year-old. But this?" I read the words again. "I wish I knew what it meant. I feel uneasy about this."

I moved to the window once more, scouring the deck. "Will you tell him you got the note?" Emme asked.

"No. But by the sounds of it, it doesn't matter."

I spotted Landon across the planks, chatting with Clarice. She didn't smile, but she didn't look bored, and that was as good as a smile from her. That man could charm anyone, and I ought to have been paying better attention to him. Tess was nearby, back to scaling fish again but within earshot of him so she could catch whatever grand tales he was spinning. My gaze lingered on her. She would be the perfect person to spy for me, because he was already used to her constant presence. If anyone could uncover what this meant, she might. But stopping it would be a different story.

I crumpled the note. "It sounds like whatever is going to happen is already in motion. I just pray it doesn't sink us all."

17

EMRIC

The air around my mother curled cold, so I kept far from her to enjoy warmth as she begrudgingly began work on another doomed raft while muttering something that sounded suspiciously like *idiotic child*. That was fine. This island was large enough to hold her anger.

I tried to focus on the calming sound of the sea and not the crack of a cutlass striking bamboo or string of eloquent curses from Arabella. A hearty dinner of smoked fish would calm her. I held a makeshift spear in my hand and eyed the water as it lapped against my knees, searching for hints of fish to use as a peace offering.

There was one thing she and I could be grateful for—my wound was healing. A dark purple scab still crusted over the place where I'd been stabbed, but I showed no signs of internal injuries or infection. That was a miracle all on its own.

"It's the island," Arabella had reminded me.

"And here I was about to thank you for your work," I'd told her.

Protective island or talented mother, either way I wouldn't die of my injuries. But even the island couldn't protect me if one day Arabella decided she'd had enough of me and ran me through. The years on Avalla had taken all the kindness out of her—if there was any there to begin with.

I wondered if I'd end up like her if I stayed here long enough. Hardened and focused only on escape, so desperate for my life back that I couldn't enjoy a blessing even if the sea brought a loved one to me.

No, I decided. The island hadn't made Arabella like this. It only brought out what was already inside her. I couldn't be blamed for that, even if I did steal her one hope.

Orange flashed beneath the waves, and I gripped my spear. In a heartbeat the creature coiled around my legs and dragged me beneath the water, and I lost the grip on my weapon. I grabbed at the fish, feeling scales tighten on my calves and climb up to my arms. Fear made my chest tighten, but I willed my breathing to come slowly to save oxygen.

Then I was pushed on the shore. I swallowed air and wiped my eyes dry to find another face grinning back at me.

"Hey, pirate."

Coral perched at the edge of the water, her bright blonde hair dripping water over her coral-orange tail, which flicked water up to me. "Sorry, I couldn't resist. Island life looks good on you."

I grinned at her in delight. "I knew you'd come." I tackled her into the water and held her close. She smelled of salt and lilies, and the white tattoo of a crown banded across her upper arm stood out in the light. She intertwined her fingers with mine, and my other hand sank into sand to keep me upright.

"How did you make it here?" I soaked in the sight of her, tightening my grip to be certain she was real.

She inspected my wound with crunched brows as she answered. "King Valian opened the way. Does this hurt? I can't believe that cursed Nightlock Thief stabbed you. I thought she'd learned her lesson about hurting the innocent long ago."

"I'm healed," I told her, still obsessed with the sight of her here and the freedom that it brought. I wanted to ask a million questions, about how she got here and how we'd get back and if the Sea King Valian was real, but instead I only knew the feel of her hand brushing my skin and the golden flecks in her eyes.

If I'd been honest, part of me feared she wouldn't come. Wait until Arabella saw I *had* used the shell wisely.

Coral nodded once, happy with how the injury had healed, then turned her gaze over the land. She let out a low whistle. "It's a beautiful prison, I'll give it that. We have sent many enemies here before, and it doesn't look to be as horrible of a punishment as I'd thought."

"It would be miserable if they were with my mother. You'll see."

Arabella remained further inland, amid a cusp of trees from which the steady clap of bamboo striking together echoed.

"Can't wait," Coral joked. Then without explanation, she moved her hand to the hip of her tail, or at least where a hip might be if she had legs, and found a crack in the scales. She plunged her hand inside. Her hand disappeared, somewhere within a slit of her tail while I tried not to stare, to familiarize myself with the oddity of scales instead of legs.

Her bright tail was twice as long as my legs were and shimmered in the light. The fin at the end spread the length of my arm. The muscle was powerful, much stronger than human legs, and I longed to know what that power felt like for myself.

"I brought you something." She brought out her hand to reveal a cloth sack, which she opened for me. Inside sat roasted shrimp. I hadn't asked her to bring food, but my stomach rolled with excitement over not having to crack coconuts or skin fish to scrape together a meal.

"You are my favorite mermaid," I said.

"I try."

I did all I could to remember manners while loading my

mouth with food. Stranded-island life didn't suit me well. It took all my strength to fold the bag with the remaining food and keep it on the beach to share with Arabella later, though if she made one more comment along the lines of *idiotic child*, I swore I'd eat the rest happily.

"Is this okay?" I asked, swallowing the last bite. "Eating a creature from the sea? No distant relation there?"

Coral blinked. "Did you just ask me if I'm related to a shrimp?"

My face heated, and I buried my head into her shoulder.

She laughed. The first laugh I'd heard in a while. Compared to my mother's grumblings, it was the most melodious thing in all the lands. "It's alright. Might want to keep away from too much sun though."

"Soon I'll hardly see the sun, once I live under the seas with you." I laid back into the water until the ends of my hair were wet. My hand settled over hers as she lay beside me. The water rippled around us with each little movement. A single freckle on her face near the corner of her eye twitched as her eyes slimmed.

"What?"

"It's just," she sighed. Her eyes fell to mine. "Are you certain? This world is yours, and it holds so much promise for you. You just got your mother back, and you have your sister. You can become the pirate you always wanted, rule over the seas, and live in the warmth of the sun. My world . . . it can't give you that."

I rolled to my side to hold her hand tighter. "My world can't give me you, Coral. If you'll have me, I want the life that comes with you."

Her cheeks dimpled with her smile. "It'll be quite the life together. And we'll do all we can to visit Emme whenever possible."

In two short months, she already knew me so well. If I

couldn't ever see my sister again, it would make leaving the land much more difficult, but the thrill of the adventure to be had beneath the waves outmatched the life I'd planned of hard work and meager food aboard a ship. Perhaps when Emme healed, she'd want to come too.

Coral gazed back at seas. "Emric, there's something you need to know about getting off this island. It's not as simple as you'd think."

"I already almost drowned once," I said. She pressed her lips tight, and I sat up. "How do we leave?"

She traced a line on the horizon with her eyes first. "I can lead you off the island and take you as far as the nearest ship. I can guarantee you'll survive, but the island doesn't like to lose its prisoners. It will take something from you when you leave."

I looked over myself. "I have nothing that I wouldn't mind losing."

She raked her hair over her shoulder and shook her head. "No, you don't understand. It can take more than physical things. It could steal your favorite memory, your ability to speak, or years of your life. There's no way to know what it takes, and once it's gone, you won't know what you've lost. Maybe you'll be lucky and it only takes your weapon. But it could steal something much more important."

"Stars," I cursed. "But you're sure you can save us?"

"I'm not sure if it's worth it."

I'd expected she'd somehow be able to drag us out of the island's reach. This blasted place was proving much more difficult that I'd pinned it for. What was I willing to lose to get away? What could it steal from me that would be too great of a loss? Any beloved memory of mine or year of my life wasn't worth spending the rest of them here. One memory of my sister and I'd still have hundreds more. One memory of Coral and we'd still be making thousands more in our future.

"It's worth it," I said. "I'll lose something to be free. I'm certain my mother will agree."

"She agrees." My mother was behind us with her arms crossed and focus fixed on the horizon. The sun was tipping toward the other side, and the surface of the water shone like glass. "I'll lose everything to get back to the sea. I assume you are the young thing of my son's fancy?"

Coral's expression soured at Arabella's tone, and she sat upright. "I'm also the thing who is saving you."

Arabella's eyebrow went up. "Are you going to drag us through the water?"

Coral extracted something from her fins again. She drew out two emerald scales attached to a string. "You'll wear this, and it will give you fins. With the blessing I received from King Valian, this island will release you as you swim with me."

Excitement grabbed me. I'd get my first taste of being a merman. Arabella looked at the scales as if she were already planning how to steal them. Coral eyed her. "Go get your things."

Arabella's own eyes narrowed at the command, but she said nothing and went to fetch her pack.

"What do you suppose the island will take?" I asked as soon as Arabella had gone.

"I don't know." She handed a scale to me, and her eyes held mine. "But I'd lose everything for you."

My heart stopped. "You'll lose something as well?"

She nodded. "I must pay the price, just as you."

Before my mother could return, I pulled Coral in and wrapped my arms around her. I shut my eyes against the harsh beams of the sun and savored her touch. "Can it take this feeling between us?" I whispered into the nape of her neck. The thought of this being ripped away terrified me more than anything.

"Maybe," she whispered back. "But it wouldn't matter. One look at you and I'd fall in love all over again."

I brushed my lips against her forehead and held her closer. "The same," I said.

I relived that memory in case it was what I lost. The memory of me shouting wildly over the side of the ship, sharing my secret about my mother, feeling furious with my sister for oathbinding herself. Then Coral had thrown herself up to sit on the ship next to me, and in an instant everything else vanished. There was only her, the most beautiful creature I'd ever seen, with skin soft as marble and eyes bright as jewels. And as she'd looked back, the faintest smile had come across her face. She'd reached out her hand to touch my cheek, and she'd won me over in that instant. A creature so lovely but so fierce.

Coral had returned the next night to find me, and the story of us began. She appeared every night after, and while I'd never been so sleep deprived, it only took one week to decide that I never wanted her to stop coming and that I'd lose my legs for her. She'd brought tales of the water and their cities made of reefs, and all I wanted was to see them for myself and experience the power of having fins.

"It won't steal away us. I know it. *We* aren't something that can be stolen."

I cupped my hand under her chin and kissed her. Kissing her now was different than kissing her before, when I would lean over the edge of the ship to reach her. Now I could wrap both arms around her back and feel her heart beating against mine.

You can't have this, I warned the island. *Anything else you can take, but not this. Not her.*

She must have been thinking this, too, because when she pulled back, there was a slight pink to her pale complexion. "We will be fine," she said softly.

I drew back and stood from the water, holding the scale in my hand. I wanted to remain there with Coral, but there was something that must be done first. Just in case. "I'll go check on my mother, then we can go."

She flicked water over herself with her fin. "I'll be here."

I retrieved the rest of the roasted shrimp on my way and wove through the overgrowth to the small hut where Arabella was emerging with her pack in hand. "Your mermaid change her mind?"

"Of course not." I tossed the small sack of shrimp at her. "Here." I went in and scanned the hut. "I need parchment and ink. Do you have any?"

She threw her head back in a laugh. "What do you think I spent my years here doing? Storytelling? I don't have parchment and ink."

I riffled through her few things. "Is there anything I can use to write with?"

"No," she snorted. "Trying to leave the island a love letter?"

I shot her a look, and my eyes were drawn to the pouch in her hand. "That's light enough."

"You just gave this to me."

"Not the shrimp." I snatched the bag and dumped the food into her hands. "I need the pouch." She didn't argue.

"And your knife."

Now she had complaints. "What's so important that you'd write it in blood?"

"Something worth keeping. I need the blade."

With a frown, Arabella drew the knife from her side sheath, but she held onto it. "It's been dulled, the pressure you'd need—"

"I'll keep that in mind." I took the blade and pressed the tip into my finger until dark red showed. Then, using the point, I wrote on the cloth. There wasn't enough blood to write much, but I put down what I could. Enough that if my memory of

Coral was taken as I crossed the island's borders, I'd find this and know she meant something important to me.

Remember her.

"Done." I flipped the knife through the air back to my mother. She wiped the blood on her dress. "Let's go."

I tucked the note into my pocket and willed it to stay there when I put on the shell and gained a tail. Twigs snapped under our feet as we left our last marks on Avalla. Had the island not been so territorial about its humans, this would have been a beautiful place temporarily.

The sand sank with each step as we reached the sea. Coral handed the second shell to Arabella.

Her lip turned in disdain as she looked over it. "I've never liked fish."

Coral's expression tightened.

"We simply put it on?" I asked. The shell weighed heavy in my hand and caught the light of the sun to turn the emerald shade into a vibrant green. I wondered what color my tail would be—something bright like Coral's or something darker. Did it take personality into account? I wondered if it'd turn Arabella's coal black.

Coral waded in deeper. "Yes, just place it around your neck. Preferably when you're in the water," she gave a sly smile. "Unless you want to flop across dry land."

Arabella trudged into the water, and I followed until the brisk waves reached our chests. When our legs could take us no further, we put on the scales.

Transformation occurred the moment the cold scale touched my skin, and my body plunged into the sea. Air bubbled in my mouth. A tingling sensation overcame my legs as they morphed together and grew twice their length. The phase between legs and tail was awkward, where my body looked distorted, but the next moment was beautiful.

Strength filled me, and suddenly I felt as if I could flick my tail once and it'd carry me halfway across the ocean with a power that legs could not wield.

The tail itself was glorious. It began right below my naval, where my skin transformed into scales the color of a sea at night. The darkest of blues met into a shimmering black by the fins at the end.

I practiced moving it up and down, floating myself further into the sea as the ground dropped beneath me. I was suspended between the surface of the water and the floor, but felt in perfect control.

I turned my head toward the warmth of the sun and prepared to resurface to breathe when I stopped myself. I didn't need air. My body craved the water. The first rush filled my nostrils. It was like breathing heavy air, but what would have killed me as a human only fueled me as a merman.

I looked up and caught Coral's eye. She watched me with a delicate smile on her lips.

"How is it?" I tested out my voice below the sea.

"Flawless," she said.

"This tail is stronger than I'd imagined," Arabella was at my left. Her makeshift dress had turned into a flowy shirt, fastened together with rope. Her tail was red and dark as blood. She gave it one flick and completed almost an entire circle around us. Her face was alive with discovery. "I could probably kill someone using nothing but this tail."

"Of course that's where your mind goes," I said.

Her mouth turned upward in a lethal curve.

"Are you ready?" Coral asked us. "It won't take long to reach outside the island's grasp, and these scales won't last forever. You don't want to be under the sea when you transform back."

Surprising disappointment surged within me that I'd be losing this tail. As soon as I made certain Emme was safe, I'd present myself to Sea King Valian and trade my legs for a tail I got to keep.

"I'm ready," I replied as Arabella gave a curt nod.

I slid my hand to the slit of the tail at my hip. An opening I couldn't see separated when my hand neared. Inside was the note, still safe. Whatever this island stole from me, I'd be prepared.

Coral turned. "Follow me."

Getting a tail was one thing, but swimming with it was an entirely new thrill. The water split as we sliced through with an unstoppable force. With one thrust, we crossed distances that would take a ship minutes to achieve. And it was effortless.

"I want to try something," I said. I tilted upward and flipped my fins twice until I'd reached the surface, then hurled myself into the air in a wide arch. I gave out an exultant cheer before splashing back undersea. "This is amazing."

Coral grinned. "I'm really glad you think so, because I don't know what I would have done if you hated being a merman."

I swam up to her. "Would you have gotten legs for me?"

She twirled in the water. "Of course." Her eyes twinkled. "But I think you'll find my world is much more exciting than yours."

Arabella was paces ahead of us, and now she called back. "When will we know we're free of the island?"

The colors had grown darker around us as the sea opened. I couldn't see the land behind us, only the vibrant floor beneath and vast blue beyond. Light splintered when it hit the surface above and swarmed around us in dancing fragments.

In a few minutes—a few glorious minutes—we'd already traveled miles.

"I'm uncertain," Coral said. "Do either of you feel like you've lost anything yet?"

I searched, but it was like combing through the sea itself. I had no idea where to start. If I lost a memory, there'd be no way to know which one. If I lost a year of my life, that was something I'd never know. Whatever the island took, it wasn't mine anymore. But we'd left the island far behind. We must be free now.

"I don't feel different," I said with a flick of my tail. "The price must not have been too high."

"Let us hope," Coral said. "Perhaps we've been blessed today."

"How far to the ship?" Arabella asked. Her earlier wonder with the tail seemed to have died off, as she now stared toward the sun.

"I can't take you all the way to the *Royal Rose*. Last I tracked, it was somewhere near Julinbor and traveling north. But there's a ship nearby that I can take you to."

"Then we'll force that ship to carry us to the *Royal Rose*," Arabella responded with certainty.

I frowned. A fuzziness clouded my brain. "The *Royal Rose*?"

Coral slowed. "Your ship. Do you not remember?"

It took a moment, but it came back to me. "Of course. I'm the captain. Yes, I remember."

But something wasn't quite right. The memory was faded, giving me pieces but keeping others. Whatever I'd lost, it was aboard that ship.

Coral slid her hand into mine. "At least it didn't take us."

I smiled, but the unease inside remained.

Coral pointed us in the direction of where the ship would be. "It belongs to a pirate named Verin."

Arabella's lips stretched tight over her teeth. "Splendid. I know that man. We'll be welcomed aboard."

I guessed the odds of her being welcomed aboard most ships were not great, so maybe the Fates had truly blessed us today. Still, I sifted through my memories of the *Royal Rose*. I remembered Ontario, the steady First. Bo, the cheerful and loud man. Arn, the young captain. Lewie, the young boy we'd lost when we couldn't get him medicine in time.

With his death came the memory of losing the others, and a sadness crept over my heart. But the fuzziness didn't fade. Something wasn't there that ought to be.

I hadn't gotten the treasure with them, I recalled. But I remembered fighting to keep it. Where was I that morning? I kept searching for the unknown something.

"Verin wouldn't defy me," Arabella was saying. "He'll take us straight to Emme, and we'll get her before it's too late."

Again, her words didn't make sense to me, and I paused. I tested out the question, almost fearing the answer. "Who's Emme?"

Coral and Arabella had swum forward, but with my words, they froze.

Was that what I'd lost? Was I meant to know of whom she spoke?

Arabella turned slowly, her hair swimming around her face like snakes. "What did you ask?"

"Emme. That name. I don't know it."

Coral swam closer and grasped my hand. Her face was pinched in worry. "Think, Emric. You remember Emme."

I tried, but it wasn't like with the ship. This memory didn't come back to me. It wasn't faded or fuzzy, it simply wasn't there.

Whoever this Emme was, she was no longer in my mind. That was what the island stole from me, and I didn't know if I ought to care. "I don't," I said. "I don't know who Emme is."

18
ARN

Ontario pointed his telescope east. "Gillen Port," he called from the helm. "We stop there for supplies and more recruits."

I hated seeing the land from the deck instead of the helm. But I stared at the familiar cut of fields all the same. My father used to take me here as a lad.

"It won't be a long stop," Ontario went on. "I swear on the stars that if any of you make us late or cause problems, you'll be dredging the hull. Understood?" This would assure the crew's obedience. That was a horrid task even when the waters were fair.

The sails were trimmed and both anchors dropped. Ontario passed Bishop a slip of parchment. "You'll collect the new inventory. Take three with you." Bishop nodded, pocketed the list, and pointed to Bo, Timmons, and Collins.

"A short trip," Ontario reminded us. "No problems."

He threaded his arms through his thicker brown coat, which made him look like a bear awakening from hibernation and hungry for dinner. He moved like a bear, too, always in rough steps and jagged lines—not to mention brash in his attack. Ever since I'd agreed not to undermine him further, that beastly rage had simmered. And I wouldn't be on the other side of his anger again.

"May I come too?" Tess asked. Her pink nose was the most visible thing from beneath the shadow of her large hat, until she tilted her head back to reveal eyes glittering with the thrill of her first adventure with us.

Ontario hesitated, then nodded. "Everyone comes."

Tess shivered with excitement. Landon stepped by her side and looked over the approaching shore where the soil turned to dark sand and feet had beaten down paths between homes. The town touched the sea, with some huts settled beyond the docks on the strips of land that rose from shallow waters.

Groups of youth gathered along the shore to help incoming ships, or to take smaller boats between the homes on the sea and the town. The harvest was over, and they would be searching for jobs. A most ideal time for seeking new recruits.

Our rowboats splashed into the water as they were dropped, and the crew slithered down ropes to board.

Emme looked warily over the edge. "I should stay. I'll only slow you."

"There will be better food on land," I promised. "But I've been thinking." I crouched at the edge of the deck to untie something that I'd made for her and held it up. By her frown, she was not impressed. I'd taken an oar and cut it down to her size, then smoothed the edges to give it a more fashionable cut for her style.

She didn't reach for it. "I'll draw many eyes with that."

"I think all pirates should carry canes," I said. "They can be handy weapons."

She sighed before taking hold of it. "You already have two weapons," she reminded me. "You don't need a third."

"My wit and my good looks?"

There was the smile. I had to work harder these days for one of those.

I slid down the rope, then reached up to catch her as she came down it. She almost wacked me with the oar. "Besides,"

I went on, helping to row us close to land as soon as she was seated. "Imagine it. A group of men with canes, no one suspecting a thing, until we raised them in attack. It'd be a new era of fighting. Cane combat."

"It wouldn't work," she countered, but her tone was lighter. "Or if it did, it wouldn't work twice."

She turned to gaze at the land where the morning had brought a frost. It likely wasn't their first one, but it was the first time this season that we'd gotten a glimpse of strands of grass caught in ice and the weak sun glittering off fields of white. The other two rowboats were ahead of us, their oars slicing through the dark water as howling wind cupped our cheeks and turned all our noses red by the time the hulls dragged on the sandy beach.

Eight hands rushed into the frigid waters to help us ashore.

"In and out with no problems," Ontario said as we shook the water from our boots, his hard expression meeting each of us as if we planned to turn feral if he didn't constantly remind us otherwise.

Bishop took off to the town with the other three in tow. The rest of us waited for more of Ontario's instructions. The eight that had helped us ashore lingered as well, and Ontario cleared his throat. "Care to join a crew?"

"What's the pay?" someone asked.

"Three coppers a week. Equal crew's cut of loot," Ontario replied.

The group fell into discussion, and in the end, six remained. "Good." Ontario nodded. "But you've got to earn it. Go to market and pocket five silvers from others. If anyone brings me twenty, they'll get double dinners for a week." They turned to run, but Ontario stopped them with one more request. "If any catch you, offer them a job too."

The six took off through the streets.

Ontario faced us. "The rest of you get yourself a fair meal

and be back within an hour. And Arn?" He caught hold of my arm and leaned close. "Check for Landon."

My gaze swept over the crew, already weaving through the docks where the knocks of pulleys hitting the deck rang across the sea and the morning mist was drifting away. Landon wasn't among them. "Where did he go?"

"I don't know. As long as he doesn't cause trouble, I don't care. But keep an eye out, will you?"

"Of course."

Satisfied, Ontario pulled away, but not before Tess tugged on his sleeve. "Can I try to steal to earn double meals too?"

His brows shot up. "You shouldn't be so eager to break the law."

"I'm eager to eat."

He stroked his chin. "Very well," he relented. "Don't get caught."

She sprang into the thick crowds. One moment she was there, and the next she was gone. Ontario leaned against a lamppost and watched the deckhands assist with the returning fishermen who rowed in, eyeing them all with a thoughtful gaze. I tried not to notice the ones who looked so much like those we'd lost, instead scanning the different corners of town in search of my own meal.

I held on to Emme to help her over the uneven path as loose rocks snagged at her boots.

She clutched the cane in her fist and drove the end of it against the frozen ground, leaning heavily on it and on my arm. A few glanced at her while they carried lines to dock, but they'd snap their attention away when she looked up. "I used to live a few miles from here, before you knew me," she said.

I paused to stare over the hills. "I thought you said you lived inland."

"That is inland."

"The sea is right here. This is barely land. You might as

well have lived in one of those huts out there." I indicated the ones on the slips of land in the sea, and that got a smile.

"I told you I used to come here with my father. I wonder if we ever saw each other."

I'd like to think that I'd remember a girl like her, but I'd been so caught up on Merelda Ann when I was younger that I hadn't the eyes for anyone else. And truthfully, many of the girls here today bore resemblance to Emme, all with dark tones and strong builds.

But it was Emme's kindness that had always set her apart, even when life was cruel to her. Now, it was her weakness and reliance upon that cane giving her a distinguishing mark.

"I came here with Landon too," I said, standing close to her so she could never question my pride at being by her side. "Let me know if you spot him by the way. He's up to something."

Emme shook her head. "He's always up to something."

"True. I just hope he still leads me to the Caster."

Emme was quiet for a few more steps, and when she spoke her voice was low. "I wasn't sure if you'd changed your mind about that."

"I think so. I'd like a name that isn't stained with 'failed captain.'"

She adjusted her grip on the cane. "What if I forget you?"

"I'd ask her to keep your memory of me intact. It wouldn't be worth it otherwise. It's exciting to imagine though, and I've already got a bit of the identity crafted. What do you think of Albany Thomas, son of shoemakers from Lemondey?"

"I like it. Simple and honest work."

I grinned. "But at night, my parents ran an illegal market for trading goods, which gives me a plethora of resources that will increase my worth on any pirate ship. Landon's crew will be lucky to have me as their captain."

"A little less honest work, now."

"But twice the fun."

Emme stopped walking to clutch the cane between her hands. A strand of her hair had fallen over her face, and it moved with each heavy breath that she took.

"Do you need a break?"

She was barely keeping upright and was digging her fingers into my arm. "You should go without me. By the time I make it to a tavern, I'll need to turn and come back."

"Then I guess I'm just here for a walk with pleasant company," I said. I almost got another smile, but it was masked by her concentration on her steps as she kept moving. I looked down the path, where narrow streets lined the way with arched windowpanes, shades of tan and dark oak, and gilded lanterns hanging from sloped awnings. The bustle of day had begun, and the modest town was coming to life. Bakers had been running their fires for hours, and the scent of fresh bread caught on the winds.

"Let's get a loaf of glazed bread from there and call it a meal," I said, pointing to a cart making its rounds by the shore. An older couple handed out bread in exchange for coins, and even Ontario was there. "You stay here. I'll go."

She nodded, releasing my arm so I could go. The paths were wet where snow had melted, and I worked to avoid the mud, but it still caked around my boots and slowed my movements. I reached Ontario's side and looked into the cart of warm bread.

"Fresh loaf?" the elderly couple asked, offering a long stick of bread my way.

I dug for coin. "Two," I replied. The money jingled as they dropped it into their pockets and handed me the loaves. I turned, but Ontario stopped me.

"I saw him at the post," he muttered under his breath.

I waited for the elderly couple to move on. "Landon?"

Ontario nodded. "He was there for something. But it could be harmless."

"Nothing is ever harmless with that scoundrel. He's not close enough with family to exchange letters."

Ontario chewed on his bread while keeping an eye on the new recruits in the thick crowd. The first of them, a man larger than both me and Ontario with calloused hands and unruly brows, returned to hand Ontario a cut bag of coins.

"No trouble?" Ontario asked.

"None at all."

"Welcome to the crew. Get your things, we leave shortly."

The man ran off, and a second recruit came back with coins. The same words were exchanged, and the second recruit left.

"Are you going to ask Landon what he's up to?" I asked him.

"No. Not my job as captain. As long as he keeps from trouble, I don't care who he communicates with."

"You won't do anything?"

"No reason to," Ontario continued as a third recruit returned. "He has followed orders so far. Hasn't even killed anyone." He raised his voice for the newcomer. "You have coins for me?"

Tess came back, almost materializing in the air beside us as quiet and still as a hundred-year-old tree. She stood in stark contrast to the new recruits who fidgeted as they scanned the crowds as if to make sure no one realized too soon that they'd been robbed. It was the first time I'd seen her so serene. Her eyes were lit bright like the thrill of thieving was a life source for her.

She flicked a blood-red pouch to Ontario. "Two dinners."

He raised a brow and looked inside the pouch. "Well done."

"We shouldn't wait for the others," she said. "The market is alert with the sighting of the *rskvateer*"—her tone changed with the foreign word—"and all are watching us."

Ontario and I exchanged glances. "*Rskvateer?*" I asked.

"It's what they call our ship," Tess said proudly. "But

unless your new recruits can take on the whole town, we'd better leave."

A fourth recruit returned.

"Very well." Ontario started to tuck the pouch away, but my hand shot out and grabbed it.

"Where did you get this?" I demanded of Tess as I lifted the red pouch with the symbol of an eagle stitched into the side and the initials KM on the bottom. The strings were fraying, but this pouch had lasted well through the years. I'd seen it many times. I'd held it many times.

Tess shifted. "Some old gentleman with short-cut hair and a cheap suit. He smelled of lemons."

"He sucks on them on long journeys," I said breathlessly, sinking into the crevice between the tents. I tied the top of the pouch shut and threw it back to her. "Return this to him at once."

She looked to Ontario for instruction.

"I said return it," I repeated harder. "He's worked a year for these wages. He'll be ruined without them."

Ontario nodded, and Tess sprinted back into the crowd.

A fifth and sixth recruit returned. "Just in time. Welcome to the crew, mates," Ontario said. "I hope you've packed your things, because we leave immediately. Grab your bags. Anyone not on this shore in five minutes will not board."

As they sprinted separate directions to fetch their things, I stared after them and thought of my father, unsure if I wanted to see him or not. Further unsure if I wanted him to see me.

It'd been six . . . seven years? Maybe longer. Would he recognize me? Or would he only see a pirate?

Ontario started through the streets back for Emme. "Pray that your father doesn't see you here, because I'm not waiting," he tossed over his shoulder.

I kept my head low as I followed after, keenly aware of every straw hat and sandy-haired man I passed, expecting any one of them to confront and grab me. He'd look at me with the same eyes that had teared up as he sent me off to join the king's navy, but this time they'd be filled with nothing but disappointment. It would be too much right now.

We reached Emme, and I gave her the bread, still trying to calm the agitation in my heart.

"How did it go?" she asked.

"His father's here," Ontario said, as he strode by us.

Emme's eyes widened, and she peered down the muddy street. "Go speak to him!"

"I can't." The top of my chest tattoo reached beyond my shirt's hem, and my missing hand allowed little room for guessing. He'd take one look at me and know. He'd curse at me, or he'd turn and walk away. I couldn't decide which would be worse. "Right now, there's a man out there who is proud of his son. I'm not going to take that away."

"Arn—"

"I'm not just a pirate, Emme. I'm a failed one."

"You're his son."

"That's why I can't see him." We began walking, and I paused to hold my arm out for her. She gave a look over her shoulder, but I resisted doing the same. "It's for the best. Let's go before you change my mind."

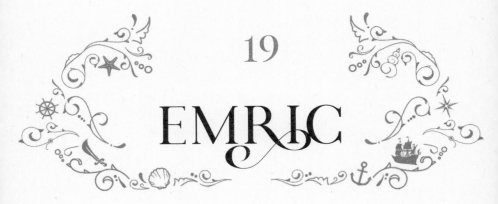

19

EMRIC

Coral and Arabella kept throwing worried looks my way, no matter how many times I told them I was fine.

"You're not, you just don't know it," Coral insisted.

"Let him be," Arabella said. "There's no need to fret over him when there's nothing to be done."

Coral frowned. "She was his sister."

"He was planning on leaving her anyway," Arabella countered. She looked down her nose at Coral. "For you."

At that, Coral quieted. I gathered all these things in my mind, trying to make sense of them.

We'd swam near a ship, and the current brought us closer to their hull. There was no more time for thoughts. A figurehead of a woman with a ruffled top carved through the waters, and the sun cast ripples of light circling the hull. Whatever the island had taken from me, it didn't touch my love for sailing or damper the extra beat in my heart as we neared the slender ship.

My skin chilled as we swam to the surface.

"It's winter here," Coral explained when I rubbed my hands over my arms. "While you've been basking in the sun, the real world here has welcomed its first snow."

"That will be the only thing I'll miss about that place," I said. She smiled, but pity resided there. I turned my face away.

"There's a magic to being a mermaid," Coral went on. "It keeps you warm beneath the sea no matter the temperature up there. But as soon as you break the surface of the water, you'll feel the cold."

"A clever way of keeping mermaids below water," Arabella commented.

"Things get . . . tricky when humans and mermaids meet," Coral acknowledged. I wondered if she was talking about us, but she was too busy avoiding my eyes for me to find out.

I was the first to swim upward.

I broke the barrier between water and sky and took a gulp of air. It tasted of salt and ice, and I instantly wished to plunge back under. My skin prickled with cold. There was no wind undersea, but here, it hissed against my cheeks.

"Tread lightly." Coral snaked closer to me. Her tail flickered around mine before whipping back to keep her upright. Her light hair molded to her sharp cheeks. While Arabella and I struggled with the transition between breathing water and air—a painful transition that I wasn't prepared for—Coral wasn't fazed. She was strong enough to keep herself up higher from the water as well, letting it slink against her waist while it bobbed around my chest.

Arabella cupped her hands and shouted. "Verin!"

"I said *lightly*," Coral snapped. "They aren't expecting merpeople to appear beside their ship, and you don't want to be mistaken for a sea creature."

"You are a sea creature," Arabella said. "Verin!"

A head appeared at the starboard side, then another. "Someone's out there!" Murmurs of confusion followed until they noticed our tails, and then awe filled their tones. "Mermaid. That one's the prettiest I've ever seen."

"What business do you have?" A new voice called. A hunky

man with a silver beard leaned his weight against the side, holding onto the riggings, squinting at us. I didn't need to be told he was the captain. He didn't merely speak—his voice commanded. That was the sound of a man who knew he was in charge.

"Let me aboard, you old boot, or I'll cast you into the water myself and drown you," Arabella yelled.

Coral gave me a look. "Five years on that island didn't change your mother at all."

"I doubt an anchor to her skull could change her."

But Verin only threw his head back and laughed. "I bring no mermaids on my ship. Swim back to wherever you came from."

Arabella raked her hair back from her face, and her voice grew bolder. "I am Arabella the Ruthless, back from the dead. You will let me aboard, or you will suffer me."

His face paled. Numerous crew members retreated. Prayers were sent up. Arabella smiled through it all. The *back from the dead* part may have been a bit much, but it got the job done. A net was thrown overboard, and while Arabella muttered about how she hated being a fish, she sat herself inside and let them pull her up.

Then they cast it down for me.

"I don't suppose I can convince you to come up?" I asked Coral wistfully. "Though, I don't know why I need to go. Let me stay with you. I'm ready to give up my legs and explore the seas." I remembered that I'd wanted to go with my mother and find the *Royal Rose* again, but as I planned to eventually stay undersea with Coral, it seemed futile. Arn had probably regained control now, and they wouldn't need me. My mother certainly didn't need me. I had nothing to tie me to above land, but plenty to lure me below the sea.

Coral placed a hand on my cheek. "You have something more important to do that needs your attention first." Her tail coiled around mine again before releasing. Her chest rose with a breath. "I know you don't remember her, but you love your sister. You told me once that she is the brightest star that walks on land, and that you'd die for her. And you almost did. It was by saving her that you ended up on the island and got this." A tender hand touched my stomach where it stung. I lifted my shirt. There was an injury there, but I couldn't remember how I'd gotten it.

"She's gone. She's not in my memory."

"You need to fight for her anyway, Emric, because she'll die if you don't save her." Coral brought her face closer for what I thought would be a kiss, but her cheek only grazed mine. Her lips neared my ear, and the softest voice whispered, "Remember her."

If only it could be so easy.

She moved away. "I'll return for you, my pirate. You won't lose me." Then she dove below before I could say anything more.

I reluctantly grabbed hold of the net and let them pull me up. Before I reached the top, I took off the emerald-scale necklace in time to haul myself overboard on my legs, weak and seemingly small as they were. I wore my familiar clothes again, though they were wet, as if I'd dragged them through the sea with me.

"How?" Verin was saying. "How?"

"My business is my own," Arabella replied coyly. "I command you to turn us east. My daughter needs me."

He held up a hand, perhaps the only man willing to defy my mother. "I can't. The king has put a bounty on pirates. I won't risk being caught."

"The king is not here," Arabella said curtly. "I guarantee you that my blade can kill you faster than he could. Turn. East."

This ship was much like the *Royal Rose* with two main masts and a sleek build to glide through the waves. The

deck crowded with roughly twenty crewmates, all staring at
Arabella whose makeshift dress was dripping water into a
puddle at her feet. Her hair was plastered against her face,
but she kept her chin high as if she noticed none of this.

Verin planted his feet. "I'm not sailing east. I'm going
north, and you're welcome to join as my crew. But I won't be
bullied on my own ship."

Arabella scanned the deck. As her face turned to mine, I
shook my head, but her eyes glazed over me. Then she took a
deep breath. "Fine. Just give us a place to sleep."

Verin let out his breath. "I'll get you hammocks."

Her hand stopped him as he started past. "Let's
dine together, Verin. It's been too long. Dinner in your
quarters tonight?"

After a pause, he gave a short nod.

"Lovely."

None of them knew her as well as I did to see the trickery
playing behind her words. And this time when she looked
my way, there was an unmistakable plan brewing behind her
dark eyes.

Later that night, I waited aboard deck as Arabella took her
dinner in the cabin. She'd spent the entire day talking kindly
to the crew. That confirmed something brewing. My mother
hadn't said *please* once, the entire time on the island—perhaps
my entire life—and yet tonight she was buckets of manners. I
got dozens of comments about how incredible it must be to be
the Arabella the Ruthless's son. *Yes,* polite nod. *It's something.*

Sure enough, just as the moon kissed the horizon, she
flung the door to the on-deck cabin open wide. She no longer
wore her dress, but pants rolled at the ankles, a black shirt,
heavy jacket, and cutlass to her side.

Now she looked like my mother. Except for Captain Verin's
hat, which she made a great show of putting on her own head.
Behind her, a body lay on the floor.

"Your captain is dead," she announced loudly. "I am captain now. And we are turning east. Any who disagree can spare me the trouble of killing them and throw yourselves overboard now."

The air stilled. The crew looked up from their tasks, mouths hanging open. Some grinning as if this was an exciting adventure. Some gulping. But one thing they all had in common: none protested.

Arabella tipped her hat at them. "What a pleasant crew you are. This will be a jolly good time. Now adjust the sails and give me the helm."

She took a few steps then turned. "Oh. And dispose of the body in a seaworthy manner."

I treaded to the rails to stare over the sea as we changed directions. My stomach was as churned as the waters. My mother was willing to kill to find Emme. And yet this unknown sister still meant nothing to me.

That captain didn't deserve this. My sister didn't deserve this. I sifted through memories and pulled at every string of my heart, trying to find the one that led me to her, and came up empty. Would it break her heart to learn I didn't know her?

Someone tapped my shoulder. "Your clothes are dry." A man the same build as me had offered a dry set of clothes while mine had the sea steamed out of them. He handed the warm lump back to me, then took something from his pocket. "I found this in them. Not sure what it means, but figured you'd be wanting that back."

He set a small cloth on top, then left. I frowned at the cloth, picking it up to examine it. Something was written in what looked suspiciously like blood. The letters were lopsided, but still legible.

Remember her.

The note was written in my own hand, the same words that Coral had whispered to me. I lifted my finger, where I had noticed a stinging cut. I stared at it thoughtfully. Then remembered. I wrote this. I wanted to remember someone, and it had meant enough to me that I'd written it in blood.

That settled it. Whoever this Emme was, I would get my memory back, no matter what.

20
ARN

The frigid water kissed our toes as we hauled the ships out as far as we dared before waiting to see which recruits would join. Two had showed so far, and they inspected the *Royal Rose* as it swayed on waters lit by the golden sun.

"She's smaller than I'd guessed," one said.

"She's fast," Ontario countered with a frown.

"And sturdy," I added.

"As long as the wages are as promised, she could be made of paper," the second one said. His mustache hid most of his mouth, but it had been combed with the attention of a man who cared for his appearances. He'd take good care of the ship while on board. He'd be a navigator, perhaps. Or physician's aid.

The first man was built like a tree and clothed in vivid colors like a merchant. The muscles in his arms feathered when he strung a sack over his wide shoulders. Likely a good fighter. He'd get the heavy work on deck. "I was only saying," he said, "that I'd thought the *rskvateer* to be a mightier vessel."

I swung my head at the name. Over his shoulder, Landon's brow pinched.

It was Ontario who laughed. "That's no *rskvateer,* mates. It's a conqueror." He shook the water from his boots as he took sloshy steps back up the pale white stones to squint over the shore.

I leaned closer to Emme so the others wouldn't hear. "By the way, I fancy the nickname. *Rskvateer.* What does it mean? Sea Lord? Slayer of Many? Mighty Conqueror?"

Her mouth twitched. "Grave ship."

My face fell. "That's fine too."

"Arn, if you wanted a fierce moniker, you shouldn't have named your ship after a flower." She grinned and ran her hands through her tangled hair. "There are the others. Let's be off."

We climbed into the boats as the final four recruits showed, all heaving from the run and carrying lumpy bags of meager belongings. We hardly fit into the rowboats for the trip back, and I gladly gave up my oar for one of them to take.

For the first time in a year, the *Royal Rose* had a crew of twenty. We were almost full.

Tess sat beside me, and I leaned to her. "You are stealthy on your feet."

There was pride in her smile. "I used to sneak rum from my parents' cellar. I got a few lashes . . . but a quick foot."

"She wove through the crowds like a ghost," I explained to Emme. "Like she's made of air itself."

Emme thought for a few moments until speaking with a hesitancy as if her words were coming against her better judgment. "Can you fight, Tess?"

"Yes," Tess answered quickly. "Well, a little." She glanced to the other men then bent close. "Not really."

"Want me to teach you?"

Tess didn't know how good of an offer that was. She didn't see Emme as the great daughter of Arabella the Ruthless, but rather the sick girl who couldn't hold her hand still enough to sign her name properly.

By the way Tess was twisting her fingers, she was finding a polite way to say so.

"At full health, Emme is one of the most competent fighters we've got," I said as hulls of the rowboats tapped against the *Royal Rose*. The crew took hold of the ropes and hauled themselves aboard. "She can teach you moves that will save your life."

Tess grabbed hold of the end of a rope. "In that case, yes." She climbed up.

I held out my hand to help Emme up. "That was nice of you to offer."

"If I can't convince her to return to her family, I might as well help keep her alive here." Emme fastened ropes to the hooks on the rowboat as I wound my foot into the loop of another.

"I'll still teach her school lessons," I promised as I tugged on my rope.

It was a blow to my pride to be lifted by the crew instead of climbing, but with one hand, it was the best I could do. It carried the added bonus of not making Emme feel bad that she also had to be lifted after me.

Ontario had already taken his place at the helm. "Welcome aboard, mates. I'll be watching you over the next few days to determine your roles on board, and that starts now. Let's set sail.

The anchors were pulled up, sails tied down, and ship inspected. Our navigator placed himself at Ontario's side to point him northbound and discuss the routes. The new members waddled across the deck back and forth, eager to help but clueless about what to do. Three of them tried climbing to the crow's nest before Landon pulled them down and shoved them in a different direction.

"Go check in with our cooper," he grumbled. "See if one of you hooligans can make barrels."

I waited until he was belowdecks before finding Tess as she was about to scale the mast to check the yardarms.

"I've got a task for you, Tess."

I swore her brown eyes actually twinkled with mischief. This girl was made of nothing but blood, bones, and aptitude for trouble. The perfect combination.

"I need you to sneak through Landon's things and keep an eye on him to find out what trouble he's meaning to get into."

Her smile dipped for a second then reappeared. "Done."

"And don't get caught," I added.

She was already halfway up the mast, her limbs crawling over one another like a spider's. She cast me a look. "Of course."

Tess was quickly becoming one of my favorite people on crew.

Pearly clouds collected across the wide sky, filtering away with the breeze, as if the sun wanted one last chance to heat the seas before winter claimed its mark. I'd take the warmth. On this deck, that was in short supply. I discarded my jacket to fold it over my shoulder as I shifted through the crew to the on-deck cabin. Three new recruits stumbled about inside, rifling through things and trying to sort them onto the shelves like they had any idea where anything belonged.

"Need jobs?" I asked. They nodded.

"Any of you read?"

To my delight, they all said yes.

"Write?" This time only two. "You'll help me be the boatswain. You"—I pointed to the third—"may find work elsewhere. Check with the lass with the octopus tattoo to see if she needs help mending ropes." He slipped away, leaving me with a girl with hair as pale as snow and freckles as red as fire and a boy a few years younger than me with a steady step that suggested he was no stranger to sailing.

I flipped open a notepad. "Count the yards of canvas for me," I instructed the girl. Then I pointed to the boy. "And you go count how many barrels of dried beans and biscuits we have. You'll find them belowdecks." He was out the door in a flash. I eased into a chair. For the first time, I was thankful for the seemingly unending well of wealth that Ontario possessed that allowed us to hire more sailors.

But just as I propped my legs up and took that first swig of grog, a hawk landed in the window. I nearly choked.

His beady eyes watched me. My fingers tightened around the cold neck of my bottle.

"Leave," I said tersely to the girl.

She turned around, noticing the hawk for the first time.

"I said leave," I repeated. "Only for a moment."

Maybe it was the cut of my voice, but she dropped the canvas to let it roll across the floor with a patter until it knocked against my chair. She yanked the door shut behind her.

I glanced out the window. Emme was within view, sitting near the prow with her legs folded beneath her and fingers working in a steady rhythm over the mass of old ropes, picking a bone needle through them. If she looked up, she'd see it: Admiral Bones's hawk.

"What do you want?" I set the bottle down and pushed to stand.

The creature held out his foot.

"No. I'm done. Your master is dead, and my oathbinding is gone. Leave me be."

He set his foot down and squawked. Then he held his foot out again.

"No." I crossed to the door.

The hawk spread his wings, bolted through the air, and latched onto my arm. I jerked, but his talons buried deeper.

I swore at him. "All right, then. Give it to me." I thrashed for his leg until finding the slip of paper and yanking it free. Satisfied, the blasted bird leapt back through the window and into the sky.

"I should have shot it," I mumbled. "Next time I will." Now I had three gnarly pierce marks along the forearm of my missing hand, and it sent shocks of pain as I eased my arms into my jacket to hide the wound.

The slip of parchment looked like any of the other messages:

dark paper, haunting sun-design seal, and the unspoken promise of nasty threats inside.

But none of the other messages made my stomach drop quite like this one did.

Arn,

I ought to take your life in payment for my father's, but I'm a reasonable man. Your dues are doubled, and you have three months to pay me.

- His son

He didn't need to say whose son he was. He didn't need to say what would happen if I didn't pay. This way, he'd cause me many sleepless nights of imagining the horrors that could be unleashed upon me by one with such a wide control over the seas.

I wondered if the son had come ashore to find his father bleeding into the sea, or his men had found Admiral Bones and called upon the son. He'd look over the books, see my relationship with his father, and want retribution for what I took from him. The Bone Legacy was now his, and that came with a large wealth, clientele list, and command over the waters.

Admiral Bones hadn't been a pirate, but he was as powerful as Arabella had been—and perhaps as ruthless. If his son had also inherited his father's tendency for no mercy, I was in trouble.

I glanced out to Emme again and crumpled the note. "It's tradition at this point," I said to no one as I tossed the note out the window.

The next three months were for Emme, and her alone. Save the girl, then save myself.

No mysterious long-lost son would take my future away from me.

21

EMME

I saw the hawk. I saw the ghost color on Arn's skin. But what I didn't see was him open the door to tell me what had happened. Instead, he called the girl back into the cabin. She obliged and started running her finger over the lines of canvases while Arn seated himself beside the table to scribble in a notepad.

Above him, Ontario stood behind the helm, staring into the horizon.

I wouldn't be lied to twice.

I left the ropes and climbed the few stairs. "Have you heard from Admiral Bones again?"

Ontario flinched. "How could I? He's dead."

"How about his son or his business partners?"

Ontario checked his compass and adjusted the wheel before answering me in a tone that was as dry as the bottom of Bo's bottles. "No, but I wouldn't be surprised if we do. Admiral Bones had more influence over other pirates than we knew, and Arn did owe him quite a lot. Any business partners will be wanting their dues."

Ontario's gaze settled on me.

"You did the right thing by killing him," he said. "He was a cruel man. You won't deal with retribution for your actions."

Admiral Bones's death weighed lighter and lighter on my conscious with each passing day, and it was difficult to tell if that was the kindness of my soul forgiving myself or the hardening of my heart, but I'd be grateful to know that the murder would carry no repercussions. "You can't know that."

He shrugged. "I'll be certain that you are found blameless," he promised. He sounded sincere. "No one needs to know who pulled the trigger."

I bowed my head in gratefulness and was about to turn away.

"Emme? I have a question for you. When will you accept that your brother is dead?"

The unexpected words were a knife stabbing through me. "I don't know," I whispered so softly that he might not have caught it. I spoke up. "I don't know. I might prefer to remain ignorantly hopeful forever, even if . . ."

That wasn't a sentence I cared to finish.

Ontario watched me steadily. "When you are ready for it, I'm offering you a permanent place on this crew."

My breath caught in my throat.

He gave a half smile. "You didn't think I'd throw you out, did you?"

"But you don't think I'll die?"

"Arn seems convinced that you won't, so there might as well be a family waiting for you when you defeat this." His smile broadened. "If you'll have us."

I swung my eyes over the main deck as the crew was busy with work, cleaning fish, repairing nets, and teaching the new recruits our ways. This was more than I had waiting for me back home. But when I thought of home, I didn't think of the sea.

"I'll think on it," was all I could say

We were interrupted as, from the crow's nest, Tess had dropped an apple and almost knocked Bo out with it. Now they'd created a game to see who could throw it back up to her. So far, they all had horrid aim.

Ontario reached up in time to catch a misguided throw. He tossed the apple down to Clarice. "Show them how it's done."

On her first try, she made it up to the crow's nest so perfectly that it landed in Tess's open hands.

"And that's why she's my quartermaster," Ontario declared.

"Because she can throw an apple?" Bo asked.

Ontario had a smug look on his face. "Tess, throw it at Clarice."

Tess chucked the apple over the edge with dangerous speed. Calmly, Clarice whipped out her cutlass and sliced the fruit in two pieces. They fell with a thud at her feet.

"She's quartermaster because she indulged you all in your game. Shows she's likable. But she's skilled enough that you won't argue with her when I ask her to carry out my orders."

Clarice took an apple half and bit into it.

"That was my apple!" Tess complained.

"I'll get you another one," Timmons offered, and soon the tossing was back on. This time, the apple almost took out Arn when he emerged from the cabin below my feet. He rubbed the bridge of his nose and laughed. It was good to hear that laugh again.

Bo had stepped away from the group, a curious look on his face. "So who's the second quartermaster?"

"There's no such thing." Ontario frowned.

"But if there were, who would it be?"

Ontario didn't hesitate to gesture to me. "Emme."

"Me?"

Arn's mouth dropped open. "Emme?"

I couldn't tell which of us sounded more shocked.

"Would anyone argue with the daughter of Arabella the Ruthless?"

The apple fell to the deck as no recruits tried for it. The

older crewmates stared at us dumbly. Only a select handful of our twenty knew that information—those who'd traveled to the fatal Island of Iilak with us.

My jaw ticked. Now anytime the new crew mates saw me, they'd only be thinking of *her*.

Ontario rested his frame against the railing, seemingly unbothered by my glower. "It's not a thing to be ashamed of," he said. "You wear her old name like a curse, but it doesn't have to be." His lowered voice was meant for only me now. "If you have a parent like that, you use any glimmer of their power for yourself until you are revered as they were."

"She wasn't revered; she was hated."

"By some, but respected by all. There's no shame in using that."

A breeze cracked at the planks, and I hoped that it would take all thoughts of Arabella the Ruthless with it and discard them over the sea where they belonged. But the crew's eyes were now wide, and I doubted they'd forget anytime soon.

Tess leaned over the edge of the crow's nest until I feared she'd fall. "I'd like those fighting lessons whenever you're ready," she said.

"See?" Ontario said. "Her name means something. Use that."

I went down the last of the stairs to the main deck just in time to spot Landon, and by the look of fascination on his face, he had heard who my mother was.

He crossed his arms and his gleaming eyes darted between Arn and me. "Now I know the reason Arn fancies you."

I scowled. "And I see more and more why Arn dislikes you."

"That's my girl," Arn said from behind me as he laid a hand on my shoulders.

Landon shrugged. "Whatever the reason, Emme just became one of the most valuable members on this ship. And any other crew would be happy to kill to have her aboard."

I'm certain everyone heard me gulp.

"And when the other ships hear that the daughter of Arabella the Ruthless killed the king? They won't dare to cross us." Landon's slow gaze studied me. "I'm suddenly very interested in keeping her alive."

"How honorable of you," I said through clenched teeth.

"How honest. Count yourself lucky. Not many of us are irreplaceable."

I didn't feel lucky. I felt like a token. I looked back to Ontario, who gave me a knowing nod. *There's no shame in using that.* But in almost the same beat, I put my hand inside my pocket to find the wolfbane pin. My reminder to never be like my mother.

"You're not irreplaceable, Landon," I said.

He angled his head suspiciously. My words came sweetly. "Without you here, who would we have to mend the old ropes?"

"Nope. Not me. That's tedious work."

"Second quartermaster," I responded quickly with a crafty grin. "You have no say."

Landon frowned and opened his mouth then closed it. He unwillingly took my place at the prow to go through the ropes and mend frayed parts, while I found a barrel to sit on.

"I think this means you outrank me," Arn whispered as he leaned by my side.

"I like the sound of that. Maybe someday I'll be captain."

He laughed, but it wasn't a full sound.

"Is that a hint of worry I detect? Scared Ontario would let me captain sooner than you?"

"I know he would. But that man won't give up his position for anyone."

"Lucky for you, I don't want it. But," I turned my eyes to his, "I do want to know what Admiral Bones's hawk was doing here?"

His stiffened then cleared his throat. "He had a letter to deliver asking that I pay what I owe."

I chewed on my lip. "Nothing about the killing of his father?"

"Seems people care more about money than relatives." His steady gaze fixated on the seas, the color matching the blue of his eyes, which were cloaked in uncertainty. Restless waters lapped against the hull in a frantic manner, likely to turn to a storm at any minute. His eyes were the same way. One breath away from chaos.

But when he looked at me, all that faded.

Maybe Ontario was right, and I wouldn't have to face punishment for what I'd done. Or it could be whoever took over the business was biding their time.

"Whatever happens, it won't interfere with our plan of finding the king and healing you," Arn promised. He continued to keep his voice low so none of the new recruits could hear us. No doubt Ontario had promised them a grand adventure on the seas and not spoken of our mission to abduct their king. They wouldn't care about me enough to risk their lives.

"You'll face no punishment for killing that man," Arn said. "And if any comes, I'll bear it."

"I wish you didn't have to do that for me."

"Emme, you are on your way to healing," Arn said, taking my hand in his. "I am on my way to destroy a corrupt man." His hand rested on my arms, bringing warmth to my whole body as his fingers stroked small circles. "You are good and kind and everything pleasant in this world. I'm grateful to have someone like you to fight for."

I let him hold me close. "You are good too."

He threw back his head to laugh. "Not even close. But I love you for thinking so."

The waves rolled more rhythmically than before, almost like they were a song and we their captive audience. The wind came from behind us to swell out the sails and drive us north, just out of sight of land, sailing closer and closer to Kvas and the king. Five days until I fulfilled my oathbinding. Hopefully six weeks until I would stand straight without holding onto rails and walk across the deck without stumbling.

Arn brought a hand to mine. "Don't worry, love. This time, everything will go according to plan."

His words had barely left his mouth when Ontario hollered.

"On guard, mates!" His voice vibrated with an urgency and command that we hadn't heard from him yet as captain. His eyes were latched onto the horizon. A ship lurked there. "I hope you can all handle a pistol."

"According to plan?" I asked Arn with a sigh, as I got to my feet to find the barrel of gunpowder.

Arn's face was pale. "That's the *Dancer*."

I whirled around and stared. "Landon's ship?"

Landon calmly stood at the edge of our ship, watching his old crew approach.

Arn cursed richly. "He played us."

22
ARN

I crossed the deck and grabbed the collar of Landon's shirt. "Tell me what they want, right now."

He ripped away. "You aren't the only ship on the seas. Perhaps they'll pass peacefully."

"Like stars they will." I threw him my pistol. "I can't load it with one hand. Load it."

He took out his powder horn and poured powder into the bore. "How small of an opinion you have in me, friend."

"You've betrayed me many times over."

"I'm a changed man." He dropped in a bullet and thrust the gun back to me. "Prime it yourself."

In the distance, the *Dancer* came closer.

The hairs on my arms stood up, and I stashed my gun at my side.

"Get ready, mates." I swung to face the crew. Tess scrambled down from the crow's nest to sloppily load her pistol, and Bo tried to show her the proper way to do it. A few volunteered to man the cannons but others quivered at the ship's side. Ontario stood stiff as a board at the helm, watching the other vessel come closer. They were a smaller craft like us, built with cedar in sharp narrow lines and trimmed with fine canvas, created to slice through the waters at unmatched speed. We couldn't turn now or hope to outrun them.

"We don't play with this ship," Ontario instructed. "When we get in range, shoot."

Landon swung his head to the helm. "That's my ship. Let's not blow it to bits."

"This is your ship now," Ontario reminded him. "And I'm not risking it. We fight."

I hopped over a crate to find Emme loading pistols. "Stay on deck near the rowboats," I suggested. "It's the safest place to be."

She looked up with a sad smile. "Look at me. I can't run. I can't fight." She held her hand up for proof, and it shook like her very bones were trembling.

I pushed back through the small crowd gathered around the gunpowder. "Landon, will they attack?"

He peered at the ship and shook his head. "No."

"Are you certain? Are you sure they won't engage?"

"They lost many of their crew hands a month ago," he said. "Then their captain. They are weak and unprepared for a fight. They will pass silently."

"But if we fire first?"

He raised an eyebrow at me. "What man wouldn't fight back?"

I peeled away and ran up to the helm. "Ontario, we can't fight. We aren't prepared."

"You might not be, but I am. I'm not letting those scumbags by without a fight."

"Emme will die if we go down. She's too weak to swim."

He quieted, and the muscles in his cheek rippled as he clenched his jaw. He drummed a finger against the wheel as I was forced to stand by his side silently while he decided our fates. From below, the crew awaited their orders. After the longest time, and when the *Dancer* was almost in striking distance, Ontario heaved a sigh and called out, "Be still. Let's see what they do."

I could have collapsed with relief. "Thank you."

He didn't look pleased. His eyes were hardened and lips slammed together. "You make me look weak."

"I make you look reasonable." I turned and descended to the main deck.

It was pure silence here, every man holding their breath as we came closer, near enough to see the star on the *Dancer* flag, and to see a figure in their crow's nest and another behind the helm. We could hear the break of waves against their ship, the sound like the marching of an army coming closer until it was almost upon us. They kept at a distance, but not far enough for the power of gunpowder.

"What did I tell you?" Landon asked. But his voice was hoarse. "Nothing."

But he didn't let out a breath. He held it like he waited for something.

Then the seas erupted.

From their helm, a woman cried out, her shrill voice piercing the skies and bringing with it a multitude of shouts that stained the air and sent us into a scramble. An ample-sized crew appeared on their deck, and the violent sound of a cannon went off.

Smoke plumed from the starboard side of their ship. I braced for impact.

The *Royal Rose* rocked abruptly. I dug my fingers into the riggings to keep upright as an unpleasant sound of wood breaking saturated the air. I stormed to the edge to glare over my beautiful ship. A gaping hole plagued the side of the *Royal Rose,* and a similarly sized one opened inside me. *My beautiful ship.*

"Liar!" I spun to Landon, then ducked as another cannon went off. "Dirty, rotten liar! You knew they would attack." I ducked again as our crew fired their pistols. The other crew fired back.

Landon stood near the cabin, hidden in the shadows of the overhang and watching the *Dancer* intently. He kept a hand on his pistol but made no move to shoot.

I raised my own weapon and aimed at him.

A second hit knocked me off my feet. Emme screamed. I

clawed at the wet deck for grip and fought to stand. From the side, Emme was bracing herself against crates and looking wildly about as the seas rolled beneath us.

I could only imagine her thoughts. And the irony of her wearing Emric's tunic was that now she might suffer the same fate as him.

Ontario shouted in the chaos. "Fire the cannons! What in the name of the dark seas are you waiting for—us to drown?"

Shouts on the other ship revealed they'd dropped their anchors to attack us—hardly the action of a ship that planned to sail past. I hit the deck as they shot again, and my tunic snagged on the rigging. It ripped under the arm.

At last, our cannons fired.

I peeked over the edge in time to see the worthless cannonball drop into the sea. They fired again. By the crashing sound and way the ship lurched, a third one of theirs   hit us.

"Ontario!" I yelled. "We will all drown!"

He leaned against his fists and buried his head in his chest before letting out a painful cry. I was worried he'd been shot until he lifted his head again. "Arms down! We will not win this." His gaze sliced over the deck, to the scrambled crew holding for impact, to the way the ship rocked, and then to me. It hardened there, with animosity so deep that it would never run dry. Then it pulled away. "Landon, climb up to the crow's nest and raise the white flag."

Landon put his pistol back in his holster and drew an arm across the sweat gathering on his forehead. "One shot and I'm dead."

Ontario drew his pistol and aimed it at Landon. His eyes blazed like I'd never seen before. He was quite the sight with smoke billowing off the chilly seas, the echoing of shots booming over the deck, our own crew in a mad struggle, and the shouts aboard the *Dancer* as they turned their ship, raised their anchor, and came nearer. His barrel stared at Landon. Landon didn't flinch.

"This is your fault," Ontario said through his teeth. "If you don't go up there, I will shoot you, and you *will* be dead."

Landon grabbed the posts and climbed while muttering something along the lines of *this isn't my fault*, and *worthless pirates*.

He made it without getting shot. Our crew had put down their arms and cowered on the deck until the firing slowed to the pace of one shot at a time. From above, Landon untied the slip of white canvas and shook it in the air.

The other crew cheered. Inside, I ached. The *Royal Rose* was never meant to be taken.

We dropped anchor and waited for them to close in enough that their hull nearly brushed ours. Around three dozen pirates gathered on their deck to mock us and claim their victory, but it was the one behind the helm that drew my attention by the way she leaned her lithe frame against the wheel and crossed her arms. She lifted her chin so the sun peeked under her hat.

"The *Dancer* is captained by Pearl," I breathed.

Emme was beside me. "The one we deserted in the Seas of Lost Lands?"

"Aye. She's not lost anymore."

Pearl's gaze met mine, and she winked.

"She was Landon's lover once," Emme recalled as the plank was dropped between ships. "They must have been in on this together." One second later, we got our answer. Pearl crossed to the railing to sweep her eyes over the deck until they caught on Landon halfway down the mast. He planted one foot on the post and leaned out to salute the crew.

"You found them," Pearl called in an impressed tone. My stomach sank.

Landon grinned, sitting on the yardarms with his arms outstretched. "The *Royal Rose*, delivered to you as promised"

He climbed down the mast to land on the deck. "I'm a man

true to my word." Though he spoke to Pearl, he looked at me as he said it. I met him with a glare.

Pearl gestured for a plank to be dropped between our ships. "Then come aboard. The rest of you will go down with your ship."

I stepped in Landon's way. "The Sea King Valian will never forgive you for your traitorous heart. He will curse your time at sea."

He brushed past. "I don't believe in the Sea King."

"Then I curse you," I yelled. "The man who was once my brother and my friend, I curse you to a lonely life spent chasing something you can never have."

He paused a moment with his back to me, then stepped on the plank without another word.

If there weren't dozens of pistols aimed at our small crew, I'd have the courage to shoot Landon now. His feet hit the other deck, and he straightened. His gaze flickered to me, but not long enough to get the proper view of my ire.

From behind, Ontario was barking orders to the crew to salvage the sinking ship. While we were going down slowly, it seemed there was a hole somewhere. I'd just gone to help them when Landon's loud voice grated into me.

"Permission to invite another aboard?" he asked Pearl. If he needed permission, he had been telling the truth about not being their captain anymore. Pearl nodded.

Landon turned to look at Emme. "I'd say enough of your family has drowned in these seas, and you'll die soon anyway." He held out his hand. "I'm offering you a chance to live."

Emme, bless that spirit, bared her teeth at him. I'd love her forever. But even in that moment, I knew what had to be done.

"You need to go," I told her.

She looked at me as if I were crazy. "I'm not leaving you."

"I'm beyond saving you, Emme," I pled with her through the painful twang in my chest. "I'll die better knowing you'll live."

She opened her mouth, but I kissed it before she could speak. "Please, live." I looked into her eyes and mustered the best smile I could. "And maybe punch him once for me too."

She studied me then kissed me back. "I'll do better than that," she whispered. "I'll find a way to save you."

She'd have to work fast. By the way the ship sat lower in the waters, we would soon sink. But I didn't say so. Instead, I lifted her hand to help her on the plank.

She gave one last look behind her, first at me, then Ontario, then she crossed over.

Some of our new recruits tried to join her, full of hysterics, but men stood at the other end of the plank with loaded pistols, and they thought better of it. Hysterics turned to madness as the plank was pulled away.

The *Dancer* drifted out.

Emme watched me as she sailed away. I went across the deck to be closer to her. "You're going to be fine," I called to her. "I promise you. You're going to be fine."

My words got lost on the seas and by the sound of their oars slapping the water as they dragged her away. Emme straightened her back and kept her eyes on me.

If that was the final look I'd get of her, I'd take it. I'd stood on the deck to watch the sight of her disappear many times when leaving her at the Banished Gentleman, but this view was different. Her dark, wild curls rippled behind her, and the corner of her octopus tentacle tattoo latched onto her collar bone from underneath the oversized tunic. She crossed her arms and held her chin high. She had turned away with such determination in her face that I had no doubt believing she'd bring that ship down.

Just as ours was going down.

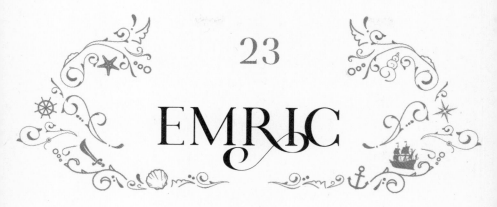

23

EMRIC

Cold wind typically calmed me. Tonight, it didn't do its job well enough. I was a chaotic mess of a man, grasping at old memories to summon the face of my sister while plotting what steps to take next. No answer felt right.

I climbed to the helm. "This is quite the ship you have, Mother," I said. I had finally started speaking to her again after the death of the captain.

"She's not bad. I'm thinking of naming her *Persistence*." She patted the polished wood of the wheel. It was as fine of a ship as I'd ever seen, crewed by a hundred men who couldn't take their eyes off their new captain, nor the blood stain of the old one that Arabella insisted not be cleaned for a few days.

Reminds them not to trifle with me.

"You should call her *Bloodied*," I said bitingly

But she only laughed. "All the best ones are."

The night hit us with another sheet of icy wind until this time my skin was cold as snow and my hair half frozen. The heat of the island was gone. I eyed the ropes. "We should go south."

"We will go to Julinbor."

"Our old home? Why?"

She gave me an odd look before facing the seas. "Before

he met his, shall we say, untimely death, the captain told me that the *Royal Rose* had been spotted along the western shore of Julinbor. He mentioned an interesting target there. If all goes well, we will find your sister and get enough gold to sink a ship."

My ears perked up. "I like the sound of that," I admitted. "And I wouldn't mind reclaiming my ship."

She didn't turn her head down in the wind or even blink. She only held the helm with a satisfied smile. Her feet were buried in the slots to show she had no intention of moving.

At my comment, she snorted. "You cannot sail on the seas and be with a mermaid. What is your plan? To string her up and pull her along?"

I glared at her. "No, of course not."

"Then you forfeit your ship." And by how she said it, that was the greatest crime I could commit. "And what do you hope to gain from a life with her?"

"She told me of great things under the sea," I said. "For one, they don't suffer such bitter winters as this. It's warmer and it's endless. There are reefs unexplored and sunken ships to pillage and kingdoms built of gems."

At this, she eyed me. "Then it's the adventure you chase?"

I frowned. "Isn't that what we all chase? That's why I wanted to be a pirate too. The adventure. I've had that one. I'm ready for another."

"But not the love?" The tone in her voice was odd.

Love wasn't a word Arabella spoke often. "What do you mean?"

"Would you choose a life with her even if you work the fields, eat porridge for dinner, and do the same thing every day until you die? Would you still take her then?"

"We could find the adventure in that too," I answered to hide a different response. In truth, I'd hate that. But that didn't mean I didn't love Coral, it meant I didn't care for farming. I'd hate that with anyone.

"As you say. But it matters not." Her voice regained its usual tone. "My daughter has become the pirate I always knew she would be. And I will find her."

"Is she ruthless like you?"

She smiled proudly. "I hope even more. But we will soon see."

24

EMME

I had to save the *Royal Rose* before she drowned, and that left no time to waste. My pistol was still loaded, but a knife would suit me better for this particular plan. The blade was cool on my arm as I slid it from where I'd stashed it in my sleeve. I pivoted to Landon as if struggling for my balance and pierced him in the side.

He let out a deep grunt and doubled over. I made certain the blade was in far enough to render him helpless before pulling it out. He collapsed to his knees in pain.

I summoned all my strength and faced Pearl. "You will release me back to my ship and offer a boatswain to assist in fixing the damage you caused."

The crew on board was larger than ours, and each of them had their pistols drawn. I didn't care for the way they pointed at me, but I stood my ground.

Pearl chuckled. "You've changed much since I saw you last," she said. "Your body is weaker, yet I suspect you are stronger." A cloak hung from her shoulders and swayed around her knee-high boots, and she kicked it out of the way to lean herself at the ledge. We didn't travel fast. We'd be here long after the *Royal Rose* sank. I could hear their frantic cries behind us as they struggled to piece the ship back together, and that sound fueled me.

At my feet, Landon inspected a blood-soaked hand. "You little witch," he growled.

"You liar," I hissed back. I raised my voice to Pearl. "I will kill you in one swift action if you don't turn us around."

She opened her mouth, likely to laugh again, and I flicked my blade at her. Had I been at full strength, that would have whizzed by her head, nicking her cheek enough to frighten her. As it was, it thudded into the wood by her hand. When she lifted it, her sleeve was caught, pinning her to the helm.

I felt grim satisfaction. That worked too. Might have been better, in fact.

I couldn't ignore the pistols of the crew. I hoped they cared somewhat for Landon as I ducked behind him. He tried to roll away, but I grabbed him by the waist, putting pressure on his wound. He yelped.

"Don't move," I warned. I looked at the captain. "Pearl, the next blade will hit your heart. Free me now and leave us be. We wish no more death between our two crews."

"Do you know how many of our friends you killed?" Pearl ripped her sleeve free. "We lost beloved souls that day." She hurled the blade to the main deck where it clattered. "We are past a truce."

"You attacked us!" I argued. I could see the crewmates of the *Royal Rose* frantically nailing boards to the broken ones, but it didn't look good. They needed to get to port for repairs. "Let me go. Now."

"I will let you live," Pearl said haughtily. "That is all I will allow."

I reached behind my back for another blade, but Landon managed to grab my arm with such force that I winced.

"Be calm."

He had the audacity to nod as if we had an understanding.

With great effort, he stood. "Pearl, love, let me see this one to the quarters and tie her up. She will come to her senses soon. I'm afraid my dearest is ill and not thinking straight." I tried to hide my shock at his words when he ran a finger down my cheek. I bit at it.

Pearl's eyes widened. "Your dearest?"

"I'd rather drown than be associated with you," I said with disdain.

"I understand you're mad that I lied to you, but that's no reason to discredit what we had," Landon said, his voice like sugar. He turned his back to the crew and gave me an intent look. "Calm. I'm not letting anyone die today."

Pearl was visibly stirred. "She's your new sweetheart?"

"Aye. Let me get her alone, and she won't cause problems for you anymore."

Pearl's gaze was like fire. She huffed and took hold of the wheel. "If you didn't lead us to them, I swear you'd be dead right now." She called to the crew, "Men, watch the ship. If it looks like it's going to survive the attack, fire the cannons again."

"No!" I jerked against Landon's hold, but he kept a surprisingly strong grip for a man who'd been stabbed. He yanked me to the cabin on deck, while I kicked and screamed against him. I got a good shot at his leg, but his strength greatly outweighed my own.

As soon as he shoved the door shut, he dropped me on the ground. "Have mercy, girl. And be grateful. Arn will live."

I stilled, keeping my feet ready to kick him again if he touched me. "What are you doing?"

"Saving you." He glanced quickly outside before rummaging through the room. It was similar to our cabin on deck, with shelves of storage and a desk with maps. He flung open the drawers to the desk to go through them. "Ah," he said eventually. "Here it is."

He kept a hand on his wounded waist as he held up parchment lined with blue calligraphy and silver embellishments. "Invitations to Winter Night."

I blinked. "How does Pearl have those?"

"They have an expert forger on deck," he explained, stashing them in his pocket. "We were taking a risk going to the Sea Gala, so I found a way to get us the invitations without it. Four should be enough."

I stared at him. He was so full of twists I couldn't keep my head straight. Was he betraying us to the *Dancer* or not? Was he loyal to the *Royal Rose*? From the distance the crew kept from him I'd say there was bad blood here, but I couldn't so soon unhear the crash of cannonballs against our hull as he'd led us into an attack. But now he waved the very thing we sought in front of my nose, sparing us from an extra trip.

"Then why not tell us this plan?" I demanded.

"I needed to know that Pearl had these. I didn't get that confirmation until this morning, and then they were upon us. If not, I would have made certain we left Gillen before they found us. Now be quiet a moment, there is one thing I still need to find." Landon knelt at the foot of the desk to roll back the red rug to unveil a brass knob to a storage compartment. He lifted it and gently reached inside.

"Thank the stars," he muttered. I'd never seen him move so slowly or hold something as tenderly as he did now with what he clutched to his chest. He briefly closed his eyes.

"What is that?"

He held it up. A thick lock of blonde hair had been tied together with twine.

"The girl that Arn killed to save you," he said, folding it tenderly into his breast pocket near his heart.

A shot of guilt coursed through me. But it was followed by disbelief.

"You mean to tell me that you let us be captured, let our

crew possibly die, let myself be taken captive, all to fetch one lock of hair?" The absurdity of it rang in my ears, but Landon's voice was like steel.

"I'd have done much worse than that for her."

"You're mad," I said.

His gaze sliced to me. "You know how much Arn loves you?" Sadness clouded his voice. "I loved Ellie a hundred times more than that. I'd let you all die to get this. But that doesn't matter now."

Landon found rope and held it up. He was moving so easily—the stab wound was obviously not as deep as I had thought.

"No." I stood to my feet and backed to the door. "Don't touch me."

"She needs to think I'm on her side," he said.

"I still think you are."

He sighed. "I can only deal with one problem at a time. You know I can force you, but I'd rather not." He held the ropes up again.

"No."

"If you don't play along, Arn dies."

I swallowed hard.

He sighed again as if I were a child he had to reason with. "There's no time."

I hated it, but I raised my hands.

Landon took hold of them and tied a loop through the bars over the porthole to trap me against it. His breath warmed my forehead as he worked, and my stomach churned at being so near to the man that I so disliked. But for Arn, I'd do anything.

"I have questions," I said.

"All in good time." He pulled a necklace from his pocket. "I need you to put this on." It was a simple gold chain with a heart locket, decorated with shells as if plucked from the ocean. "But don't touch it."

He hurriedly glanced over his shoulder. "No time to

explain." He pushed my head down and laced it around my neck. It hung long enough to sit halfway down my chest, resting against my brother's tunic. "A word of advice? When Pearl comes, don't speak."

"I still have questions," I hissed.

But he was already out the door, slamming it behind him.

I craned my neck to see out the porthole for a glimpse of the *Royal Rose*. It was the wrong angle.

"I should have stabbed him harder," I muttered.

But through the window, I could see Landon throw his arms open to welcome Pearl as she came down from the helm, but she only shoved him. His arms dropped. They spoke in heated voices where I caught a few words such as "traitor" and "this wasn't the plan." Finally, Pearl stormed away, and Landon sat at the foot of the main mast to whistle a tune. Before long, a bearded man sat down beside him.

Landon whistled while the *Royal Rose* sank. And he didn't return for me.

I'd felt hopeless before, but never so confused. And never so desperate.

I tore against my bonds until my wrists were raw and my breathing patchy enough that my lungs burned for air. I kicked at the walls. I screamed. I cried.

All the while, Landon sat and whistled that dull song. The bearded man left his side as another joined him.

I hung my head. *I'm sorry, Arn. I tried.*

The beating of waves was my only reply, and it sounded like a death march.

More tears fell to the floor as the door opened.

I whipped my head up as Pearl stepped in and closed the door behind her. She kept her back to me for a moment, breathing deeply before turning around.

She placed her hands around the generous curves of her waist and tilted her head. "So you're Landon's new lover."

I kept my mouth shut. She stepped closer. "I would have expected you to be with that other pirate, but Landon is a difficult man to turn away from." Her eyes snagged on my neck, and she reached out. Her laugh was etched in pain. "He gave me a necklace like this too."

Without hesitating, she ripped it off. I winced.

Her fist closed around the locket. Hatred filled her voice. "You can stay tied up in this room for all I care. I'd kill you if I could. At the next port, I'm leaving you. You'll never be a part of this crew."

Her hair whipped me in the face as she spun for the door.

"How did you get off that island?" I blurted out.

She stopped. "Landon's ship passed by on the way back. They were miserable after you slaughtered so many of them." She glared at me. "I had to pick up the pieces of them myself. Then they lost the treasure"—another angry glare—"and Landon was too absorbed in his sorrow to lead a crew."

"So you tracked us down to make us pay for the lives your crew lost?"

"No," she said. "First I went back to Aható and made those men who'd trapped me pay. I freed the women they'd stolen and gladly killed the rest, starting with the man who'd been my husband." While my blood chilled, she continued, "Then I tracked you down. With the ruin of the *Royal Rose*, I have my redemption."

"That's not redemption," I said. "It's simply more blood spilled into the ocean."

She gave a dry laugh and reached for the door handle and then went still.

From outside the window, Landon watched us intently.

Pearl slowly turned back around. She stared at her hand. Black coated the tips of her long fingers and stretched down to her palm, spreading longer every moment and growing darker until it rivaled midnight. It curled around her wrist, creeping up her arm, snatching at her elbows, and latching onto every crevice of her skin.

She dropped the locket. It clanged to the ground.

She lifted frantic eyes.

"What was on that locket?"

"I-I don't know," I stammered.

Landon slipped into the room and unsheathed a long-tipped knife. He crossed to me. The dangerously sharp tip sliced through my bonds. "Quick," he said, giving me a hand. Pearl sank to the floor as she tried to speak, but only gurgles came out.

The black spread to her neck. It was the fastest working poison I'd ever seen. I thanked every star that Landon used a slower one when he poisoned Arn.

Pearl thrashed when we stepped over her, but soon, she made no movement at all. I tried to control the rolling of my stomach. By the time we reached the door, Pearl's eyes were ash-colored and lifeless.

I might have vomited if Landon wasn't dragging me out the door.

He threw me toward the middle of the deck and called for attention. "Crew, I have unfortunate news. Your captain, Pearl, was laundering your goods away and swindling you from right under your noses. But I've taken care of the problem." Landon indicated the lifeless body. He spoke quickly so there wasn't time for questions. "I care not who you pick as next captain. I find I'm feeling merciful and plan to rescue the *Royal Rose*."

There was murmuring among the crew. I swung my gaze to the seas where the *Royal Rose* still floated. She was much lower in the water than I liked, but she was there.

"In the name of the dark seas, Landon." A man stepped forward to stare at the heap that was Pearl. I was trying hard not to look. I wouldn't be able to keep from throwing up twice. "Must you always bring death with you?"

"I'll work on that." Landon nudged me forward. He raised a gun to point it at the bearded man who he'd been speaking with earlier. "Manty, you'll come with me."

The pistol wasn't needed, as the man was already untying the rowboat. With his sleeves rolled up to his elbows and arms covered in tattoos, he undid the last of the knots. The boat dropped to the water.

Landon pushed me toward the boat. "Get in. See if we can still save your precious pirates."

"We can't let you go." A brave man came forward. He was tall, narrow, and courageous as I saw no weapon at his side.

Manty crossed his arms. Manty was tall as well, but wide with muscle and face set hard like stone, built from sharp lines and rough cuts.

Landon stood, looking pleased, next to Manty. "Care to argue with us?"

Manty cracked his knuckles for dramatics. I was grateful he was on my side.

The other man backed down without another word.

Landon clasped Manty on the shoulders. "I like you. You'll be very welcome aboard. Now come." He winced as he swung himself over the ship and down the line into the rowboat. "Another crew needs me to save them."

The rough ropes cut across my palms, and I slid too quickly down into the rowboat, then gripped the sides as Manty dropped beside me. As soon as our feet hit the deck, Landon was rowing away. I took up oars and helped him, pulling as fast as I could.

Mercifully, the *Dancer* adjusted its sails and pulled away with no further challenge. The sight of them leaving should have helped me breathe better, but the air still caught in my throat as all I could see was the vision of my crew drowning. It spurred me to row faster.

Landon spoke through labored breathing. "Well, Emme,

I'm certain Arn will want to shoot me as soon as he sees me. You don't mind too terribly if I put a blade to your neck to keep my own?"

"I do mind."

He paused rowing long enough to flash the forged invitations to Winter Night. "Do you want these or not?"

I frowned. The blue letters were my ticket to healing. "Fine. But if there is one drop of blood, I'm letting Arn shoot you."

"Fair enough." He leaned to Manty. "They aren't friendly with me on the *Royal Rose*. But that'll all change soon enough."

From behind us, a man shouted over the waves. "Don't come back to us, Landon. We've had enough of you."

I tried not to notice the way Landon's expression splintered, but it was so much like Arn's that I had to stare. Both men desperate for their ships back, and both willing to betray others to get what they wanted.

This time, Landon hadn't betrayed us. But next time it could very easily be Ontario lying dead in his quarters, or Arn with a bullet in his belly. Landon glanced at me, and I gave an innocent smile hoping it masked the emotion underneath. It was Ontario's voice earlier that told me to be like my mother, but now it was my mother's voice that spoke in my head. *You trust no one on the seas, for the waves have a way of turning alliances until they are soaked in deceit and all honesty is drowned.*

Any decency in Landon had drowned long ago. It was only a matter of time before it drowned us too.

25

ARN

The shouts grew louder with each passing minute.

"Where are the blasted nails?"

"I've got them!"

"More boards?"

"We are running out."

"The ship is going down."

"We're all going to die!"

It was hard to tell who was saying what. It was equally difficult to tell who was helping and who was merely running around aimlessly, offering up their final prayers while casting uneasy looks at the water.

One of the new recruits, Quincy, proved himself an excellent carpenter. *"I don't know much about fixing boats, but I can make great cabinets. I reckon I can mend some holes,"* he'd said.

"You can turn this whole ship into a cabinet as long as it floats," Ontario had said.

"They are just going to shoot at us again if we don't go down," I'd said as I tore open boxes to find nails and a mallet.

Ontario's nostrils flared. "I swear I'll kill you before we drown."

I paused in passing him the tools. "What did I do?"

"I wanted to throw him overboard! But I'll settle for you."
He jumped belowdecks, and there was no chance to apologize
for once again trusting Landon.

"I'd wanted to kill him on the Island of Iilak," I mumbled.
"That would have solved everything." I should have done that.
I should have taken a cutlass to his chest before anyone could
argue and have been done with the whole thing. My crew
would still be alive, and Emme would be healed. Landon's
mates wouldn't have attacked us, and we could be done with
his schemes.

Amid the ongoing shouts, a new cry came. "A boat
approaches!"

I threw myself at the rails to look.

"It's Landon!" Bo exclaimed. "Shoot him and be
done with it!"

"No!" I quickly intervened. "Emme is there." Landon had
a blade pressed to Emme's neck. I fumed. His crooked smile
gleamed as bright as the blade. "Once she's away from him, we
kill him. I don't care who does the deed."

Timmons, Bo, Collins, and Bishop volunteered. Tess
watched anxiously.

Ontario appeared above deck with his breeches soaked to
the thighs. "We need more planks, mates!" he called out.

"Landon's returning!" I called back. Ontario jerked his head
to the boat, then stomped to my side.

"We kill him this time," he growled.

"Agreed."

They got close enough that I could see Emme's face and
noticed it lacked fear.

Her hands were free at her side, not grasping his arm or
fighting to free herself. "No one shoot! Landon is helping us."

Ontario and I groaned at the same time. "I still say we shoot
him," I muttered.

"We still might," he said.

"Don't shoot," Emme repeated. Landon pulled the blade back to help row closer, but he stayed right behind Emme, and she spread her arms out to protect him.

I gave the *Dancer* one last look as it sailed north. That was the ship I planned to take once Emme healed. It was impossible not to compare it to the *Royal Rose*, which had more polished wood and the promise of new sails. But this other ship was faster, and that held more value. Less room for storage, so it needed more stops. But clearly ample in a fight.

It also wasn't sinking.

The shouts from below had quieted. Either they were under water or no longer feared we'd drown, I thought callously.

Ontario tossed a bucket to Tess. "We are alive, for now. Get to work emptying out the mess."

Her shoulders slumped as she cast a look to the rowboat, now at the hull, but obeyed.

"She likes being where the action is," I said.

Ontario's jaw was set. "I do not need children around when I murder someone." His dark eyes were flames of anger. "That man almost took down my ship."

"Just wait until Emme is clear."

"Throw us a rope, will you?" Landon was craning his neck to see us.

Ontario grabbed a rope and made a loop for Emme. "We only want her," he yelled over the side. "You and the giant can sail back!"

The large man gave Landon a sideways glance, and Landon whispered to Emme. She nodded and announced, "I don't come up unless he does." Her words might have been a dagger in my heart. But then she put a protective arm again in front of Landon, and that hurt worse.

"Why?" I demanded.

"Throw the rope, Ontario." She avoided my gaze.

Ontario tossed the rope, while Timmons, Bishop, Collins,

and Bo all stood dutifully behind us with pistols drawn. The others had formed a steady stream of buckets being brought up and tossed into the sea, and we lifted with each round.

The ship leaned westward when Emme grabbed hold of the rope. She tucked her foot inside the loop and pushed from the hull as we dragged her aboard. Without acknowledging us, she threw the rope back over.

The large man climbed up next, then turned around to pull up Landon.

"He can climb himself," I said. But when Landon toppled over deck, he winced. He clutched a hand to his abdomen where the thin fabric of his blood-stained tunic was sliced and stuck to his stomach.

"I might have stabbed him," Emme said offhandedly.

"I'll recover," Landon grunted.

Finally, Emme wrapped her arms around me in a trembling embrace.

Quincy poked his head above deck. "We've sprung another leak!" His clothes were soaked, and his hair matted to his rounded cheeks. He swung his head in search for Ontario. "Cap, we need more planks."

"All the inventory is belowdecks. Take from the bunks if needed. It's high time we get hammocks anyway."

Quincy disappeared. It now sounded like chaos below there, while above deck was stiff silence. Landon kept to the railing in the shadow of the larger man, who quietly stood expressionless. It was as if he were a statue standing exactly where he belonged.

Emme became the mediator between us all, and she motioned for the pistols to be lowered. No one obeyed.

"Landon killed the captain of the *Dancer*," she let us know.

"He also almost killed us," Ontario pointed out.

"Not so, mate. I saved us. More importantly," he nodded to Emme, "I saved her." He pulled papers from his pocket.

"What are those?"

"Invitations to Winter Night. We don't need to go to the Sea Gala."

"You got these from the *Dancer*?" I asked, swiping them from him. The crisp paper was thick enough to not bend beneath my touch, and the silver lining shone as if the moon was trapped inside.

"Manty forged them." Landon jutted his chin in the direction of the statue next to him.

I stared at the man large enough to rival a horse. "You're an artist?"

"My father was an artist," the man replied in a voice as grating as tree bark. He was all rough features and muscle, with a beard so thick that I couldn't see his chin or the top of his worn-out jacket.

"Was your mother a bear?" I asked.

Emme jabbed my side.

Manty didn't mind. "I can make more of those if you want." He gestured to the invitations.

"Deal. You can stay. Landon, you can jump back into the sea."

"The Sea Gala would have been crawling with foes more formidable than the likes of us." Landon talked as if I'd said nothing. "For the entire sea is on the search for not only the king, but a princess on the run. It seems the kingdom of Az Elo is missing their precious Princess Calypso, and they say she will be there at the gala."

"Poor place to choose to hide," Ontario said.

"She's evaded the king's grasp for three years. I think she'll do fine. But the price on her return is high enough to capture the attention of many pirates."

"What is it?" I asked.

"A thousand silvers." It was Ontario who answered, his voice far away. In the next beat, he was speaking with such determination that one would think we didn't already have enough ahead of us. "We should get her."

Panic flashed through me. "We can't. We aim for the king."

"We can get both."

Landon laughed dryly. "I just went through a lot to be certain we avoided the Sea Gala. We show up there, especially you with that face tattoo," he pointed to Bo, "and we will be arrested for piracy in King Unid's domain. She isn't worth the risk."

Landon had a strong point, but silver had a way of making points irrelevant. That much silver would satisfy my debt. It'd buy a nice ship. It would buy security.

But it wouldn't buy time, which we didn't have for a side mission.

"I tried to deliver a princess to the king of Az Elo once," I said. "It didn't go well."

"You survived. You were accepted onto a respectable crew."

"Let's get the king, then worry about a princess."

Timmons still held his gun with both hands. "Can we shoot him?"

"Yes," I said, at the same time that Emme said, "No."

Ontario sighed heavily through his nose. "You can make more of these?" He held up the invitations.

Manty nodded.

"The *Dancer* was coming for you in return for what happened on the Island of Iilak," Landon said. "I removed the threat and got us what we needed." He regarded Timmons uncertainly, a hand bent to his holster in case he had to fight.

Ontario drummed his fingers on his arm, then relaxed his jaw. He turned without a word and hopped belowdecks. We heard the rumbling of his voice, then a few moments later he came back up. Whatever news Quincy had must have been good because the tension was gone from his face. "You stay. But you are on thin ice."

Landon smiled as if he'd just been granted the ship. "Understood."

Ontario went back belowdecks as Landon and I eyed each other.

"Did you stab him good?" I turned to Emme.

"As well as I could," she sighed.

"That's good enough for me."

I headed to the on-deck cabin to begin the unpleasant task of recording what inventory we had left after the flooding, but Landon caught my sleeve.

"I wouldn't betray you again, mate. After what happened on that island, I won't be crossing you."

But the island wasn't the first time. The first time, he'd left me in the dark of night, sailed away with the crew that had been my family, and left me as a slave to another ship. I'd lost a lot then. I lost even more on the island. And now? I looked at Emme. I had more to lose than ever. I yanked my sleeve away. "Twice was enough for me. I'm not going to let it happen again." The downcast expression on his face wasn't enough to stir my pity as I left. That man cared little for anything, and if he was trying this hard to make me believe he wanted a friendship, then I feared for what tricks were forming in his mind.

The wan moonlight accomplished two things tonight. First, it settled like a shroud over the frigid waters until they were covered in webs of frost—as if we sailed on a bed of ice. Autumn was gone. Winter was here.

Second, it cloaked the air in a ghostly color that perfectly set the mood for the midnight meeting in the cabin.

Ontario clicked the door locked behind him. "I left Emme at the wheel."

"So she can steer but not me?" I asked, rising from the seat at the table where I'd been waiting. I'd finished going through the inventory hours ago, and it wasn't as bad as I'd worried. We still had enough food left to last through Winter Night when we could replenish at Kvas, enough lines to last the winter, and enough wools to keep warm.

Ontario's oil lantern gave a warm umber glow to the small room that sent shadows dancing as he hung it on the hook. The sides of his hair were beginning to grow out so his tattoos couldn't easily be seen. "I'm not worried Emme will fall in love with captaining and try to steal my ship."

"She might," I said.

"Doubtful." He took my seat. "It's a wonder we still stand."

The lower cabins were stained with sea water that would leave a foul stench in the air for months to come. But we'd survived.

"Landon almost ruined us." I looked out the window to the helm where Emme stood with a steady gaze fixed on the midnight-blue waters. She was so relaxed that you'd think she was home.

"He still might." Ontario pressed his hands on the table. "We can't trust him."

I tried to guess at what he wanted to do. By the pinched muscles in his face, he was done with having Landon on crew, but our next moves had to be seamless if we were to get rid of Landon before he could learn what we intended and turn on us.

I glanced out the window again. Emme wasn't at the wheel. Instead, Tess was in her place, looking thrilled.

A breath later, the door opened. Emme appeared in the doorway. Red tinged her nose and cheeks, and she let down the hood of her thick cloak.

Ontario stood.

Emme shut the door behind her. "We need to get rid of Landon."

Ontario and I shared a glance before he smiled at her. "I like you more and more every day." He stepped aside. "Have a seat."

26

LANDON

I coiled the lock of Ellie's hair through my fingers as I stared out the porthole. Most of the cabin slept behind me, but my mind was madness every time I closed my eyes until all I saw was death.

So I didn't close my eyes. I stayed awake to fight off the nightmares. I stayed awake to stay sane.

I put the hair to my lips and kissed it. Ellie was the one who had calmed me on nights like this. She'd been the one to calm me the night I first had the plan.

"It's risky," I had said, crumpling the paper into a ball and throwing it across the cabin. "It won't work."

"Nonsense." Ellie kicked her feet from the table onto the ground and fetched the paper. She uncrumpled it. Her finger traced my writing until it was smeared with the fresh ink. "It's brilliant. Let someone else get the treasure for us, while we sit back and do nothing."

"We might not be strong enough to take it once they have it," I told her. We had docked at the Island of Iilak the night before, but none of us were foolish enough to go ashore. Or none of us were brave enough. We were outmatched in a place such as this and sorely unprepared to face a ghost.

"They won't be ready." She laid the paper in front of me

and perched beside it on the table. "We'll be richer than anyone else on the seas, and you and I will buy an entire island to ourselves. We'll take our winters there and live on the mountains with a fire that always burns in our hearth and a table that's always full."

She reached out and took my hand. That one touch gave me courage.

I looked at the paper again. "It's still risky."

"For our future." Her hand lifted my chin until my eyes met hers. "It's worth it."

It wasn't worth it. It wasn't worth it at all.

A dirty tear ran through the strands of her hair—the only token I had left of her, and it would never be enough. I tucked it back into my pocket and quickly blinked my eyes dry as someone squirmed in the cots behind me.

A moment later, Tess was at my side. Arn had been right. She was stealthy. She practically melded with the shadows as if she were born of them. But I'd discovered her stealth before he had. Where the others saw a child, I knew her as something more.

Her mouth reached my ear.

"Arn asked me to spy on you."

I broke into a smile. At last, something was going right. I could taste my fortunes turning already, and by the break of Winter, I'd be doing well again. He was too predictable. I played with the hair in my pocket as I made another promise to Ellie for revenge.

I whispered, "I have an assignment for you."

"Anything," she said. "For my sister, I'd do anything."

I gripped her hand. "Ellie would be proud to see the woman you're becoming."

Her lips peeled back into a grin. "Tell me what I must do."

27

EMME

Ontario and Arn stayed in the cabin discussing plans, then met again the next night. I watched them from behind the wheel as the bond tightened between the two of them until it resembled something close to what it once was.

A few others crewed with me through the night, and while they glanced often at the two men meeting in the cabin, they didn't enter, and they didn't ask questions.

It was well before dawn when Ontario opened the door and went belowdecks. Arn also emerged, rubbing at the space between his thumb and finger. He neared the rails to check what could be seen of the plains of Kvas. We were almost upon it. The king was within our reach.

Arn came to the helm.

"Ontario said he was tired, so he went to his cabin for the night. He finally granted me permission to steer, so there must be some trust built there."

I held the wheel tight. "You'll have to fight me for it."

Arn chuckled. "If you enjoy captaining, then don't let me take it from you."

I let go. Arn took a deep breath as he stepped to the wheel and ran his hand over it.

The truth was, it was harder to let go than I had thought.

And even harder to confess that. My body was failing me as more strength left my muscles each day. But when I slipped my feet into the notches on the deck and gripped the rails in hand, I didn't feel weak. I had the strength of the ship at my command, a strength that battled the might of the sea, and it felt good. It felt powerful. The control I'd lost over my own body was found in the control of the ship, and I savored that it moved where I wanted it to go.

But I'd give that up for Arn. Because when he took the wheel, it didn't look like him taking control of something. It was him finding the parts of himself that he'd lost. Arn was made to captain.

I situated myself at the back of the helm to trace my fingers along the worn-out rails that carried cracks, scraps, and buckets of memories. I touched the rough edge of the deepest groove. Arn had almost kissed me here, and I'd ruined it by catching my blade on the oak.

"That's my favorite spot on the ship." Arn twisted to watch me. "That one chip in the wood. It's my most treasured scrape."

It was like a scar on the ship, bright in color and too obvious to ignore. It was a wound that reminded us of who we used to be before the turmoil of the sea molded us into something new. Had little Lewie even died when this had happened? Had we been haunted yet? If I pressed my finger in deep enough, could I find a hint of the innocence we used to have?

"I was so worried when I scratched the *Royal Rose*," I confessed. "I thought you'd never forgive me."

He raised a brow before facing the seas again. "I hope you don't find me that cold. There are many things I care about more than my ship."

"If Landon had nicked it, you'd have run him through on the spot."

His breath vaporized in the cold as he gave a little snort. "I'd be happy for the excuse."

His golden hair was paler in the dull light of night, and the ribbon that held it back fluttered at every breeze. His hold on the wheel was so firm Ontario might have to wrestle it away in the morning.

But perhaps not. The two had come to an understanding.

"Will you kill Landon?" I asked, flicking my eyes over the deck. Tess sat in the crow's nest, and Clarice watched the riggings.

Arn took a moment to reply. "No." But that one word was dark and filled with emotions. Sadness? Vengeance? Something mixed with the two threads and set hard like stone. "But we will leave him at Kvas when we sail."

"That's merciful." I was relieved. Landon would have resources to forge a new path. Their kindness in sparing him was proof that not all pirates were ruthless.

Truthfully, I thought they'd create a plan fouler than that. Ditch him at a tavern with a blade in his chest. Throw him overboard during the night when no one was on deck to hear his scream. I shivered at how easily those two ideas came, blaming the pirate's influences around me. What had Arn said those months ago when I'd asked him if he'd ever killed? *What did you expect? I'm a pirate.*

"And are things patched between you and Ontario?"

Another long pause. "I doubt they will ever be. He still makes sure to remind me that he's in command." He ran a hand over the wheel. "And now with Admiral Bones's son seeking me, I fear my path to captain may be a long one."

Even though I knew what his answer would be, I dared to venture, "You can leave it. Admiral Bones's son would never find you on the sheep farm with me. We could invite your father to live with us and craft a simple life in the fields."

He gave a tight smile. "That sounds lovely."

I withdrew a little. That wasn't an answer.

I coughed. "At least you have the friendship back with Ontario."

"The second Landon is gone, any bond between us will likely uncoil and give way to bitterness once more," Arn said. "I have no future here as the captain I once was."

The hatch opened, and Landon climbed above deck. His hair was a tousled mess, and his knickers were rolled to his knees despite the bite of the winter wind. With each movement closer, Arn stiffened until he was as tight as the ropes holding the sail.

"The stars grow brighter each night, don't they?" Landon came to the helm and rested against the rails with his head leaned back to stare at the open sky. I cringed as he brushed the special spot in the wood, not wanting it blemished with the touch of him.

He brought his gaze to me. "Tell me, have you ever experienced Winter Night?"

I kept close to Arn. "Of course. Back home, we used to have festivals where we'd bake treats and exchange them at dusk. One treat would have a pearl inside, and if you found the pearl, you got to be king or queen for the night."

Landon waved the story off. "No, I mean, have you ever experienced it on the seas?"

I shook my head. "Is it different here?"

Arn spoke up. "Everything is different here. But Winter Night is one of the best displays of beauty you'll find. Even the stars celebrate." He pointed upward. "They'll turn to pale blue and multiply until it looks like snow coming from above. The belly of the sea will glow white, and special fish come to dance beneath the waves."

"Swimming Sequins," Landon said.

Arn shot him a look. "I know what they are called. These fish are claimed to be good omens for any who catch one. They're meant to grant a year of prosperity and fortune. That night, many of those living on the coast will venture out in hopes of ensnaring one themselves."

It made my story sound dull by comparison.

"It's unfortunate that it's the one night we won't be on the sea," I said ruefully.

"But fortunate that the seas will be crowded if we make our escape that night," Landon pointed out.

Arn pinched his lips together.

"That is the plan, right?"

Arn ignored the question. "What of the Caster? You still seek her?"

"That's the only reason I'm here."

"Do you know how to find her?"

"I'll manage."

Arn faced Landon. "Do you know where she is or not?"

Landon smiled as if pleased to rile Arn. "Why does it matter to you?"

"Because when you go, I want to go too."

Landon laughed. "You want to be certain you recognize me when my identity has changed?"

"Yes," Arn confessed. "But I want a new identity as well."

Landon's mouth snapped shut. Then his eyes narrowed. "If you do that, you can't undo it. Your crew won't remember who you are, and all traces of the poor boy who became a navy man turned pirate will be gone."

"Aye. That's the point."

Landon stepped from the rails and crossed his arms. "Your father won't remember his only son."

Arn's expression remained unchanged. "I'm aware. It's a price I'm willing to pay."

Landon shrugged. "Fine. Take a new identity then. But two things you should know. One," he glanced to me, "a new identity will be far more convincing if you are married."

"Why?"

I tried not to notice the edge in Arn's voice.

"Because the Caster needs something to ground the identity in. A marriage to a real person gives it an unbreakable bond."

I would have given anything to not be standing there in that moment to hear Arn's silence or see the smirk on Landon's face at his unease. Landon allowed us the moment of discomfort before continuing. "And second. Your father losing his memory would be a terrible price to pay."

He started down the stairs, timing his words with the ringing of his footsteps. "But don't think that's the only price Caster will demand. Toying with this sort of magic isn't cheap."

28

EMRIC

The Sea Gala looked as if they'd tried to build a village on the ocean and mastered it perfectly.

Planks of birch wood held up entire huts, with floating pathways connecting them to each other. Swallow-tailed banners of gold and maroon lined the sides, their edges slipping in the waters each time someone walked uneasily across.

I could spend all day watching nobles attempt to traipse across the sea.

Broken waves snapped at the hulls of decorative ships set in an arch around the main podium. In the center, a large platform held a hundred of the richest nobles in Julinbor, all ready to celebrate the coming of winter and the king and queen's anniversary.

Captain Verin claimed he hadn't come here to seek out Calypso, but his ship told other stories. He was prepared with the right fixings to tailor this ship as a celebratory vessel, lining the yards with banners of purple and yellow, and outfitting the crew like honorable folks with plumed hats, double-vested jackets with tails, and clean breeches to tuck into their heeled boots. We hadn't all been able to attend the gala, but with five invitations, Arabella, myself, and three more had come along. Two girls, one tall and narrow with eyes closer to gold than brown and a nimbleness in how she moved that suggested she'd be an excellent spy. The other was built with curves and a smile that could dismantle a man quicker than a blade.

The third was a man charming enough that even Mother smiled when he spoke.

My mother chose her close allies well. Stealth, strength, and charm. Then there was me, who she claimed was an erratic mess.

"I'm worried I won't know her when I see her," I said, adjusting my coat over my jacket.

"I will," she declared. "But here's a trick. If any girl says hello to you, that's probably your sister." Her sarcasm wasn't helpful.

We stood on a wide cargo boat that transported groups of ten to the party. Musicians with flutes played a welcoming song as we pulled near.

"You told me she's sick, right? And that the blood of one who loves her can heal her?"

Arabella looked taken back. "You remember that?"

"I don't remember her, but I remember bits of that conversation on the island. Yet I've been thinking, how am I to heal her if I don't know her? For surely in order to love her, I must know her."

Arabella had no response.

Our boat touched the edge of the platform where two men reached to help us out. Mother offered a grateful hand and winked at the nearest gentleman who turned red in the cheeks. She laughed and kept on. She'd tamed her curls and clothed herself in a sweater of black wool overtop a tight dress, painting her lips dark red and pinching her cheeks to invite color in, and more than one man looked at her when we arrived.

Tables were set up along the perimeter, half to offer food and half—I suspected—to keep drunk partiers from falling off the end and into the sea. They'd imported trees and stuck them along one side, painting their branches white to mimic snow and hanging glowing bulbs from them. Guests danced in the middle, and others mingled in a circle around them.

"The seas have never been so loud," I commented. Large huts were attached to the main stage by narrow walkways—some dressed up, obviously for the elite, while others were simple for servants to use. I'd search every one of them in hopes of finding my sister.

I took it all in. I'd miscounted before. There must be several hundred people here. I kept lingering my gaze on young women with dark hair. *Looks like me but with your coloring,* Arabella had said. That's all I had. And Arabella hadn't seen her in five years.

I'm looking for you. I'm meant to heal you. I willed my words to find Emme and bring her to my side.

Arabella walked into the crowd like she owned the room, while the others melded into groups with ease. I kept to the edge, walking along the tables, locking eyes with others for long enough to tell that they didn't know me, then moving on.

My path crossed a woman near the edge, keeping as close to the sea as she could. She held an empty glass between her fingers that she stroked with her thumb. She appeared around my age, but her hair was like the day instead of the night, and her eyes were too bright to be related to me. Or maybe they were dark. They shifted the longer I looked, one moment appearing as blue as the waves and the next as green as the grass from back home. I shook my head. Her dress didn't change colors, a silky, silver gown that hugged her body while she poured herself a slender glass of sparkling cider. She brought it to her lips, which she'd painted dark brown, and took a long sip. Through the glass, the lips appeared red now. Then orange as a fire.

An enchantment of sorts covered her appearance. That meant trouble.

I went to move around her, but her melodic voice stopped me. "You've been staring at everyone as if searching for someone to kill."

I almost choked. "That's not my intention."

"No?" She leaned against the table and took another sip. A scar in the shape of a diamond lined her pinky. "They why are you prowling?"

I took a glass and poured myself a drink. "Forgive me, I simply never know how to behave at such events."

She chuckled, but it was more a sound of boredom than anything. "So polite." Her own eyes roamed over the crowds in the same manner mine had, shifting a little to see a face better before going to the next one.

I planted myself next to her, where together, we'd look more like a couple watching the crowd than suspicious individuals hunting for prey.

"Have you been to the Sea Gala before?"

She half turned to glance at me. "Once," she replied. "When I was a small girl." Her attention continued to rummage through the crowd. "You?"

"Never. And I never will again."

Now she looked at me fully. "Don't enjoy parties?"

"Don't enjoy formality," I said back. A girl over her shoulder caught my attention, but her gaze slid over me without any interest. When I looked back at the girl beside me, she'd returned to facing forward.

She nursed her drink in silence.

I spotted Arabella leaning close to a gentleman while he puffed up his chest with the excitement that came with the attention of a beautiful woman. If he had any information for my mother, she'd pry it from him easily. *Look for the proud ones,* my mother had always said. *They like to claim that they know anything and will spill many secrets to prove it.*

"Did you come alone?" I asked the girl.

"I will also leave alone." Her tone was curt.

"No, stars, I didn't mean it like that." Heat flamed my cheeks. "I'm looking for a girl I used to know."

"I see. I guarantee you, sailor, we haven't met before."

I flexed as if her words had punched me. "Why do you call me *sailor*?"

She rolled her shoulder up in a shrug. "You are one of the few who do not stumble even as the ground moves beneath us. You come from the sea."

"You don't stumble either."

"I do not walk." She gestured to the table she leaned her side against.

"Ah. So not sailor. What should I call you then? Ground dweller?"

That amused her enough that she gave a faint smile. "You may call me Raven."

Raven was a name for a girl of my father's heritage. One with bronzed skin and black hair who worked the fields and could fight like a lion. This girl was a whisp of a thing with the essence of the sun trapped behind her skin, and her hair the shade of the silver moon. Raven didn't fit her.

Raven's gaze fixated at the furthest north point.

A large hut bobbed at the end of a long pathway, the birch wood almost white like snow and the roof made of glass so sunlight reflected from inside with a hundred brilliant colors.

"The ice jewels?" I asked.

She nodded and took another drink.

Those jewels were fabled to have been forged from ice in the northern mountains, guarded by trolls and strong enough to crack bone with one hit. In the older days, armor had been crafted from it for the king, though it hadn't been finished before the men needed to leave for war. In the king's pride, he'd taken the armor early so he could lead the troops in their certain victory, fastening the sides of the breastplate together with chain. An arrow had found its mark, and he died in that armor. That breastplate now sat in glory among the jewels.

Outside the hut were two guards. And beside them was the other three of our crew, laughing like they were all old friends.

I checked to see if Arabella knew of the gems, but her back was to them. She looked over the shoulder of the man she spoke with to one of the others on our crew, who gave a slow nod, then slipped away.

Arabella put her body close to the man. It was only because I knew her well enough that I checked her hand. Sure enough, she was pressing a blade to his stomach. He gulped and followed her direction toward a small hut.

"Excuse me." I swallowed hard and set down my drink.

"And me," Raven said. "The person I seek is not here." She made for the boats that went back to land as I hurried after mother. I might not recognize my sister, but I could be fairly certain that the lanky gentleman with a trimmed beard, wrinkles by his eyes, and sun-stained skin wasn't her. That, or else my mother was dreadful at giving descriptions.

Arabella compelled the man down a pathway to one of the smaller huts. Inside, she shut the door. The path to get there was nothing but a few planks tied together and strung over the waves, with a rope to hold onto. I almost lost my footing more than once.

At the end, I stumbled into the room. There were crates of supplies and jars of oil surrounding my mother. Her blade was still drawn and at the throat of the man who'd fallen to his knees in a begging posture.

She grinned like she'd been waiting for me and was so pleased I arrived. "Emric, my son, meet Darren. Darren was just about to help us."

His face said that Darren was just about to vomit.

I shut the door and crossed my arms as Arabella turned her attention back to the cowering man.

"Tell me everything you know about the *Royal Rose*."

He lifted his chin away from the blade. "They attacked us last week. They killed our captain, stole one of our men, and ran off."

Arabella brightened. "And their crew? Did you see a lass named Emme?"

He pulled back again from the blade. "She was one of the two who killed the captain. She also stabbed our old captain."

Arabella's blade lowered. "Ha! That's my girl! Hear that, boy? Your sister is a fighter. Where does the *Royal Rose* sail now?"

"Rumor has it, they plan to kill the king."

Not even Arabella could hide her surprise there. "My daughter was strong enough to kill your captain, and now she will take down a king." Undeniable pride marked her tone.

But my chest sank. I'd been hoping my sister was like me, perhaps not the best of people, but still good at heart. But it seemed she was like Arabella instead.

The man paused. "Is that all you needed from me?" Hope gleamed in his eye.

She brought the blade back up. "One more thing. Move aside."

He ducked to the right. She reached past him for a clay jar of oil. "It's been a pleasure."

He kept rigid until she'd crossed to the door and opened it, then he relaxed. I followed Arabella across the platform and back to the main party. "I'm surprised you didn't kill him," I said bitterly.

She moved along the edge to the northern hut. Then she winked at me. "I could kill a man a hundred times. But the dead cannot spread tales of how I have returned."

Then she walked down the planks, turned north, and marched directly to the ice gems.

As she moved, she poured the oil on the unsteady ground that almost tripped me as I hurried after her. Three guards stood post by the gems, and I kept expecting them to tell her to stop until we got closer and I realized they were our crew mates. They nodded once to us. "The rowboats are ready."

From behind the hut, two rowboats bobbed in the water with more of our crew.

"How were they not seen?" I asked.

Arabella grinned. "They are more concerned here with who is sneaking on from land, not with fishermen passing by." But several bodies bobbed in the water to indicate that a few had spotted our crew, and it hadn't turned out well for them.

"You cannot hope to steal these. Everyone will see you."

Her grin deepened. "I'm counting on it."

She dropped the jar of oil with a loud crash, and a crewmate handed her a torch. She lifted the torch high to draw attention before tossing it in the middle of the path.

Realizing what she was about to do, I leapt for her, but it was too late.

There, in the middle of the path, the wood burst to roaring flames that ate at the makeshift ground quickly, burning a hole between us and the rest of the party. Arabella cut the ropes that served as a railing, and we began to drift backward. No, we moved too fast to be drifting. I looked behind us. The rowboats were pulling the hut.

The flutes stopped their music, and the crowd gasped. Guards rushed to the edge of the main platform, but Arabella held another torch and lifted it high. "Shoot and the torch falls, and all these jewels will end up at the bottom of the seas."

These jewels were prized by the nobles. They wouldn't risk losing them.

They weren't prepared for a fight here. I saw no crossbows.

They were only nobles, uncomfortable on the water, and a few meager guards to keep the peace.

We weren't their biggest concern anymore. The fire had engulfed the pathway and hit the podium where the guests were. It began to burn. Screams rose as they fled the fire.

It was chaos. Two minutes ago, this had been a perfectly lovely event with white skies, crystal blue seas, music in the air, and laughter all around. Now smoke pillaged the day, the crackling of flames replaced the music, and laughter had turned to horror. Behold, my mother's influence.

Arabella shouted above the noise. "Tell all that Arabella the Ruthless has returned, and she searches for her daughter."

She lowered the torch. I choked on the air. "Did you even intend to find my sister today?"

Her expression held no apology. "No. But we got something invaluable, and now Emme knows to find us." She hopped into the rowboat to help, leaving me behind with the gems and a sickening feeling in my stomach that if my sister was anything like my mother, I wasn't going to like what I found.

29
EMME

We slid past the gala with no complications, after removing our flag in favor of a merchant's sails. Our inventory now sat displayed on the main deck to convince any observer that we carried goods in for the Winter Night celebrations. It wouldn't have mattered. So many ships passed on the seas that we could have sailed the bleeding rose flag and none would have questioned it. The *Royal Rose* was not so well known yet that it'd raise suspicion.

"That changes this week," Arn declared. "After that, we will be feared."

"The great *rskvateer*," I said. After we took down the king, that name would be richly appropriate.

The wind snagged at my braided hair and lashed at my cheeks. I meticulously counted each of the blades strapped to my wide belt and practiced drawing them out. Two at my waist. One in my sleeve. One in my boot. The one in the loop at the back of my pants. I guarded them all beneath a reddish cloak of thick wool. Fitting for what our task was.

"Two nights until Winter Night," Arn said.

"I'm ready," I said. The land drew closer. Banners promising the finest winter treats and vendors bedecked in jewels and blood-colored rouge painted the shores. A man of portly size stood guard at the docks, collecting taxes from those who came into harbor. We sailed past to find an open berth many meters north.

Bo threw the rope to the dock. It landed with a thud that reminded me of a battle drum. It sounded for us.

"I will get him for you," Arn reminded me.

"I will be ready in case you can't," I said back.

We lowered our sails and dropped the gangplank. One by one, we stepped across.

I'd painted my lips a saturated red today and ran my tongue across the texture to taste something other than the bitterness inside my mouth. With each vendor who glanced at us, I expected to hear a cry of alarm, but their eyes grazed over us with no other curiosity than whether or not we would buy from them.

We had a few coins to spend so we would blend in with the crowds. I planned to buy hot cocoa, tartlets, and a strand of bravery if I could find it. The pounding of my heart was surely louder than our footsteps as we crossed the docks.

Ontario led us down the path. He wore a rounded brim hat and slim jacket that couldn't have been warm, but the tinge of cold only made his warm skin glow. Mittens covered his hands, and he knocked them against the wood at the tax collector's booth. "Berth ninety-six."

The man bent to see our ship. "Two silvers, please." He held out his hand. Ontario exchanged the coins for a ticket.

"Many thanks." Ontario didn't have to hide his accent, and neither would I. Half the crew would need to keep silent if they expected anyone to believe they were local, but even without speaking, the tax collector gave the pale-skinned Arn a long look.

"Hold up," the collector said. We stiffened.

Ontario had intentionally placed the lot of us from Julinbor near the front to cover the others. Landon and I, along with

the group we'd recruited recently, went without hats, while
the others kept their faces low behind crates that they carried.
They pretended to struggle with the weight, but I'd heard
Ontario order they be kept empty to carry supplies back.

Ontario didn't look concerned even as the collector
scrutinized faces. "We bring tablecloths from Njor for the
festival tables," he said. He waved Clarice forward, and she
and Timmons shuffled with their crate. They made a great
show of making it look heavy. "See for yourself."

I held my breath as the man cracked it open. Ontario
winked behind his back.

The man frowned. "It's tablecloths."

"As I said."

He poked at the cloth, then studied us. This time, his
attention settled on my weakened form. "And you chose her
to help deliver?"

Ontario bent toward him as if the two of them were about
to share in a joke, but he hadn't the decency to keep his voice
down. "It was her dying wish to see the castle. We pity her."
He straightened as I flushed. "Do you care to check the rest?"
he went on. "I'm sure the line won't mind waiting." Ontario
started for another crate, but at the mention of the line growing
behind us, the man ushered us through.

"We brought tablecloths?" Arn asked when we were far
enough away.

"We *have* tablecloths?" was my question.

"I know we have two." Arn adjusted his hold on his crate
with his stubbed arm. "Unless my inventory is off."

"We have two and a stash of old ropes." Ontario knocked on
the crate triumphantly. "It was a gamble, but I wasn't worried
at all." Still, he wiped sweat from his brow. "Now come. Let us
find decent lodging for the night." He peered down the path.
"Preferably as close to that castle as we can get."

In the distance, the Kvas castle stood like a white mountain on a canvas of wilted green, surrounded by fields and forest alike. It stood a mile walk from the massive town, the entire way lined with carts bumping past each other on the road with their wheels getting caught on fallen banners and their owners red in the face from the cold and long walk.

After a moment, Ontario frowned. "We don't dare cross that path tonight and be caught on the wrong side when the sun goes down. We'll find rooms in town and scope out the castle tomorrow. Whoever comes up with the best plan will sleep in the captains' quarters for a month."

"I made the invitations," Manty said. "Does that grant me the captain's lodging?"

Ontario chuckled. "Those were the easy bit. I don't fear getting in. But as soon as their king is taken?" He lowered his voice and peered at the castle where a black gate opened. Swarms of people trickled inside. "We will get in. The trick is to be on this side of those walls when that gate snaps shut."

His focus swung to the seas, and he let out a low whistle. "Good thing we didn't go there."

We all looked. The Sea Gala was on fire.

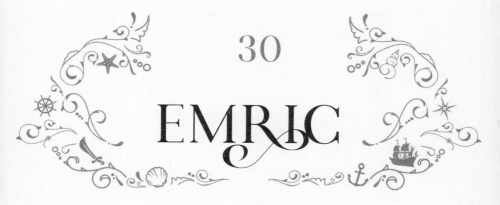

30

EMRIC

Arabella counted the number of fine vessels in this port as if any were for her to pick. "So many fools drunk on mulled wine, their bellies full of cobbler and minds caught on the festivities," she mused from the helm. "Their ships would make a fine addition to my fleet."

The air smelled of cider and sawdust as we came closer to land. A long string of ships docked outside the bustling town. "You have a fleet?"

"I used to." She steered us past the ships, past the open berths and busy causeways. "Someday, I will again."

We'd dragged the jewels to the ship where the hut was pulled behind like a dangerous trophy. But Arabella and I needed to get off on land soon so the crew could get away. We wouldn't be safe around Julinbor for a while, and very soon they'd send ships after us.

A bitter flick of wind came from the north, and I turned my back to it. My eyes snagged on a vessel. "Stop."

Arabella couldn't stop, but she turned to where I pointed. "That one, with two masts and a yellowed flag. Berth ninety-six."

She squinted. "Small, but agile. It's not the finest ship but it would do. After we find your sister, we can steal it for you."

"We won't have to," I said, staring at the *Royal Rose*. "It's mine."

I tried to press its image into my mind and call up the memories that came with it. She was on that ship with me. But all that came was a vague idea of brown hair and burnt skin—the only description my mother could give for someone she hadn't seen in five years.

I prayed Emme would call out to me if she spotted us in the town. Or else I'd walk right past her and never know.

"She's here then." Arabella spun the wheel to turn toward a berth.

"I thought we weren't going to dock until much further south."

"I want to get my daughter back. We will dock quickly, then be off. Prepare to jump."

The crew noticed the change of direction and trimmed the sails. Meanwhile, I stood on deck watching the *Royal Rose* grow closer. It appeared to be abandoned, and I yearned to take control of it now, sail off on my own and have my ship back.

I missed being captain. It had lasted for only a short time, but I loved every splendid moment of it. And unlike my mother ever did, I'd earned the position rightly, before I'd been tossed to the seas and gobbled up by the waves. I'd trade my dinners for the week to stand behind that wheel, just for a moment.

I wouldn't retake the ship just to leave it once more, and if Coral was my destiny, then the ship was no longer mine. But now that I could see it, my chest tightened at having to let it go.

It seemed a cruel fate to not remember my sister. But I believed it crueler for my heart to desire two things equally, when neither side could meet. Someday, I reminded myself, I'd lose my legs and my chance at captaining the strongest crew the seas had ever seen. Or, a small thought intruded, someday I'd choose the seas over Coral.

"Which of these ships should we steal for your sister?" Arabella's head turned from side to side as she inspected the ships. "Berth seventy-two? The three of us can sail side by side like an impenetrable wall."

"Or you two may sail, and I shall swim beneath you," I said, biting down against the lure to make that vision come true. We could be a force on the seas.

"Weak," she muttered. "But that's of no matter. Emme will be like me." From under her breath, I heard her words. "Almost there, my daughter. Then we shall rule the seas together."

The quartermaster crossed to us, pulling on the ends of his mustache as he eyed the land warily. He stood close to Arabella, closer than most dared, and she took note of that as he asked, "Will you return to us?"

"You won't easily be rid of me," she said. Her tone had lost its usual sharpness. "Stay away for a while, then pick us up in two weeks at Kaffer Port. I have a contact there. You know the town?"

The quartermaster nodded. I puzzled at why that town sounded familiar and fuzzy at the same time. Another memory to which Emme must have been attached. I was beginning to think that island took more than its fair share.

We neared the berth. Arabella gave up the wheel to come to the prow with me. "A little closer," she directed. They got us as near as they could, then we jumped into the sea.

Freezing waters swarmed us, soaking through our clothes and to our skin as we kicked for shore. The docks were so busy that only a few would notice as we approached like fish. With luck, they didn't yet know of the stolen gems and the crew could sail freely on. The ship had turned round and made for the distance.

We pulled our soaking bodies to the rocky shore.

"Think they'll return for us when this is over?" I asked.

"I hope not," Arabella stated. "The entire fleet will be looking for them. I don't want to be anywhere near them. I didn't leave empty-handed though." She opened her pocket to show me five icy jewels flashing with sparks of white light. "If you were smarter, you'd have grabbed some too."

"I'm not cutthroat like you," I said. "But I'm not daft." I opened my own pockets to show her the gems I'd grabbed. Her smile was the proudest I'd ever seen her of me.

"You're a pirate through and through. We'll make something of you yet," she said. "Now it's time to find your sister."

31

EMME

Each pound of our footsteps stirred up aging dust in the wine cellar below the tavern, and I toed a line between teaching Tess how to fight and risking her breaking a hundred-year-old bottle of red wine.

"It's probably not a hundred years old," Tess said between grunts. I'd placed her feet in the dirt and taught her how to brace herself against the impact of a sword swung by a man three times her size. "That's just what the tavern says to drive prices."

"I know. I used to work at a tavern. But believe me, the tavern owner won't accept that logic as an apology if we break anything. Go again." I had her drive against an old barrel, using the blunt end of her cutlass instead of the sharp one.

Her eyes rounded as though I'd just told her I used to work in a traveling circus. "Your life is so exciting. Daughter of Arabella, worked in a tavern, lives on a pirate ship."

"I'm sitting because I haven't the strength to stand for more than a minute, and I'll likely be dead in two months," I reminded her. Her smile fell. "Be content with what you have."

She tightened her grip and drove again.

"What about you?" I asked her. "What life do you leave behind?"

Her blade faltered before she lifted it higher. "A family in debt and a farm too beaten down to prosper. And my parents too prideful to see it." Her next strike was harder, and it chipped the side of the barrel.

"I'm sorry." I really was. "No siblings?"

She wiped her brow. "Just me." With her next strike, she nearly toppled over her feet.

"Steady," I warned. "That barrel isn't fighting back, but a person will. Poor footing will leave you dead faster than a ship sinking."

She adjusted, then went again.

The door opened, and Arn came down the stairs. "Tess, the crew is leaving to inspect the castle. If you plan to go, now is your chance."

"Is the sun up already?"

He nodded. Tess hid her cutlass behind a long cloak and fastened the clip under her neck. Her copper hair stood out against the forest green of the hood. Despite her panting breath, her eyes flashed with exhilaration. *I could go again,* they seemed to say. *I could fight all day.* She looked nothing like me, and yet it was like peering into a mirror. A young girl, desperate to become someone, training hard to prove her worth. I hadn't been much older when I'd stopped trying to please my mother. Just in time to lose her.

Tess hurried past Arn on the stairs, only to halt at the top. "You aren't coming?"

"It's too long of a walk." I rose to my feet.

"And you, Arn?"

"I staked out the castle last night, watching their guard rotations. I need rest before tonight's ambush." He paused, making eye contact. "And, Tess?" I could hear his whisper plainly. "Have you found anything?"

She shook her head. "But I'll keep looking."

"Good. You can go."

Tess scrambled away, leaving a slice of light from the crack of the door as the sky flashed orange. Arn came down the stairs, rubbing the bridge of his nose in weariness.

"What was that about?" I leaned against the hilt of my blade for support and felt it sink into the dirt.

Arn's tunic was as deep red as the wine around us. The boards of the stairs creaked as he came down the last of them and examined the bottles. He picked one and rubbed the label. "I asked her to look into Landon for me. Is there a bottle opener?"

"Put that back," I said. "Are you sure that's wise?"

"Wine is always a good idea."

"No, I mean to ask Tess to spy on Landon. What if he finds out?"

He reluctantly put the bottle down. "He seems to have taken a liking to her, so I'm not worried about it. She can come up with a good lie."

"She's twelve. She needs someone to look after her."

His brows shot up. "She said she was fifteen."

"Thirteen, at most." I reached for the barrel to brace against. "It's hard not to worry about her."

He took my hand in his. "Look at you," he said. "Worrying for others when you should be taking care of yourself."

"I can't help it. Promise me that if I die, you'll take care of her."

"You're not going to die."

"Promise it anyway," I pleaded, squeezing his hands with the weight of my sincerity.

"Okay, I promise. But I won't let you die."

I gave a half smile. "I'm almost tempted to believe you."

He cleared his throat and shuffled his feet. "However, since you brought it up," he said slowly, licking his lips between each word as if tasting them to be sure they were the right ones. Then he'd stop and try again. "What I mean is, not that I'm worried you'll die, but just in case." He exhaled. His hand went to his pocket. "Emme, I want you to marry me. Soon."

My mouth fell open. In his hand was a dainty ring, embedded with three blue stones.

"I thought it looked like the sea," he said as he twisted it to inspect. "With the band swirled around the gems like that. It's not much, but—"

I looked at him suspiciously. "Did you steal that?"

He clamped his mouth shut.

I tore my eyes away from the beautiful ring. Mother never wore one, and she'd insisted we not spend money on frivolous things, so it was easily the nicest jewelry I'd ever been given. Still, I pushed it away. "Who do you think I am that I'd wear a stolen ring?"

"The wife of a pirate?" he asked hopefully.

I closed his fingers around the ring, hiding the glint of blue. "You should give that back."

"Fine. I'll return it to the owner as an early wedding present to you."

I swallowed.

He stepped back with a stricken look. "You'll marry me, won't you?"

There was an ache inside, writhing. Unknown clouded around us for our future, for my health, and for what these next few days would bring. Deeper than that was the unknown about why he was asking.

He'd never mentioned marriage before. *But the second Landon tells him that it could help grant him a new identity . . .*

Even so. "I love you," I said, for it was the only thing I knew to be true.

Though the words were kind, he straightened like they'd stabbed him. "I never thought hearing that could hurt so much, but I could swear that means no."

I didn't cross the space between us. "It's not a no. I simply have follow-up questions."

"There's the response every man wants." He shoved the ring into his pocket and kept his hand there, stiffening his back until it looked like he'd melded a shield around himself. Protecting his heart from me.

"I just want to know if this is because Landon said a new identity works better when anchored in a marriage."

"No."

He answered too quickly. Or would I have taken a slower answer as a false one? I rubbed my temple. "You've never even talked about marriage. I didn't know you wanted that."

The dust in the cellar thickened, bringing the walls in closer with it, until I was certain the room wasn't large enough to hold our emotions. They'd come exploding out, leaving us shattered.

He smiled, but the joy didn't extend to his eyes. "What did you think I was doing courting you?"

"In truth, I hadn't realized you were courting me. This is the first I'm hearing of that."

"I . . . kissed you."

I had to laugh. "That doesn't replace asking me."

He took a heavy breath. "I'm asking you now." The silence between us was as deep as the distance. "Do you want to marry me or not, Emme? Because I'm asking you to be my wife since I might not get the chance to ask again."

I loved that Arn wanted to marry me. But I didn't want it to be because he thought I was dying. I didn't want it to be because the man he hated said he should be wed. I didn't want it to be for anything other than he was unable to breath without me as his wife, and that he would willingly give up everything in the world to be with me.

Because that was the way I felt about him.

I'd give up everything, my quiet life on the farm, the safety of land, to be with him. I'd make plots and probably wear a stolen ring if it meant I could be with him. I'd spend sleepless nights by his side at the helm just to hear his voice and be near to him. I would spend my final, dying days, chasing down a king and a healing nut, just to amuse him, because I didn't want to say good-bye. I was surviving each day solely on the sight of him, living from touch to touch, wanting nothing more than that.

And it might be vain, but stars, I wanted him to want me like that too.

I stood. "I hope you get the chance to ask again, Arn. And I'll say yes when I know that you're asking for no other reason than that you love me."

"What in the name of the dark seas does that mean?"

"I don't know. It's too complicated." I put a hand to my stomach. "I'm famished. Can we just get nourishment and focus on the next few days?"

When I walked past, he caught the edge of my cloak. "I do love you," he said, and it was as if all the sadness of the world wound itself into those words.

I gave a small smile. "And I love you, too."

He helped me up the stairs. "There's a fine establishment around the corner where you can get food alone. I've seen guards this morning and need to see that they don't poke through our rooms."

He turned to leave, and my heart twisted. He headed for the rooms above the tavern while I faced the icy blast of morning air and ghost-like streets shrouded in hazy mist. A clocktower chimed in the distance, ringing long after the door swung shut behind me.

My fingers traced across the hilts of my blades again. Waist, boot, sleeve, belt. Waist, boot, sleeve, belt. Find the king, deliver him to Serena, find the healing nut. I repeated the mantra in my head as a promise that when that was done, I'd convince Arn to ask me again.

The clocktower struck the ninth toll when I turned the corner of the streets, maneuvering my hand along the wall to keep myself upright. I could be grateful the streets were mostly abandoned so none witnessed my poor movements. It was getting worse. If someone asked me to walk in a straight line, I wouldn't be able to do it.

A hint of chipper voices drifted through the crisp air, followed by laughter and the chime of a brass bell over a door as it swung open. A sign hung on hooks over the slender entrance with such a pure white and saturated blue that it must have been painted recently, and when I lowered my gaze, drops of the paint stood out on the wooden slab outside the door. Crates of pinecones trimmed the windows, scents of cocoa and fillets blended in the air, and lit candles adorned the tables inside.

I went to sit at the nearest one.

The tables were carved from logs, but only the bark had been removed and the edges polished, leaving the lumps behind. They were turned upward and placed about the room, at least three tall trees' worth of sliced logs supporting chilled drinks, steaming teas, and long coats as folks rubbed their hands together to relieve the chill.

"Ale?" A server came with an apron tied to her narrow waist and hair coiled into a bun.

"Water," I replied.

She nodded and returned in a matter of moments. "Let me know if you want anything else." She gave a side glance to a table opposite mine before checking in with others.

I followed her gaze over the brim of my cup. A lass sat in the corner with a hood pulled over her head, eyes covered in its shadows, feet propped on the table, and a loud hum buzzing in her throat. From the way she tipped her head back to drink from her cup and laughed though no one was there to tell her a joke, I guessed she was intoxicated.

The sun wasn't even fully over the horizon yet.

The crew should be nearing the trail to the castle now, preparing to scope it out for our ambush tonight. The window wasn't positioned toward it, but I glanced out all the same.

"Such a fine day, wouldn't you say?" the girl across the table asked in a loud tone. Her gaze slid over me with no real direction.

"We ask for quiet in this establishment," the lass who served me replied with a cold look over her shoulder.

The drunk girl ignored her. She checked out the window while taking another sip. Then she threw the cup across the room. Half the guests jumped at the noise, which seemed to please her. "It's an even finer day than I thought, for we have royalty in our midst!" She stood to her full height, which wasn't much, and strode to a nearby table where a gentleman was eating with his back to the room. He stiffened as she drew closer.

The girl swept into a low bow.

"Your Majesty."

"Quiet, you," he gestured her away. "I don't know you."

"But I know you!" She checked out the window again before looking around the room. "Ah, this will do. A crown for the king of Julinbor."

My breaths came shallow, if they came at all. I moved my fingers to my knives. Waist, boot, sleeve, belt.

The server grew impatient. She put her hands on her hips. "Quiet, or we'll have the guards take you. There's to be no nonsense around Winter Night. Today is a holiday."

That only fueled the other's volume. "My mighty king, I bow at your feet."

The Fates had blessed me. Finally. We needn't scour through a guarded castle in hopes of finding the king. We needn't flee a castle while a band of guards came for our throats. We only needed to ambush him here, as the king himself sat in the corner, simply attired and drinking from an ordinary goblet.

Had I not been so exhausted, or perhaps not as desperate, I'd stop to think further. I'd wonder why he was here instead of at the castle. But my mind offered the idea that he was enjoying peace before the chaos of celebration, and I accepted that greedily.

There wasn't time. He could leave, and this would be ruined. Already the man had taken enough of the girl's bowing and gathered his cloak to depart. I stood quickly and slipped out the door to press myself against the outside wall and breath heavily.

Waist, boot, sleeve, belt.

My fingers curled around the blade at my waist.

Arn wouldn't be able to take him for me. I'd do this alone. I'd prove that I could still do some things for myself.

My stomach clenched into knots so tight that I feared they'd never loosen. *Think of the story Arn told you. Think of the wicked ways of the king. Think of how others are coming to kill him. If you don't draw the blade, someone else will.*

Think of Arn. You do this for the chance at a life with him.

I bit down hard on my lip until the metallic taste of blood washed over my tongue.

His heavy footsteps came, and the king turned the corner.

Again, a wiser lass would have searched for guards. She would have remembered how Arn told her guards patrolled the streets and been wary. She'd have noticed them outside during one of the times that the drunk girl had glanced out the window. She'd look for them now in the shadows.

But I didn't look. I drew my blade and I advanced.

The bottom of his long cloak brushed my feet when I stepped close, and the soft ground gave way to dim the sound of my footsteps. I lifted the blade in the air. My sleeve tumbled to my wrist, and the morning sun glistened off the steel still stashed there.

He's a wicked man. He sold his daughter away. He's your freedom.

I only needed to knock him unconscious. Once we delivered him to Serena, she would determine his fate, and I'd have my freedom from this binding tattoo. I let adrenaline course through me as I watched him move down the path. His hands patted his pockets and adjusted his hood, while I lurked behind him like a shadow. A dangerous, hesitating shadow. At the corner of the tavern, he paused near a sturdy cart overflowing with bundles of spinach and crisp kale. He stood beside a wide booth with faded paint and dirt-coated wood, where he transferred the vegetables from the cart to neat rows on a table.

I stopped silently behind him. My fingers curled tight over the hilt.

It is weakness to not strike first, my mother taught me.

He deserves it, Arn's voice said in my head. *He is wicked, and you are good.*

He's your only chance at a life, my own voice said.

Then a louder voice rang out. *His life is not yours to take.*

He transferred more bundles while I wrestled to make the move as my conscious chose a wildly inappropriate time to speak. It'd had months to convince me otherwise, and it hadn't. I couldn't choose a different path now.

I reared the hilt with a shaking hand as tears fell down my cheeks. My teeth gnawed together.

You will be the cause of much bloodshed, the old woman had told me.

I'm not a killer, I'd said back.

I lowered the blade to the folds of my cloak, my reflection in the metal staring back at me, jaded at the edges. My grip loosened. I wasn't a killer. If I brought this man to Serena, I'd be bringing him to his death.

My clarity found me then. I could go to my grave content with goodness.

But the Fates had never been favorable to me.

In the moment I chose to lower my blade, a wild horse attached to his cart trampled close, flipping his mane. Perhaps his eye saw my blade and predicted danger. He might have been spooked by a rat. Either way, the beast reared his head, then kicked.

His back hooves struck the king on the chest, and he fell into me, sending my blade clattering to the ground. We were allotted one moment of painful silence where his expression crumpled in confusion and my heart thundered in my chest. Then the village exploded into chaos.

Shouts came from all directions. First, from inside the establishment next to me, where I'd raised the blade in full sight of the windows. I'd been so foolish. Faces pressed against the glass to see what had happened.

They wouldn't have seen the horse. All they saw was the man on the ground, a sickly pool of blood, and my knife beside it all.

Guards drew their swords and came from all angles, looking over the man and coming to the same conclusion that any would: I'd killed him.

"Stop," they called. "Murderer!"

I ran for my life.

My feet moved sturdier than they had for months. Fear had an odd way of stabilizing me. I wove through the street and turned down a narrow path where celebratory flags whipped my cheeks as the shouts multiplied behind and the thunder of footsteps urged me faster.

Just as I twisted around another bend, I slammed into someone's chest.

Strong hands seized my arms, and I found myself looking into brown eyes, narrowed with determination. The man wore a tunic the bright blue-and-cream colors of the king, a badge of rank, and eyes that said he'd kill me on the spot if I resisted. He jerked me hard enough that I lost my footing, and he dragged me down the street.

"I've got her!" he shouted

"Let me go," I pleaded. "I've done nothing wrong." I kicked at loose rocks and banks of snow, but his hold didn't waver.

"You killed farmer Malcom," he replied in a sharp tone. He yanked me to my feet. "You killed a good man."

I stared dumbly back. "I didn't."

"I saw you standing over his body," he said. He pulled me back to the shop. A small crowd gathered around the king, but they separated as we came closer. Other guards filed in from the streets with hands on their weapons to form a circle around me.

"Is he dead?" someone asked.

"Dead," another confirmed. "The farmer is dead."

"A farmer?" I asked in a dry voice. The guard didn't reply.

No. Please no. Not an innocent man. If I hadn't stalked after him . . .

All earlier stability fled my body. I'd been responsible for the death of an innocent man. I'd already struggled with the idea of killing a cruel one, but this? This I would not forgive myself for.

There was no redemption for this act. I deserved the fate I'd receive.

A farmer. He was a farmer. My knees buckled, and the guard jerked me upright.

"Call for the wagon! We take her to the castle."

"Take this one too." The server from earlier grabbed hold of the drunk girl and pushed her out the door. Her face was white as she stared at the body. "This one's been causing trouble."

The drunk girl didn't appear drunk anymore. She gaped at the farmer and tripped down the stairs, clutching the fabric of her tunic around her stomach and muttering something under her breath.

Two guards rode up on horses, one white as snow and the other black as night. They were fastened to a small wagon, with bars on the door and a canopy above it. One of the guards dismounted to fumble with his keys.

"In they go. Always more trouble around Winter Night," he complained.

"Wait," I begged. "Please." I kicked against the guard, but he held fast. I was no match for him.

"You can plead your case to the jailor," he said.

"I'm sick. I'm not in my right mind. I mean no harm."

The crowd on the street grew larger as I screamed for someone to help. I begged for my life.

"We've no pity for murderers." The guard's voice was colder than any winter frost.

His hand went to my waist. I thrashed harder. With nimble fingers, he found my other stashed blade there and dropped it onto the dirt. He picked me up as if I were nothing and threw me inside the wagon. I banged my elbows against the hard floor.

They threw in the girl next. She picked herself off the floor and stood back as the door slammed shut. Once the lock turned, she sighed.

But not with defeat. There was a suspicious tinge of relief there.

I couldn't share the emotion. I threw myself at the door. My hands wrapped around the bars to pry at them.

"I'm sorry," I shouted. "I didn't mean to cause harm! It was the wrong man anyway!" I was fairly certain that wasn't the right thing to say at the moment, but I'd lost control of all thought. The wagon began to move.

"They won't free you," the girl said placidly.

"Please," I shouted again. The crowd stared after me.

Through their faces, I found one that made my heart drop. Arn stood back from the others. He looked at the fallen man then at me.

He sprinted after the wagon. Nearby guards yelled for him to halt.

Arn jumped to grab hold of the door and clung to the bars, staring back at the guards who chased him.

"I thought it was the king," I said. My vision blurred with tears. "I thought it was the king."

He breathed fast. "I oathbind myself to you, Emme Jaquez Salinda, in promise that I will find you again."

"Arn, what—"

He winced as the oathbinding must be imprinting itself on his skin. Then he sighed. "Now as long as I have this oathbinding, it will lead me to you."

I choked on my tears. "One of these days, we need to stop oathbinding ourselves."

He grinned. "I'll work on that."

Guards reached him and yanked him from the wagon. He let go willingly.

The guards took his shoulders then pushed him away, but he was only looking at me.

I wasn't certain I was breathing anymore. I cried silent tears as my body shook with fear and Arn grew further away. But the look on his face was one of such sincerity that I let myself believe that this wouldn't be the end.

He'd find me. Or I'd break out on my own. Either way, the daughter of Arabella wasn't going down easily. And I still had three blades left. Boot. Sleeve. Belt. I wouldn't be taken down.

32
EMME

The girl kept to the back, seated on the floor with one leg propped up and the other stretched before her. She wore tight pants tucked into boots and a tunic the color of a sunrise beneath a black cloak. Now that the hood was back, I saw her golden hair in all its glory. It was long enough to go down her back and wrap to her front where she twisted one end between her fingers.

A mark stretched over her little finger. A scar in the shape of a diamond, reaching from the base to the tip.

"I keep going over it," she remarked. "Why do you want the king dead?"

"I don't," I replied, then couldn't contain myself. "Why did you say that was the king?" I pressed my eyes shut to keep out the image of that poor man trampled on the ground beside my knife.

She shrugged. "What do you want from Sea King Valian?" A knowing smile played on her lips. "After all, that's why someone would be after King Unid right now—to fetch a pretty prize from the king under the sea. What would you ask him for?

I began to wonder how many people were aware that Sea King Valian was asking for the head of the king, and how much competition I had to reach him. To think, an hour ago I thought I'd gotten him. Now I was on my way to what would likely be my death.

"It doesn't matter now, does it?" I clamped my mouth shut and watched out the window. The town was in the distance now as we'd climbed higher on the countryside. We must be approaching the castle. The cobblestones were smoother here, and the wagon didn't bounce as much as we turned east. For a moment, all I could see was the sea, and it sent an ache to my heart.

The open, shining sea was a symbol of independence I longed to taste again. "Was this your goal?" I asked her. "To act drunk so you get thrown in here?"

She shrugged again.

"It was a foolish thing to do."

Her reply was so soft that I barely heard it. "We'll see."

The wagon halted, and I was thrown off my feet. A key clicked in the lock, and the door swung open to let the sunlight warm us. Two guards reached inside to grab my arms with bony fingers and drag me out. "This one is the murderer."

I could have fainted at those words. Boot. Sleeve. Belt. I recited to keep my mind sharp. Two to free myself, one, if needed, for the king.

We had stopped in a courtyard at the back of the castle where thorns dug into the stone walls, heavy drapes covered all the windows, and bare trees littered the path with fallen leaves. A wide arch marked the entrance to the castle, where two gargoyles sat on either side of the door almost like omens of death. They bared their teeth at us. Beside them stood two more guards.

A bitter wind licked my cheeks.

The guards let go of my arms but left red marks where their fingers had dug through my flesh. They reached for the girl. "This one is the drunk."

She let them pull her from the wagon with a halfhearted protest, eyes sharp on our surroundings. I doubted they missed a thing—not the way the trees cast shadows like spiderwebs over the cobblestones or the leaves swept beneath high hedges or the way the only exit of the courtyard was a single, ironclad door with a heavy lock. Behind us, the gate snapped shut, and men took their posts. Two guards outside the gate, two guards inside the courtyard, and two guards to lead us. Two girls against six men.

"Let's get them inside," one of the guards huffed. Their breath crystalized at the tips of their noses as the barren trees rattled around us. They grabbed our arms again and got us inside with minimal effort.

The iron door closed behind us, and suffocating darkness drowned me. A shiver spiraled down my spine with a sense of fear unlike anything I'd felt on the seas. The seas were exactly what I wanted right now. They were open and free and welcoming. This was stifling, cold, and pungent with death.

But this was where I needed to be, I reminded myself. This was where the king lived. We were pulled south to a narrow hallway and the mouth of a dark tunnel. A steel door, layered with spikes sharp enough to pierce a man, barred the entrance.

The guards stopped. "You'll stay here."

I squinted through the darkness at a doorframe built of steel and a small room behind it with a sliver of a window to let in light. I wished the window would take the smell out, but it was likely stained into these walls.

The guard turned the key, and the door scraped against the ground like claws. He shoved us inside. My eyes adjusted to the darkness well enough to see six cots, layered in two rows, and a lone bucket in the corner.

I waited until they'd turned their backs to run. I slammed my feet against the stone to drive forward with my shoulder and barrel through them. For a sweet moment, I thought I had a chance, but that illusion crashed as they yanked me backward, and a tearing pain rippled from my shoulder. They threw me on the ground, sending a jolt through my entire body.

"I don't care to kill you, miss," one warned, "but I will. The likes of you deserves no pity."

I recoiled at the harshness before remembering what I was in his eyes—a murderer.

I winced at the pain in my shoulder while he unhooked a board from the wall. A parchment had been stapled to the slab. Beside it, he took down a jar of ink and dabbed a quill inside. "It's regulation for prisoners to sign in upon entry."

The girl laughed. "You want to know our names before you kill us?"

"You'll get a trial," he snapped. He shoved the board at her. "Sign."

She hesitated before scribbling something down and shoving it back. The man remoistened the quill then passed it to me.

His brow raised at how shaky my hand was. "What's the matter with you?"

"It's Paslkapi." When his puzzled expression deepened, I sighed. "I shake. A lot."

Content, he stood back.

My eyes roamed over the page where the girl had signed her name, Raven, on the line. I had to brace the board against my stomach to hold it with one hand, but that wasn't the problem. I gulped.

"Hurry up," the man said. The other ran his fingers through his beard while casting looks down the quiet hallway.

I brought the quill to the page and tried to write the E. I accomplished a line that waved as harshly as the roughest storm, and several dots surrounding it where my hand couldn't keep the quill against the page. I tightened my grip and tried again.

My E wasn't legible. It was a lie to even call it a letter. The next letter was even worse.

"I can't," I whispered. It was another thing that I'd lost the skill to do. With each lost ability, I lost another piece of myself, until I'd have nothing left.

My father had spent his final days in bed, unable to eat for himself. I was quickly nearing that.

"You don't know how to write?" the guard asked.

"No." I shook my head. "I physically can't." Humiliating tears soaked my cheeks.

He gently pried the parchment and quill away. "That'll be fine. Your sentence will be easy to decide, so your signature isn't as vital to our logs." He stepped from the room and closed the door.

I stood like a statue, staring at the last moments of my life.

"I'm such a fool," I whispered. I should have abandoned the mission and spent my final days on the sea with Arn instead of chasing down death masked as hope. I should have accepted my fate. I should have lived before it was too late. I placed a hand against the door. When I found a way to break free, I would stop chasing the king. I'd live.

"My grandmother had Paslkapi," Raven said in a kind voice. She sat on the cot with her hands crossed. "My mother didn't, so my odds are better. It usually doesn't present until you're older."

I slid my back down the wall. "I'm unlucky like that."

"I'd say so. Were you going to ask the Sea King Valian to heal you?"

That idea hadn't occurred to me. But it wouldn't have mattered—Serena's oathbinding would have killed me if I didn't fulfill my oath, so even the Sea King Valian couldn't save me.

"No," I replied simply. "But finding King Unid was a step I needed to take in order to heal. It won't matter now, though."

She went to the door and inspected it. "Good," she said. She looked over her shoulder at me. "Because I'm going to kill King Unid as soon as we get out of here."

33

ARN

In a snug room above the tavern where the air tasted like mulled wine and the walls smelled of burnt oil, I held three papers in my hand. Each read more disturbing than the last.

Ontario dragged himself into the room behind me, eyeing the bed longingly. He'd been up late with the crew as they scouted the castle, and hadn't had time to sleep since. He wouldn't get that chance until tomorrow. At my long face, he raised a brow. I extended the papers. "Have you seen this?" I passed one to Ontario. The top was torn where I'd ripped it from a post outside, the parchment crisp and smelling like the coming winter.

He frowned at it. "We knew it was dangerous to come."

His tone wasn't worried enough. It should be. I pointed to be certain he saw the hefty reward on our heads.

"Fifty silvers for the capture of pirates." That ought to strike fear in even the bravest of us. One silver coin was enough to lead men to do traitorous things. Fifty coins . . . hungry men would sell their soul for less.

Ontario studied the demands. Someone had made a rough drawing of a pirate's hat on the front with a cutlass running through it, pulling it apart at the seams. The message below the sketch revealed the bounty on our heads. An idea came to mind. "Perhaps we trade Landon in for the money instead of abandoning him here."

Ontario rolled the parchment up and handed it back. "That's more than he's worth." Sweat speckled his face, worsening as I told of how Emme had been involved in the injury of an innocent farmer and been taken to jail. The man had been taken to the town doctor where, last I heard, he was poised to recover. For Emme's sake, I hoped he did. She'd be much harder to free if she was killed as punishment.

The next paper weighed heavier in my hand. "Admiral Bones's son reached out again," I said dryly. "His ability to locate me must be admired."

Ontario's expression was impassive. "What does he want?"

"Money. Retribution for his father's death. Two things I can't provide."

He checked out the window in the upstairs room of the tavern where we waited for the crew to finish their meals. Outside, the town was ablaze with jolly folks and festival commencement, while our band of pirates was a tangle of nerves and differing ideas on how to get to the king. The sun had almost set now, painting the sky all shades of orange, so we allowed the men a proper dinner before meeting again to smooth out plans. That's what we said, but there were no plans to smooth out yet. We had nothing.

"It might be best to leave the seas and go inland where he can't find you. I hear Emme has a farm."

"She had a farm," I corrected. "But I'm not giving in." I shoved the newest letter, filled with the same threats, deep into my pocket. That left one paper. This one was interesting—not to mention easier to focus on than the matter we couldn't solve.

I checked that the door was still shut. "Tess found this among Landon's things this evening." I passed the paper to him. The corners were crumpled and the writing smudged but legible, but the message clearly requested a meetup, complete with a time, location, and date—for tomorrow.

Ontario turned it to see both sides. "Who is he meeting?"

I took it back. "I don't know. But I'll follow him to see. Perhaps it's the Caster."

"I doubt it. Could be a trap."

"But he didn't give it to me. Tess found it."

Ontario shrugged. "Still. Be careful. Or don't go at all. I say we free Emme and get as far away from here as possible. How well can you track her?"

My new oathbinding tattoo was hidden beneath a thick, wool sock and brown boots, but the sting of it remained. It didn't look like my other one, which had thin lines and rough turns, forming a cyclical pattern as crooked as the man I'd made the deal with. This one curled in a nicer design, but it was darker in color and covered most of the flesh up to my ankle. How it appeared didn't matter to me. I needed it to do what my other one had done for Admiral Bones. I needed it to track. "I tested it before. It gives me a sense of where she is. On the seas, that would work well enough to tell me her location, but I worry that it won't lead me to the right room in a castle. I know she's there, I just can't see where exactly."

Ontario frowned. "It'll have to do. Could you oathbind yourself to the king at a distance as well? Let us track him?"

This was a new thought. "Do you know the king's middle name?"

"I do not."

"Then probably not, but I can try." I cleared my throat. "I oathbind myself to King Unid Everson with the promise that I will find him and destroy him." My foot didn't burn with the binding ink. "Didn't work. I'm not surprised. But finding the king isn't our problem. It's getting out."

Ontario ran his hand along the shaved side of his head. "Everyone has a different idea on what to do. Create panic and take him in the mayhem. Abduct him in the hallways where we can run. Lure him to the courtyard so it's the shortest trip out of the castle. Steal him at night from his bed. All fine ideas, but weapons are stripped from guests upon arrival, so there's one issue. The king is always guarded by at least six attending soldiers, so there's a second issue. And none of us are fast enough to outrun the bullets that will surely chase us once we knock him out.

I stared at the castle on the hill as the oathbinding burned to remind me that the one I sought was inside there. The King and Emme. Two impossible tasks with a great ticking clock over it all.

And I needed to find the Caster. Not to mention uncovering what Landon was up to.

"Whatever we do, we need to make it fast," I said. "I hate the thought of Emme locked up in there." I pressed against the window. "I promised her I'd protect her."

"She doesn't need your protection," Ontario said. "Her body is weak, but her spirit isn't."

I knew that better than anyone. I'd just opened my mouth to say so when I snapped it shut. A new plan formed in my mind. It was only the bare bones of something . . . but it could work.

"What if we don't kill the king or break Emme out?"

"Then we accomplish nothing."

I turned to Ontario. "What if Emme does it from the inside? If she demands to see the king, they unlock her for us. She binds him, and we are there to get her out."

"It sounds just as complicated as any other plan."

"But they wouldn't expect her to do anything. She can get close without us, and unless one of our men is secretly an expert locksmith, we need them to let her out. All we do is wait on the side."

"I don't know." Ontario pursed his lips and stared past my shoulder at the window. His eyes narrowed and skirted back and forth as if going through the layout again. Long hallways, they'd said. High ceilings. White marble and wooden mantels and fires in half the rooms. Guards at every other corner, most chatting with members of the court or sampling the treats they'd imported to the courtyard.

"It's a festival. It's going to be chaos. Surely we can pull this off."

"We will do our best." Ontario placed both hands on the sill, but his gaze dropped from the castle to the streets outside the tavern where we stayed. I stared at the corner where Emme had been arrested. If I'd gotten there sooner instead of being so caught up in my damaged pride that she'd turned down my proposal, I could have spared her from this fate.

Ontario suddenly unlatched the window and swung it open. A chilly wind blasted through the room.

"What are you doing?" I reached to close it.

"Don't touch that." He slammed a hand against the glass and leaned out so far that he could fall.

Over his shoulder, I checked outside. The streets had come to life with lanterns, vendors selling all kinds of goods, and musicians with bagpipes sitting by the warmth of establishments. Most people moved aimlessly in their wandering from shop to shop, but a cloaked couple caught my eye with their rigid steps and tendency to keep from the crowds.

It wasn't until a breeze snared on one of their cloaks that we got a proper look at the man's face.

It was Emric, and he was very much alive.

His head turned to every person that they passed, his hand tucked into his cloak where the form of a cutlass was. He moved differently than before, less confident and more wary, but it was the same man. A man who ought to be dead.

"He drowned," I blinked. "How did he survive that? There were no other ships to pull him aboard."

"Perhaps his mother had something to do with it," Ontario said in a displeased tone.

At that very moment, I saw her.

Now I noted the resemblance between her and Emme, or what Emme had looked like before the disease weakened her. She had the same rounded cheeks and sharp chin, the same gleam that said if she was given the chance, she could take over the world.

Her head lifted, and Ontario and I ducked from sight. I pressed my back to the wall and took a deep breath.

"It's my ship." Ontario gave me a sharp look as if them being here was personally my fault and meant to hurt him. "I earned the right to captain the *Royal Rose*, and he can't have her."

"That's right," I realized with a grin. "Emric has a claim to it, being as it was his when he drowned."

"No." Ontario pushed from the wall. "It's my ship. I swear, no pirate has ever had as much trouble keeping his ship as I have." He stormed out of the room.

"I highly doubt that," I said to myself as I followed after him.

A thought slammed into me like a wave. Emme would be thrilled. Although she held onto hope, she thought she was the sole survivor of her family. But apparently she had her mother and brother back. She should know. She should be here.

I strode from the room and rounded down the rickety stairs that spilled into the dining room of the loud tavern below where our crew congregated.

"Come along, friends," I announced. I barely caught myself before saying *mates*. The image of the bounty poster was burned into my mind along with the cruel methods they could use to kill us or how many people would gladly turn us in to get that silver. Emric and Arabella likely hadn't seen how much pirates were wanted for yet. If they had, they wouldn't be wearing their cutlasses so boldly. Arabella especially would make a fine catch to deliver to the king.

The crew stood from their plates as Ontario shoved open the door. The bartender gave us a suspicious look.

I gestured outside as naturally as I could. "There's a show to watch."

The crew took the hint to follow. And there was Landon right at my heels.

Ontario darted around the crowds until he planted himself in front of Emric. "You are meant to be dead."

Being captain had made him cold. His desire to keep his position had turned him desperate.

But Emric was the same man as before—an endlessly energy that a few months ago I'd wanted to toss into the seas. He smiled from ear to ear and barreled Ontario into an embrace.

Arabella stood aside with crossed arms as she inspected each one of us. I straightened as her gaze landed on me for mere moments before pulling away.

"It's good to see you," Ontario said with minimal emotion. "How—?" But Emric had already turned to me, shaking my hand vigorously.

"Emme's missed you," I told him. "You have no idea how much she's missed you."

"Which one—where is she?" His attention hesitated on the group behind me.

"She isn't here. She's been captured."

"When?" Arabella's voice was hard like rocks, and her focus never stayed on one place for too long—it went from us to the people around us to the castle at her back.

"This morning. She almost killed a man and was caught. The guards took her to the castle."

Arabella turned on her heel and headed in Emme's direction.

"Wait," I called after her. "What's your plan?"

"It's a mile walk," she said over her shoulder. "I'll think of something." She picked up her pace. Emric lifted his hand to us and took off after her, while Ontario and I exchanged looks.

"I'm not pleased with this," he grunted.

"Looks like we have a mile walk to let them know that," I replied.

Ontario faced the crew. "Come with us. Looks like we break Emme out tonight. With luck, we will be sailing away before the sun comes up."

The sun already hung low in the sky, but it was a decent thought. At least it'd give us something to hope for as we marched to what could easily be a disaster.

It took Ontario and me several long strides to fall in line with Emric and his mother. Half the crew followed, and the other half ran to arm themselves with knives. But by the time we were one fourth of the way to the castle, everyone had caught up to enjoy the silence as Arabella was frustratingly tight-lipped about her years of absence.

"Frankly, I could care less where you've been," Ontario finally said, giving up. "Have you ever broken into the castle?"

The path was cleaved through the hill, but every so often it broke to give a glorious view of the sea, and Arabella's eyes were on the water as often as they were on her footing. "Three times," she replied.

Emric faltered. "Three times?"

"Where do you think I got those nice swords for you and Emme to practice with?" Arabella gave him a wink. From behind us, the entire crew was a disordered mess as some tried to get near Arabella and others slinked back.

Ontario kept right at her heels, unbridled by fear. She noticed it and gave a wry grin as he pressed on. "And how do we free Emme?"

"We kill any guards we find and walk right in."

Ontario dug into his pocket. "We have invitations. Let's not make this messier than it needs to be."

She stopped and glared at him. "And how many times

have you broken in? Or do you merely think you can do this better than I?"

"I didn't get lost for five years," he replied with admirable courage. "And I'm the captain of this crew."

Emric's brows raised as he looked to me. I shook my head.

Arabella gave a dry laugh as she continued up the path. "My son is the captain. You are just holding his place."

I was certain that if I pried back Ontario's fingers from his tight fist, I'd find grooves dug into his palm from his nails.

"We should form a coherent plan." Emric thankfully intervened as a harsh wind funneled through the trees.

Arabella sighed and glanced over her shoulder. "Are any of you brave enough to simply walk into the castle and fight?"

In our entire crew, Tess alone raised her hand. I wished she wouldn't have. Tess had a promising future, and I didn't want Arabella to notice that and take an interest in teaching her whatever dark, twisted ways she had. Arabella's gaze softened slightly on the young girl.

"Good. You will be with me when we face the king. But there won't be a fight." She snatched her hair to one side and pulled down the shoulder of her tunic. She had a black tattoo of a crown on it. She righted her clothes to explain. "It's not uncommon for kings to have . . ." she searched for the right word, "hired hands on the sea. People like me who are willing to do their dirty work for a handsome pay."

Emric stared at his mother in shock mingled with disgust. "I swear, I don't know you, woman."

She grinned like he'd given her a compliment. "You'd need a lifetime to understand someone as complex as me. But the important part is I'm certain the king will be grateful to have his faithful soldier back, enough so to give me my daughter in return." She continued up the path. "If this works, we won't need to draw a blade."

"Hear that, Arn?" Ontario said, too loudly. "Your girl will be safe."

Arabella's back stiffened, and her withering gaze slid over me. I didn't care for how her lips turned down.

Emric's attention snapped to me as well, and after a while, he fell back to speak with me. "Do you love my sister?"

It was a rather abrupt question, but I had no problem answering. "Yes."

"More than anything?"

He knew that I did. "How did you survive?" I asked him instead.

He waved my question away. "I need to know," he insisted. "Do you love her more than you love anything in the world?"

The intensity in his eyes grew sharper. "Yes," I finally admitted. "I asked her to marry me today."

He visibly relaxed. "Congrats, mate."

"She said no."

His smile fell. From ahead, I swore Arabella chuckled.

"Well," Emric raised his voice. "I'm not certain she needs to love you back for it to work. Arabella?"

The woman didn't answer.

"She does love me. I've no doubt about that." I studied him. "What are you asking for?"

His reply was eager. "You can heal her. Tonight."

I froze. Ontario froze. Landon ran into my back. He quickly recovered but turned his face away from Emric to keep on.

Ahh, Emric hadn't seen him yet. That was a reunion that wouldn't go down well. "What do you mean?"

"Arabella told me if blood was spilled from one who loved Emme more than anything—enough for her to rinse her hands in, it would heal her. Your love will literally heal her."

The breath was knocked from my lungs. Hope mixed with frustration that the answer could be so easy. "Is that true?"

"I've never heard of such a thing," Ontario said as he stepped around me.

"But it's true," Emric stated. "Tell them, Mother." When

Arabella didn't reply, Emric ran up to her side and put an arm out to stop her. "Tell them it's true."

She pushed past him. At his expression, my chest fell.

The sky was turning as red as her hair as the sun faded away, signaling how little time we had left if we planned to free Emme and get the king tonight. But Emric had no apparent intention of moving until Arabella answered him.

She sighed. "I needed you to be hopeful that if you got off the island, you could save your sister. If I hadn't told you that, you wouldn't have fought so hard to be free. I needed to be free."

Bits of their story came to view. Trapped on an island. Emric somehow went there too. She'd lied to save herself.

The muscles in Emric's jaw feathered. Quick breaths came in little puffs that vaporized in the cold air as he shook his head slowly. Then he lifted stormy eyes. "You lied to me. Again." He spat. "You used me to free yourself."

"You don't even remember it," she said dismissively. "You can't pretend to be hurt now."

That bit of the story, I couldn't understand.

"I remember this!" He swung a hand to his chest. "I remember the ache that always came when you proved that you cared more for yourself than for me. Five years stranded on an island and missing your children, yet all you can think about is that." He thrust an angry finger in the direction of the sea. "That's all you care for."

She marched past him. "If that were true, I wouldn't be here searching for my daughter."

After a moment, he angrily trudged after her. The rest of us exchanged uneasy looks before following.

"I will stay for my sister." I heard Emric's terse voice say. "Then I'm done with you. Perhaps I'll see you again in five years."

It was the fury of Emric and the rage of Arabella that led us to the castle as the hours ticked down.

34

EMME

Raven messed with the door for what seemed like hours. Then the window. Then she clawed at the walls until her fingers bled. She collapsed to her knees, pounded her fists against the stone, and screamed.

"They'll let you out in a few days at the most," I said.

She looked up with a frown. "I hate small spaces."

"Then you shouldn't have gotten arrested for pretending to be drunk." I sat with my back against the wall and legs dangling off a cot, picking at the loose hem of my cloak. Raven had no cloak, only long black pants tucked into boots that cut off at the ankle, wool socks bunching together over the heels, and a knitted top in the same mocha shade as her thick brows, which were currently drawn low in frustration.

She snatched a locket from around her neck and opened it. Slowly, the tension in her expression lessened.

I buried my cheeks into my knees as the winter wind filtered through the bars of the window. "Lover to get back to?" I asked as a distraction.

Raven shoved the locket back under her sweater. "No," she scoffed. "Children to fight for." Her next words surprised me. "I rescue lost children."

I studied her better now. She was about my age I guessed, a

deep tone to her voice and stiffness in her shoulders. She drew out the locket again.

"What children?"

"Any abandoned in the towns, any lost ones looking for a family. Any who feel without a purpose. I bring the children aboard and train them to survive at sea. I have thirty-seven younglings on a ship, and they need me to return."

After a few moments I found my voice. "Do they have anyone to care for them right now?"

She rubbed the edge of her locket with her thumb. "The older ones will step up until I return."

She said it with such determination it was as if she'd seen into her future and knew she'd be free soon, but the way her foot tapped told me she was more worried than she let on.

"So what would you ask the Sea King Valian for?" I asked. "A family for the children?"

"We are a family," she shot back. Then softened. "No, I'd ask him for three jars, one of apples that never run out, one of roast that never empties, and one of water that never dries up."

Her request was undoubtedly more righteous than Serena's. If I got the king, all it would do was let a scorned mermaid back into the seas.

"And if you can only have one of those?" I asked.

"The water," she said without hesitation. "But I plan to ask for five to make three seem reasonable."

I laughed. The sly way she'd said it and the smirk on her face was so much like Emric, that for a moment I had him back.

"What would you ask for?"

I pushed my stocking down so she could see. "Nothing. I'm oathound to someone who asked me to get something for them. If I don't, I die." She stood to come closer and examined the tattoo, where the ink had grown darker with the urgency of the task. Her fingers reached but hesitated before touching, then they pulled back.

"I've never seen one before. It'll kill you if you don't get it fulfilled?"

I nodded. "But clearly, I'll be dead within months anyway."

She retook her place on the ground as I rolled my stocking back up. My shoulder felt better now, only tender as I moved to the door. The bars didn't budge when I pulled, and the door only gave the quietest of rattles on its hinges. If Raven couldn't make this door move, then I stood no chance, but she was polite enough not to say anything as I gave it a few tugs.

Suddenly, the grating sound of metal against stone in the arched hallway sent me backward and Raven to her feet. She tucked the locket deep into her shirt.

The guard with gray eyes who had led us in here approached. Two others stood behind him. "You." He pointed at me. "The one who can't write."

"Emme." I gulped.

"Come this way." He swung his point to Raven. "If you try to flee, I've permission to run you through."

She rolled her eyes. "I was drunk. Killing me sounds extreme."

"You'll go free if you behave."

She held up her hands and dropped against the bed. Content, the guard unlocked the door. Behind him, the two others stood with hands behind their backs and hard looks set on me. One had bronze skin like mine, and the others were dark, but their mouths were all set in a similar straight line, and their eyes all watched as I stumbled out of the room.

The guard with the gray eyes held out a hand for me.

"No cuffs?" I asked.

"Do you need them?"

"No."

Boot. Sleeve. Belt.

He gripped my wrist, but the angle which he held me from—underneath instead of overtop—indicated he was more concerned with keeping me upright than keeping me from running away. The other guards stopped and waited for us to catch up again as they checked the corridors.

Meanwhile, I was too busy plotting to enjoy the view.

It was my first time in a castle, excluding the lovely hours I'd just spent in that damp, pungent cell, and the start of winter must have been the height of the castle's beauty. The last autumn leaves clung to the trees with their red hues starkly contrasting the pale spread of the sky, and all the windows were open to catch the last favorable weather before they'd be locked up. I had to stop at one of these windows, and my fingers brushed the damp residue on the sill.

"Come along." The guard tugged.

Inside, the castle was already dressed for winter with fires blazing and thick rugs rolled out that swallowed my shoes practically to the ankle. We crossed by halls trussed up for the festival, winding staircases overlooking the sea, long corridors where everyone stopped to stare, and finally to the threshold of a room.

It wasn't the throne room. It was one tall door carved from oak with the design of a tree inside, symbolizing our main trade item. The guard let the knocker fall, then stood back.

Another guard opened the door.

Beyond him snapped the warm crackle of a fire, a small table set with an untouched glazed ham and mulled wine, a scatter of papers and a wax seal, and a line of guards standing at attention for two figures seated at the table.

They stood as we entered. I didn't need anyone to tell me I was looking at King Unid and Queen Isla.

Now that I'd seen him, I wondered how I'd ever thought the farmer was the king. This man had broad shoulders, a thick build, full head of wavy hair, and eyes that said he was kind enough to be loved by the people but fierce enough to lead them into battle.

The queen was every bit as majestic. Strong arms, thick brows, and an expression that said she owned the room and we were all simply moving according to her will.

I came to them as a criminal, but I fell to my knees as a loyal subject at the feet of my monarchs.

"Rise, child," King Unid said in a tone I couldn't determine. The guard helped me to my feet.

Queen Isla came forward with narrowed eyes that took in every detail about me, and I waited for her to discover my blades. I kept as still as I could manage as she walked a slow circle around me, close enough that her skirt brushed my legs, until she came to the front again.

Her hand shot out, and she snatched my chin.

I grunted. She pulled it closer until I could see the birthmark on her cheek and the dip in the tip of her nose.

She ran her other hand through my hair.

"Daughter of Arabella," she whispered. "What a prize we've found."

She let go, and I stumbled back.

"What did you call me?" I asked breathlessly.

"It is a queen's job to know her enemies," she replied.

My heart pounded quicker. The awe I felt a moment before shifted to fear. "I'm not your enemy."

"No?" She looked to the guards, then back at me. "Were you responsible for the death of a man in the square?"

I hesitated. *Yes, but that was an accident. I thought it was your husband instead.*

A guard stepped forward, one with the blackest hair I'd ever seen. "Actually, that man lives, Your Highness."

I exhaled with my entire body. That guard was my favorite person at the moment.

If the farmer hadn't died, then I shouldn't die for the crime either.

Queen Isla didn't miss a beat. She hardly gave a passing

glance to the guard, who lowered his head and returned to the stiff line at her side. "When I tell the story, he died. Brutally. And this pirate," she jutted her sharp chin in my direction, "was the one who did it, because she is as her mother is. Ruthless. Bred from nothing but a savage hand and stone heart." She crossed back to the table and plucked an apple from her plate. "She will be our example to the seas that we will not relent in our mission to rid our waters of such thieves. And she will be an example to her mother."

My mother is dead, I thought, but I was physically too tired to speak.

The king didn't move, nor did he acknowledge the guard who'd said that the farmer hadn't died. That was the bit that they should be focusing on. I hadn't killed anyone.

That they knew of.

"I'm no pirate," I managed to say. "I grew up on a sheep farm in the small town of Gollins. And I'm clumsy." That part was clearly true. I couldn't stand still without shaking. "I honestly meant that man no harm and am deeply sorry for any damage done. I don't even know who Arabella the Ruthless is."

It should have worked. My accent and coloring were from Julinbor, my physical condition clear, and the break in my voice as tears came should soften their hearts. My mother had lighter skin, wild red hair, and a temper that didn't match mine at all. But my shirt must have been loose at the collar, for the queen reached to pull at it.

"These tattoos say otherwise." She let go to grab my wrist and shove the coat sleeve up. Thankfully my hidden dagger was stashed against my other arm. The one she peered at had a tattoo of coral wrapping around the skin, and she grinned satisfactorily at it before dropping my hand. "You're a pirate, and your tattoos match hers. I'll make certain they are on full display when we execute you on Winter Night."

Any strength in my body gave way at that moment. I fell to my knees in earnest. "No."

The queen turned to the line of guards, where for the first time I noticed one man was more decorated than the others. He had three ribbons pinned to his chest and silver cuff links that caught the light through the frosted window. His jaw was set, and he didn't move.

Queen Isla raised a brow at him. "Is my ruling unclear?"

He shifted his gaze between her and King Unid.

The king placed a hand on his wife's shoulder. "I approve the ruling. She will be hung in the square at dusk in two days."

"No," I said again like a helpless child. "I didn't mean to do anything."

The king moved on as if I were nothing.

The queen brushed roughly past me with a grip on her husband's arm. But in that brush was a whisper. "My word should be enough." Then in a louder voice, "I'm going to prepare for our dinner."

In desperation, I grabbed at her skirt when she passed again. Her brows raised with bemusement, but she didn't pull away.

I looked at her from my knees. "Kill me, and you have the wrath of the seas coming for you. The daughter of Arabella the Ruthless is loved."

She tore out of my grasp. "Try me."

Her footsteps echoed away, as my arms were lifted by the guards to drag me back to the cells. "You're making a mistake." I braced my feet against the floor while the king retook his seat.

"My queen's word is final," he said without a look my way. He motioned for the captain to join him at the mess of papers on the table.

"I'm just a girl," I protested. "I'm going to die in a few months anyway." I kicked against the guard's hold, but even with half his strength he outmatched me. He hauled me out the door.

The disbelief of my sentence numbed me, but it was the disregard of the king that made me angry, as he placed his elbows on the table to dine with the captain as if I were a passing thought that had already taken up more of his time than he liked.

My life meant so little to him that I didn't even get a pitiful last look, and the queen had hardly stayed long enough to give her ruling.

No one else would free me.

Boot. Sleeve. Belt.

In times like these, I had one trick left to play, and I played it well. I dug my feet into the ground, threw back my head, and let out the saddest sob I could. The dramatics of my cries might have been fake, but the tears streaming down my cheeks were very real—made of fear and desperation.

"I don't want to die," I cried. I used my shoulder to blow my nose. "I'm so scared."

The three guards escorting me shifted. Perfect.

My moans grew louder. They shut the door so the king didn't have to listen.

"And I don't get to say good-bye to my family," I wailed. I sniffled in the most unflattering way possible. "I'm going to die alone."

"You think you can handle this?" one of the guards asked the man who held me, though his grip was decidedly looser than it was before.

He shot them a look, and I cried harder.

"Fine," he mumbled. The other two scurried off, leaving me with only one overwhelmed guard to escort me. "Come along. You can cry in the cell."

I could have danced with joy. But instead I continued crying. Mother had told me that tears made men uncomfortable. *"Not as uncomfortable as my blade,"* she'd added. *"But it's worth remembering."* In a moment, the guard would be uncomfortable because of both my tears and my blade.

I might not be in this situation if it weren't for my association with her, so it was only fitting that she got me out.

He led me through the corridors and to the back of the castle where the air was colder and my cries vibrated off empty stone walls. He unlocked the first door to bring me to the dark entrance of my cell.

Raven pressed a face against the bars when she heard my hysterics.

"Back up," the guard said in a disgruntled voice. "All the way to the wall."

I winked at her. Her eyes flickered as she obeyed him.

He gave me a glance as he let go to twist the key into the lock. I cried in return, hugging my arms around my chest and sobbing wildly. He rushed his movements. I tried not to think of how this was likely my only opportunity to escape as I reached for the familiar hilt of the dagger up my sleeve.

The key turned in the lock.

I brought my blade up and struck the hilt as hard as I could against his temple. It met with a crack.

They keys clattered to the floor as the guard fell into a lump at my feet while the door eased open. Behind it, Raven stood with her jaw dropped open.

The man stirred.

"I'll take this," Raven said. She bolted from her cell and took the blade.

"Don't kill him," I said.

She repeated my motion from earlier, but much harder. He gave one last grunt as his eyelids fluttered before he stilled in a contorted position on the ground. This time, he didn't stir.

"There." She flicked the knife back up to me. "Easiest

prison break I've ever done. Well, second easiest. Top five, at least."

"You didn't do anything," I said, wiping the remaining tears from my eyes and sheathing the blade at my wrist.

"True. Second easiest, then." She prowled like a tigress through the halls, her long limbs moving like a vapor that had drifted in with the morning and hadn't the good mind to leave when day came. She was silent, one with the shadows. Her frame pressed against the wall at the top of the stairs, and she peeked into the courtyard.

I kept at a slower pace and had no hope of matching her stealth.

From behind, I looked over her shoulder. The courtyard we'd come in from at the back of the castle was still nothing more than barren trees, leaf-riddled paths, and the hissing of wind in the cracks of aged cobblestone.

I almost bumped my head against an oil lamp. It wasn't lit, but the residue of scorched stone was still there. I held it to brace myself. "There's no one there," I said. "I say we run for it."

"The wall above us has guards that patrol. I saw them on the way in," Raven said. "And there are guards stationed at the doors." Raven reached for something in her pocket and sighed. "I hoped not to use this."

"What is it?"

"A sleeping potion." She put it back into her pocket. "But now isn't the time." She grabbed me and led me back into the tunnel.

I dug my heels into the ground. "Why are we going back there?"

She let me go to clutch the arms of the guard we'd knocked out and dragged him through the open door of our cell. "We will wait until the festival starts at dinner tonight before leaving. The guards will be pulled closer to the front, and we can drug the few here then leave out the back. But first," she dropped the guard and wiped her brow. "First I am going to kill the king, and you are going to live."

"Or we can run now."

She raised a brow. "Can you run? You can hardly walk. And if we leave now, our path will be too heavily saturated with guards." She pushed the guard under a cot. "No. We wait until the prime moment. I happen to know the king and queen take a private dinner to celebrate their anniversary in a small garden on the south side."

"That's an odd thing to *happen to know*."

She gave a sly grin. "I might not have been truthful about who I am." She threw a thin blanket over the guard to hide him. He'd wake eventually. We didn't have forever.

The itch to run was overwhelming, but I hesitated. "Can you guarantee that we get to the king?"

"I can guarantee more than that. I'll guarantee his head. But that hinges upon us choosing the right moment to run, and that moment comes when I say it does." She sat herself down and propped a knee up, keeping an eye out the window in the meager light. It was almost night, Winter Night, and the country would be celebrating. The night we had all hoped to make our escape. If Raven came through, we still would.

I sat beside her. "I want to know who you are."

"Follow my plan, and I'll tell you."

35
ARN

We stopped among the last trees before they gave way to dying fields at the mouth of the castle. The drawbridge was open, and lines of people crossed it, dressed in varying shades of blues, silvers, and whites. They'd celebrate in the castle with a feast and dancing, then move to the boats down the shore in hopes of catching a Swimming Sequin. When they moved to the water, we wanted to be moving, too, and with both Emme and the head of the king in our possession.

"How many invitations do you have?" Arabella asked. She hunched at the tree line, watching the castle like a lioness.

"I thought you didn't need those," Emric replied. "You're apparently so valuable to the king that he'll give you whatever you want."

She shot him a deadly look.

"One real, four forged," Ontario replied. He touched his breast pocket but made no move to hand them over.

"Give me the real one," she demanded, holding out her hand. "And I will return with my daughter."

Ontario still didn't move.

Her tone intensified. "Do you wish to see my daughter die in the time it takes you to form a new plan?"

Ontario slowly reached for his pocket and removed

one invitation. He gave it to Arabella. "You get one hour before we come."

She held the invitation firmly and strode to the castle.

We kept low as we watched her navigate through the field to the line outside the bridge, but by the time she'd reached the door, she was deep in conversation with a gentleman she'd come upon, and it appeared as if they had journeyed together. She flashed her invitation and was ushered inside, where she disappeared into the dense courtyard.

Ontario let out his breath. "The forged invitations worked. Well done, Manty." He handed me another. "This is a real one. Follow her."

I took it uncertainly. "What good am I?"

"I trust Arabella's word less than I trust the seas." He pushed me into the clearing. "You have one hour—I mean it this time—before we follow. Bring Emme out safely."

"And the king?"

Ontario shook his head stiffly. "Not tonight. I'm not sending men in there until we have a plan. I won't let any of them die because we were rushing."

His words tore at a deep wound, reminiscent of another plan that we didn't think through that led to the death of our men. Ontario kept a tight expression as he spoke, his eyes locked on the castle, and it was that moment that showed me he was a good captain after all. It's a man's instinct to run forward when the thing he wants is in front of him, but it takes a smart man to bide his time.

I took the invitation. "Are we certain Emric wouldn't be a better option? Emme will be relieved to see him, and she and I left things uneasy."

"You go," Emric encouraged. "I'll see her when she's free."

"Emric is not oathbound," Ontario pointed out. "You can track her better. Now go before you lose Arabella."

I took off for the castle and didn't slow until I reached the looming iron bridge. The air smelled of wet mud, withered leaves, and smoke. The sky came in shades of light blue to rusty orange. Soon it'd be dark, and the only light would be from the lines of torches plunged into the ground.

People crowded around me before the guard at the gate. He carried his head high. He had the best job in the castle tonight. Everyone was excited to see the man that would let them into the party. He barely glanced at the invitations as he nodded each person inside.

I kept my arm tucked into the folds of my cloak so he didn't notice my missing hand and hoped he didn't spot the golden tattoos of waves along my collar. I idly wondered if I could turn myself in and get all the silver, then find a way to free both me and Emme. Before that plan could take root, I was at the gate.

It was tall and made of iron, and there would be no way to get out once it was shut.

"Invitation?"

I held mine up.

"Welcome to Winter Night."

And just like that, I was in.

Dainty paper snowflakes hung from trees around the courtyard on branches that had been painted silver, and rolls of blue cloth coated the ground. Fake icicles hung from tables that clattered as folks bumped into them, especially the table along the west side, where a giant bowl of spiced cider had been set up. From the other side, the courtyard let out to a path that led down to the ocean, where they'd gather later in hopes of catching a Swimming Sequin tonight, thereby gaining prosperity and good fortune.

Arabella wouldn't have gone that way. She'd have turned right and headed straight into the castle. Two doors were opened to get inside, where a dance was held under white lights. There were so many people here that even with Arabella's red hair, I hadn't the hope of finding her.

But I didn't need to. I knew where I was going.

My oathbinding burned like a thousand fires on my foot. *You are so close*, it whispered in a haunting voice for only me to hear. It drew me to her. *She's here.*

It turned me east, where double, wooden, arched doors led to a wide corridor. The path laid out before me like a silver trail on the ground for me to follow, guiding me to her, and each moment it burned brighter than the next. I ignored the guests whose shoulders I grazed as I followed it like a rope pulling me along. Her very essence was attached to this trail, like if I touched it, I'd touch a piece of Emme.

I shivered. Admiral Bones had had this close connection with me when I'd been oathbound to him.

"Sir." A hand was on my chest, and I glanced up. A guard wearing a white coat and thick black beard stood at a doorway, looking at me questioningly. The silver trail led beneath the crack to what I suspected was outside the building.

I thought fast. "Outhouse?"

He nodded and let his arm drop. "Keep your invitation handy. You'll need it to get back in."

With luck, I wouldn't be coming back.

I slipped out the door and into the chill of night. The day had vanished quickly, and stars already peeked through the dull sky. My feet made a scuffle along the path as it wound along the castle, surrounded by stone on one side and a tall hedge on the other, where roses must have grown in the summer. Now those colors were gone, and it was quiet. Much too quiet.

I stepped lighter. The trail intensified.

It was almost solid silver by the time I rounded the northeast turret and found a narrow gate. The courtyard inside was nothing but barren plants, but the trail glimmered. *She is here. Fulfill your oathbinding.*

I would have, had another figure not slipped through the path.

She came from above, descending the stone like a spider and dropping lightly to the ground. The moonlight gleamed off the visitor's red hair. So much for going to the king to ask for Emme's release.

I hunched into the shadows to wait.

36

EMME

I grew impatient. "Can we go yet?"

"No."

"The festival has started."

"Give it time," Raven said. "If we leave now, there will be guards waiting for us."

I stood on my toes to peek through the high window of the cell. "It appears empty."

Raven sighed. "You are less patient than my children. The courtyard may be empty, but the path we will take is not. I swear we will leave the moment it is safe, and that is not now. Do you want the king or not?"

I settled down, but my jittery feet couldn't be stilled. They begged me to go out the door that was unlocked and to find Arn. Yet Raven held herself with such calmness that I forced myself to trust her knowledge.

One hand fidgeted with her necklace, the other held the key. I was tempted to wrangle it away from her, and if I thought I had a chance, I'd have done it. I kept an eye out the window, but there hadn't been movement in forever. We were too far in the back for guards to come by often, and one sick girl and one drunk girl didn't warrant much watching.

While I was gazing at the key, I missed the first sign of movement, and a scratch came from the window near my head.

I jumped from the bed. Raven froze.

A boot appeared first, wedged between the bars of the window. A calf followed, as the person knelt. The length of wild curls came into view, and a face with a slow spreading smile.

It must have been hard to see us through the small space. It was difficult to see her. Difficult enough that my mind turned her into someone else.

She exhaled, then spoke with a triumphant tone. "I've found you at last."

That voice sent chills up and down my spine. "Mother?"

She placed both hands on the bars and tugged. "Let's get you out of here. My ship will be returning soon to fetch us."

"I'm losing my mind," I said to Raven.

She was white like a ghost. "That's your mother?" she whispered.

There was another tug at the bars. "Now is not the time for explanation. Now is the time to fight. The king won't be happy when he sees me. I stole a great wealth from him before I went missing."

Her sleeves were rolled at her elbows, her black wool sweater paired over a gray dress, and her lips painted red. She hadn't aged a day. I dug my fingers into the bed near me as if that could clear my head. She remained at the window, digging along the sides. "I stashed a key here ages ago."

"Are you the daughter of Arabella the Ruthless?" Raven asked me, voice hushed. From where she stood, Arabella couldn't see her.

I nodded slowly.

Raven took a breath. "She was also at the Sea Gala yesterday."

"You are dead," I said to Arabella. "You died five years ago, after you pretended to be dead, during which time you let me believe you were dead. Now you aren't dead again?" That sounded chaotic, even to me. My mind was unsettled.

"I'll explain once you're free." Her fingers dug through the dirt. "And I'll want to hear all about your adventures on the seas."

Even without my disease, I wouldn't have been able to keep from shaking, but right now, I could hardly stand still. I moved forward to touch her. She was real. This person before me was not a ghost.

"How can this be?" I whispered.

"Not all things that go lost will stay that way," she said. Riddles as always. This really was my mother. She took my hand from her wrist and held it in her own—not in a tender way, but inspecting how much it shook. I pulled back.

"I hear you killed a captain," she said.

"No, I was an accomplice in that. I've never intentionally killed anyone."

Her smile fell. "Then what are you doing here?"

"All I want is to heal this disease so I can live," I said. My voice was an echo in my ears, joining in the confusion.

Arabella moved back from the window to take in the full sight of me, as my head swam with a million questions—too many to ask. She looked over my face. I'd been just a girl when she saw me last, with no real direction in life and still not grown. She'd been gone so long that I had both grown and begun to wither away.

She wasn't seeing the best of me, but from the disappointed look in her eye, she saw all she needed.

"I planned to ask you to rule the seas with me," she said. "But can you even lift a cutlass? Do you possess the strength to aim a pistol, or the strength of mind to pull the trigger? Can you lead a crew of a hundred men?"

At my silence, she gave a dry laugh. An ache pulled at my heart.

"I was told stories of how you were mighty! I thought you

were someone to be feared. Tell me daughter, does anyone fear you?"

Arabella loved the seas most of all, even as the waters had drowned her. Five years without her children, and she'd been stripped of any love that remained, leaving only a bitterness in her words and disappointment that I wasn't who she wanted. It seemed my mother had been returned to me for the sole purpose of reminding me of that.

From the side, buried in the shadows, Raven's eyes glittered in sympathy. She opened her palm to show me the key.

I could show it to Arabella, show her the man under the cot, tell her how we planned to be rid of the king and heal my disease. That would please her while leaving an empty hole inside me.

I set my jaw. My mother wanted the daughter that she'd raised. I didn't want to be her.

"I choose to be loved instead of feared. Emric was the same way."

Her hard gaze kept on me. "Emric still lives, and there are strands of me inside him that he doesn't see yet."

I staggered. "My brother is alive?"

"Your brother fought hard to return to the seas," she said. She'd given up messing with the bars to peer through them with narrowed eyes. "But the boy is too soft to rule over them. And my daughter," her eyes went from my feet to my wobbling knees to my shaking hands that held onto the cot to stabilize me, "my daughter is too weak to captain at my side."

"I have Paslkapi," I said.

She leaned back. The sliver of moonlight showed enough of her disappointment. "You are trapped in a cell with barely a crime over you, too weak to break yourself free, too weak to kill a man, too weak to even stand."

Raven extended her hand again, but I didn't take the key.

"This is not the daughter I was promised."

I bit my lip to feel pain different from the sting she was piercing me with. "And you were never the mother I needed."

"No. I wasn't." She stood and shook her head. "Two children, but no heirs to follow after me. I cannot linger when the key I once buried is clearly gone. Hanging is an honorable death. It'll go quicker than the one currently waiting for you."

Then she left me. Again. This time, not to fake her own death, but to willingly leave me to mine.

I waited until she was gone to breathe again.

"Had I known who you were, I could have told you that your mother lived," Raven said in a small voice.

"Nothing would have made that any easier." I blinked my tears away. "Can we go now?"

Raven nodded.

"Good. Let's get to the king and be gone from here. There is nothing in this country left for me."

37

ARN

Arabella didn't know her daughter well enough to hear her pain, but Emme's voice shook with it. I heard it all. Then I saw Arabella turn to leave.

That wretched woman. Only a fool would leave Emme.

Luckily, I had the perfect way to repay her, for while I could hear her, she couldn't hear everything I was doing. She didn't hear the creaky door open from the top of the turret, nor the clatter of footsteps coming down the spiral stairs. She didn't know the guards were coming and would be upon us soon.

But I did. I cleared my throat, prepared my best Julinbor accent, and willingly opened the door to them.

Two guards were dressing in their livery when I came into the small room. They reached for their swords.

From down the hall, two more guards carried a torch. "The boats will be leaving soon," they said before they spotted me.

When they did, they whipped their hands to their pistols as I held up mine, letting them clearly see the one empty hand and the other missing one. Their focus snagged on my nub of a wrist, and I watched as the edge went out from their stance. "Please," I stumbled over my words like a lowly farmer. I pulled a crumpled parchment from my pocket. "Silver bounty for pirates?"

At that, the two guards in front of me fully relaxed. One was tall as the door with a thick build and features similar to a mangled wolf, while the other was dark-toned and handsome. They hardly glanced at the paper. "We know of it."

The other two guards came near. "What's this?"

"Do you know of Arabella the Ruthless?" I asked.

It was the darker toned one who nodded first as he folded his old tunic away and straightened his festive scarves beneath this coat. "She stole the ice gems yesterday. King's all in a rut about it."

I leaned toward them. "She's fifty meters from us right now. Snuff your torch and you'll catch her."

The four guards hesitated with their eyes shifting between me, each other, and the door. "It's no trick," I promised and stepped aside. "She'll walk by in a moment. Your king will be glad to have her as his prisoner."

After a moment, they snuffed the torch and poised in the shadows of the doorway.

"She is trained." I kept my voice at a whisper. "Be careful."

Arabella's tall shadow crossed the fields as she drew closer. She turned away from the castle before crossing our path, but upon seeing her, four guards jumped from the turret to go follow. I waited with my back pressed to the wall to see how she would fare.

She had only the time to draw a blade before they grabbed hold of her.

She didn't make a sound as she slid her cutlass from its sheath and swung. The guard closest was dressed in bracers that stopped the blade from reaching his neck, and the one beside him drew at pistol.

At its lethal tip, she froze. She stared down the barrel.

"Tie her," one guard said.

Arabella reared her head and knocked it against the guard who tried to approach. The one holding the pistol wavered.

He knew as I did that the king would want this prisoner alive. Arabella used that to charge him, betting he wouldn't fire.

He didn't, but the guard beside him did.

The bullet went into her shoulder, and she screamed.

They all flanked her, stripping her weapon from her hand, and she was seized.

One removed a scarf to bind her wrists. "Our king will be very pleased."

She gave a laugh. "Your king will let me go before the week ends."

She might be right, but that guaranteed we could leave Julinbor with no problems from her. And it would give Emme some satisfaction. If not her, then me.

I slipped out the door and along the shadows with my face tucked into my cloak as they brought her back up the hill. "Your reward?" one called out to me.

I picked up the fallen jacket from the ground. I'd gladly take the reward, but they'd catch me as a pirate myself before I could claim it. I masked my voice as well as I could so Arabella didn't turn me in right there. "I think I'll just take her coat. The garb of a pirate will sell nicely."

After they had gone, I crept through the courtyard to the window bars and lowered myself. "Emme?" I called through the window. "Are you there?"

The door was wide open. The cell was empty, and a silver trail remained in her place, one that led into the heart of the castle.

Something about it all looked like a very bad idea. Bad ideas are what pirates live for. When I checked, the entrance to the cells was unlocked and unguarded, unless the sleeping men slumped on the ground could be called guards. They didn't stir, and I suspected something aided their deep slumber.

The silver trail glowed. *Follow us to find her.*

I put on Arabella's coat and followed inside.

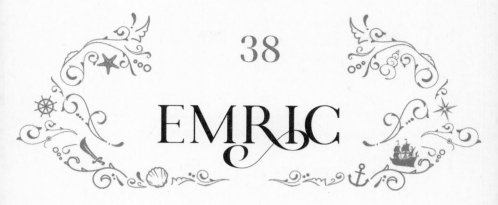

38

EMRIC

We waited beneath the trees while the crowds in the castle shifted from the courtyard to further down the hill. "What are they doing?" I asked.

Ontario glanced up from the stick he was whittling. "Going to catch Swimming Sequins."

I didn't know what that was, but I turned my attention back to the castle.

Ontario scraped the edge of his stick a few more times before snapping it in half. "She should be back by now."

"I'm used to waiting for her. She'll come when she's good and ready."

I'd hoped the memories of my sister would return when I was among the crew, as if they carried a piece of her in them and would help my mind to remember. But as I searched their faces, I couldn't find her. Besides, many of the faces were new, and there was nothing of her in those that were familiar.

"What are you all getting from this? Stealing any treasures inside?" I asked.

Ontario shook his head. "Nothing like that. We are only here for Emme."

I tried to imagine anyone risking their lives for my mother, but her crew was much more likely to celebrate her leaving than wager their necks for her. Honestly, I doubted anyone would do that for me either. "You must really care for her."

He gave a half smile. "We all do. You both were welcomed aboard from your first day."

I tried to pull a memory from that. Had she worked with me at Farrold's Trading Post and come aboard then? Why had I joined the *Royal Rose* to begin with? Those memories were fuzzy, so they must have included her. But they were out of my reach.

I hung my head. "I don't remember her," I admitted.

Ontario sounded shocked. "What?"

I checked to be certain no one else heard. "When I supposedly drowned, I ended up on an island where our mother had been captive for five years. But to leave the island, it demanded a sacrifice. I didn't know what it would be for me, but it took Emme." I rubbed the note I'd written to myself in my pocket. *Remember her.* "I lost all memory of her."

His eyes widened. "Yet you still came here for her?"

"My mother is determined to have one child who rules on the seas with her."

Ontario was still, then he laughed. "Emme is not that child."

"But we heard that she killed a captain."

"I don't know about that," Ontario said. "But I know that she is the kindest person on this crew, and likely on the seas. I've spent only a few minutes with your mother. Emme is nothing like her."

A pang hit me, one laced in the closest thing to emotion that I'd been able to feel toward Emme since losing my memory. I'd been working on the assurance of what my mother told me without questioning if her words were truth, but here was a very different account from someone who knew her, and it was one that I desperately wanted to believe. I asked to be certain I heard him right. "She's not coldhearted?"

He chortled. "Emme? I doubt anything in this world could make her coldhearted."

My relief couldn't be measured. I felt it like a huge tidal wave slamming into me, knocking the air from my lungs. *She is good. She is like Father.*

At that moment, a shot cleaved the air, followed by a scream.

Ontario swung his eyes to the castle. "What was that?"

The relief inside shriveled up and gave way to fright. "That was my mother," I said. I grabbed my pistol and started off.

39

EMME

I looked behind us as voices rang through the night. "Did you hear that?"

"Not relevant to us," Raven said. She didn't turn. "We keep going."

She knew the route well enough that she didn't even use the halls, but instead crept through back rooms and secret panels in the walls. Sometimes it'd be a door behind a tapestry, or an entrance veiled by a rug, and once a drafty tunnel that went under a fireplace.

Raven kept flinging her hand back to check that I followed, and I stumbled to keep up with the fast pace.

"On the other side of this wall is the gardens where the king and queen will be," she said. "We'll be coming up in the gardens."

"And what's our plan then?"

"You've got a knife, right? We use it."

I ran into her back. She grabbed my hand to steady me, and her fingers were cold. "We are here." She pressed my hand against the stone in front of her. "This opens to the gardener's shed."

"How do you know this?" I asked.

"I once had a thing with the prince," she confessed. "If we both get out alive, I'll tell you about it."

"Now you're on your way to kill his father?"

Her smile was sad. "Times have changed." She pressed against the door gently, and the stone scraped against the ground as it opened.

The light didn't come all at once. It was a slow stream that showed bit by bit, first the jars of seeds and bags of dirt on one side, then the cracked window, then the tools gathering cobwebs in the corner. We crawled to the window to peer out.

The garden was set like a fairy tale with tiny lights hanging in bulbs from trees, sheer cloths draped from the branches, and paper snowflakes strewn about the floor. It must have taken a large team hours to cut all those snowflakes out, and all for one dinner between King Unid and Queen Isla.

They sat at a small marble table in the middle of the garden, with no guards in sight.

"Where are the officers?"

"It's their anniversary," Raven reminded me. "It's the one day a year they have a private dinner."

"That's convenient for us."

"Mostly. We still need to get by Queen Isla, and she scares me more than the king." She took the dagger strapped to my arm. "You stay here," she ordered. "You'll only slow me down."

She stood, but I grabbed her sleeve. "I can help. I'll cause a distraction."

Her brows shot up. The black of her eyes almost overpowered the blue as she stared through the window at the layout of the gardens. She nodded slowly. "That's a decent idea. Okay, you go that way," she pointed north, "and make noise. For the sea's sake, not too loud. We don't want it attracting the guards. I'll sneak up on the king from that way." She pointed to the hedges that still clung to their leaves.

I took the blade from my boot. She stared at me. "For my own knowledge, how many of these do you have?"

I grinned. "Just one more."

"Good." She slipped out the side door.

I was exhausted, but I gripped that dagger and made my way into the garden. With each movement I checked through the thick bushes and caught glimpses of the king's red coat or the queen's dark hair. Moonlight glinted off their goblets as they raised them to their lips. I traced my hand along the back of a bench to guide me to a dried-up well.

King Unid was saying something to Queen Isla, and they laughed together.

This weather-stained marble bench would be as good of a place as any. I gave Raven a few moments to get into position, then reached down for thick twigs.

I snapped one. Then I snapped another.

The laughter stopped.

I snapped a third.

They said something that I couldn't hear, then came the unquestionable sound of chairs scrapping against the stones.

I shuffled my own feet in response.

This would be an excellent way to leave me, I thought. Raven could run now, and I'd be trapped.

The slender form of Queen Isla advanced, shifting as she peered through the bushes. They were just dense enough to hide my face, but open enough that they'd see hints of my gray coat.

King Unid was slower. "Is someone there? Can we not have one private meal?" He buttoned his coat and grumbled as he took a final sip from his glass.

The crack of leaves underfoot sounded from across the garden. They whirled around.

King Unid drew his sword with a loud slicing sound from the blade against its metal sheath. I wound in front of the bushes to see Raven advance like a tigress with my dagger clutched in her hand. The queen grabbed a horn from the centerpiece, lifted it to her lips, and blew. It sounded long and loud, like death bells. For us, that's what it was. Another horn signaled from inside the castle.

They had a private dinner, but they weren't defenseless. The guards were coming.

I tightened my grip and ran for the king.

Raven held her dagger fearlessly, even in the face of the king's sword. At the last moment, Raven slid and held the blade sideways in front of her to catch the sword as it clashed mere inches from her face. From there she rolled on her back and twisted her legs in a move I'd never seen to wrap them around the king's wrists. Still keeping the blade firmly ahead of her, she yanked her legs down.

That would have disarmed others, but the king merely slid his sword back, and Raven had to withdraw quickly to avoid deep slices in her calves.

The queen held her own sword, retrieved from beneath a thin sapling, and wrapped her fingers around its hilt, keeping an eye on Raven. She sighted me.

When our gazes met, she gave the faintest smile. I shivered.

I kept my blade tucked at my side until Raven lost her footing on the slippery stone and bashed her knee against the ground. She rolled out of the way. The king's next strike narrowly missed her chest.

She reached for her dagger. He kicked it away.

I grabbed at the hedge beside me and used it to stabilize myself as I took aim and threw my blade at the king.

He hardly looked my way when he flicked his weapon to deflect it. It clattered on the ground at the queen's feet.

Raven's eyes were wide, and her chest rose quickly in the face of the king's sword at her neck. I fumbled for the blade in my belt.

"Run," Raven shouted to me. "Use the tunnels."

From the distance, the march of guards grew closer.

Queen Isla drifted to the king's side. "Finish this, my love."

But there was hesitation in his eye.

Queen Isla had none of that hesitation.

She placed herself behind the king and swung her weapon with sickening speed. Her aim was not for Raven.

With a cracking sound I'd not soon forget, her blade cut through the king, and he fell dead at her feet.

The king was slain.

His hand rested over Queen Isla's shoes as if reaching for his wife. With her lips turned down, she nudged it away with her foot.

I placed my palm to my stomach as it roiled like the waves while Raven scrambled to her feet. She hunched in attack position, but there was a tremor in her hand as she held her dagger.

The queen approached the table where she'd been seated moments before and yanked the black tablecloth away. Her back was rigid, but she didn't waver, not even as the dishes shattered against the chairs and stone ground. She wrapped the cloth around the king's head and tied it in a knot.

She held it to Raven. "This is what you seek. Take it."

Somewhere close by, a door scratched against the ground, opening. A flurry of stomping boots foretold the guards rushing closer. Raven grabbed the makeshift sack and bolted for the shed. I turned after her but paused.

Curiosity overcame my horror. "Why?"

Queen Isla tilted her chin upward. "A queen answers to no one."

I couldn't tell if that was her ignoring my question or answering it.

She'd been second in command. But now, she was first.

She took the control she wanted, and we were an excellent excuse for it.

"You should have run, girl," she chided in a cold voice that shook me from my thoughts. She tossed her blade at my feet just as ten guards hurled themselves through the maze of hedges to halt at the sight of the blood. Their faces washed of color.

Even if I had run, I wouldn't have made it. Raven, however, had disappeared.

"Pirates have killed the king," Queen Isla declared suddenly.

The guard at the front pushed some of his men back. "Sound the main alarm," he commanded. Two officers turned, but the queen's voice caught them.

"No. Wait. I see we have a gift."

From the east side of the garden, other guards were coming. They didn't move with urgency like the first, but they dragged someone along behind them. Arabella appeared on the other side of their rough rope with the skirt of her dress torn and her hair a tangle of curls that twisted each direction as she scanned the garden like a hunter examining its prey. Even bound, my mother was frightening. Blood soaked her shoulder.

"My queen," the guards said, their heads held high enough that they failed to see their fallen king. "We bring you the captured Arabella the Ruthless."

Queen Isla put up a hand. "You can see we are in the middle of something."

Now they saw the king and went ashen.

"But the timing of this is wonderful," Queen Isla went on. "Guards, I present to you the cruelty of pirates." She indicated the king's body. "For too long they have gone unchecked at our borders, and now is our time to rage war against them."

The guard at the front stepped forward almost regrettably. "Words cannot express my sorrow, Your Majesty. We'll call in our fleet to patrol the waters."

"Not patrol." Her voice carried a lethal edge to it. "Fight."

The guard didn't waver. "This is a large decision. Let us bring it to the council."

"No." Her voice sliced through the air. "I am your monarch. I will be obeyed. The only meeting we will have is to plan our strategy, and that is final."

A queen answers to no one.

The guard bowed, but the look in his eye said that wasn't the last of it.

Queen Isla turned her feral gaze to me. She smiled. I hated that smile. "Though perhaps I am wrong. Perhaps pirates are not as cruel as we think. Let us play a game, yes? Test your heart." She held those in the garden enraptured when she spoke, and she stepped around her husband's body to come nearer to me. I drew to my feet, using her sword as both support and potential protection. She stopped a few paces from me.

"For the crime of murdering our king, you shall be killed. But you are clearly to die anyway from whatever ails you. I give you this choice. You can be free to live your final days in whatever manner you like, and your mother will be taken captive instead. Or you take your mother's place. One of you will go free, and you'll choose which one." Her expression told that she knew how wicked of a deal this was.

Silence fell like a heavy cloak over us, weighing heaviest on me. Flickers of uncertainty passed my mother's expression as she yanked against her bonds.

"She is a child," Arabella yelled. "She cannot make that decision."

Queen Isla held up a hand. She whispered for only me to hear, "Let no one answer for you." Then her voice raised. "If I am wrong that pirates are coldhearted, then your daughter will take your place. But if I'm right, then even the love a child has for her mother won't be enough for this creature to give up herself."

I peeked to the shed where we'd come in. Raven would be long gone by now. As was the head, which was my one ticket to survival.

The queen tapped her foot. "My mercy grows thin."

She didn't want me to give up myself. She'd want Arabella as her prisoner and me, who she knew didn't commit a crime, to go free.

But if I chose to not take my mother's place, the queen would prove to everyone that pirates are heartless.

My eyes turned to my mother. Earlier she'd left me to die. Now her fate was in my hands. For always being so strong, she'd never appeared so helpless as the ropes on her wrist held her up.

I shut my eyes as my heart twisted into a thousand cruel, unrelenting knots. When I opened them, I looked to the queen. Raven had told me she feared her the most. I should have listened. Or better yet, I should have fled.

"If Your Majesty is offering mercy, I choose my own life."

There was murmuring among the guards. My mother was deadly silent. She'd chosen her own path. I wouldn't go down because of her.

"As I suspected." Queen Isla faced the guards. "Pirates know nothing of sacrifice. Take Arabella and string her up to a pole for the night. Let us celebrate the victory with the kingdom before she hangs in two days." Her attention slid to me as my blood chilled. "You better leave now. The next time we meet, I won't have an appetite to play games."

I turned. As my back faced her, my mother's bellow hit the ground in a mighty roar that shook me to my bones. I didn't look back as I fled.

It was only when stone gave way to frozen grass that I realized exactly what I'd done. With me on the run, Queen Isla had the excuse she needed to hunt down pirates under the guise of searching for her husband's killer. If she had me killed tonight, she wouldn't get the war she craved.

I slipped my cold hands into my pockets where they struck something. I pulled it out. The wolfsbane pin stared back at me to echo the old woman's words. *Through either your life or your death, much blood will be spilled.*

She'd been right. Unintentionally, I was the catalyst for war.

My people. My home. The seas that I'd come to love. They were all in danger now because of me.

I threw that pin deep into the fields. Then I turned back to the castle.

The snap of a twig stilled me. Then the rustle of leaves as a figure moved across the hill. They stopped when I turned, just to break into a run in the next breath.

I clutched my cloak as my pulse quickened. The queen had changed her mind. Or my mother had broken free and was coming after me. Both terrified me.

"Emme!"

Arn's soft call was the sweetest sound I'd ever heard.

His coat flapped open as he dashed across the field, darting in and out from the jagged shadows of trees until he'd found me, scooped me up, and held me close. He smelled of sweat and pine. His hair fell unevenly to the side in his bun, and his face was frantic. His arms tightened around me. "You're alive," he exhaled.

"Barely," I said, but already I breathed easier.

"You scared me to death. Promise no more random stabbing of gentlemen we meet in squares?"

I managed to smile as he put me down. "I'll do my best. How did you find me?"

He gestured to his foot. "The oathbinding. I thought the

trail had broken earlier, but it led me to you in the end. I can feel it going away now."

I stole a look behind him at the looming castle. The alarm hadn't gone off yet, but the courtyard was ablaze with light. I could picture them setting up the pike in the center and tying my mother to it where she'd stay in humiliation as the kingdom came back from its hunt on the seas for the magical fish.

Arabella's look wasn't one I'd easily forget as she was dragged into the gardens. Neither was Raven's as she held onto her prize and left me alone. "I fear my chance of breaking my oathbinding is poor."

"We can still find a way to get the king."

"I don't think so. He's gone."

"He'll come back." Arn kept me in his arms, rubbing his fingers over mine. His well of hope would never run dry.

"No, you don't understand. The king is dead, and his head is gone. I'm done."

40

EMRIC

The overgrowth crunched underfoot as all attempts of secrecy were gone. I tore through the fields in search of Emme, Arabella, or Arn. With luck, I'd find them all in the same place. With greater luck, they'd have taken care of the king and we could leave these shores. I didn't care for the bounty they'd put on our heads.

"We shouldn't be here," I had told Arabella as I read the wanted poster when we came ashore.

"Only fifty silvers?" She'd laughed. *"I'm worth much more than that. For fifty silvers, the king can have my boot."* And she'd marched on.

But as time passed, I wondered if the king had gotten ahold of more than just her boot.

I aimed for the stone surrounding the castle and hoped a guard had left one of the white gates unlocked. If not, perhaps I could scale the wall unnoticed.

"Emric, wait." Ontario took hold of me. "Look." He pointed. Outside the gates, a figure stumbled through the darkness. "I think that's Emme."

A voice from behind us said, "Someone else is with her." He was right. Another figure moved behind the first with more certainty and stealth.

"I think she hears him," the voice said. "Is that Arn? He's talking to her." There was a snort. "And now he's hugging her. That's Arn."

I twisted to see who spoke, but the details of his face were hidden beneath his cloak in the darkness. "Who is speaking?"

The man went still.

"That's Landon," a girl's voice said.

My jaw tightened. I drew my cutlass. "What in the name of the dark seas is he doing here?"

He stepped back as Ontario drew his own blade to block mine. "Be quiet!" Ontario warned. "You'll alert the entire kingdom."

"Good! They can hang him. Did you hear there's a bounty for pirates? We've got one right here."

"I could turn you in just as fast, mate." Landon put a hand on his pistol. "But while you've been gone, I became part of this crew, so there's nothing you can do. Crew's code and all that."

"There's no such thing," I said. I turned my blade to the side. "Ontario, you have one minute to explain why that man is on my ship before I run him through."

"*My* ship," Ontario countered. He shoved the cutlass aside. "And I made a deal with him, so it would not be honorable to harm him."

"Honorable?" I couldn't believe what I was hearing. "That man has no honor! He slaughtered us with no warning. He poisoned Arn. He gets no forgiveness from us."

"Yes, how did Arn survive that? I've been meaning to ask."

I frowned. The details of that fight were like sea fog in my mind—all blurred at the edges with darkness blotting parts out. I sheathed my blade with deliberate force so the sound of it cut through the air. "I will go nowhere with this man."

"He's part of the crew," Ontario stated firmly.

I marched away through the thick grasses. "Then I am not. I care only for my sister."

"I think she's safe. Arn is with her." Ontario had followed me, staying in the shadows. Landon, to my disgust, stayed with him.

I peered through the dark. A third figure moved behind the other two, and they didn't appear to notice. "I'm going to deal with you later," I told Landon and sprinted for my sister.

The two figures looked up as I got closer. I kept my focus on the third behind them, who recoiled as I drew near.

"Emric," Arn hissed when I'd almost reached them. "Be quiet."

"Emric?" Emme gasped, and I got my first look at my sister.

She would have looked exactly like my mother if Arabella had darker skin and hair. But slowly, other differences came out. The way she held onto Arn like he was supporting her was something Arabella would never do—she'd rather melt on the ground than need someone to brace her. The tears that came to her eyes were different too. Arabella hadn't shown an ounce of that emotion when I'd appeared on the island. Emme broke from Arn and flung trembling arms around me.

She held me and wept.

But even as I held her, any memory refused to be summoned. I buried my head into her shoulder as she cried.

"How?" her voice shook. "How did you survive?"

"It's a long story," I told her.

Emme pulled back and wiped her cheeks on her sleeve.

I recognized it. "Is that my tunic?"

"I needed a way to feel close to you after—" she stopped. "You can have it back if you want."

My heart warmed. "No. That's okay. You can keep it." Another difference. Arabella was never so sentimental. Emme was vastly different from the ruthless girl I'd been promised. I looked over her shoulder "Where is Arabella?" I asked as the rest of the crew formed around us. The figure in the distance melted further back.

"She was captured."

"She abandoned Emme," Arn said. "Luckily, Emme broke free afterward. I say we leave Arabella."

"I second that," Ontario interjected. "Let's be gone from here. Where is the king?"

There was a pause before Emme answered, "Dead."

Ontario shifted. "Do we have what we need?"

Emme shook her head.

In the distance, the figure advanced slowly. Based on the narrow frame, I guessed it was a girl. "If you're looking for trouble, you'll find lots of it here. Be gone," I shouted.

She didn't stop. Instead, she held something up. "I believe you'll be looking for this."

At her voice, Emme gasped. "It can't be."

The girl stepped closer where the darkness couldn't veil her features. Her hair stood out first, shining like the moon. Then the sharp point of her lips and slender tilt of eyes, and the glint off her necklace.

In her hand was something wrapped in cloth. She held it up. "I bring you the head of King Unid in exchange for passage on your ship."

Disbelief rippled through the crew. Emme put her hands over her mouth, and Ontario drew his brows down.

"You brought it to us?" Emme asked.

"I told you." She dropped it at Ontario's feet. "I need passage on your ship to find mine. I've been gone for too long."

"But the children," Emme protested.

The girl had clasped Emme's hands. "You need this to remove the oathbinding. After that, save yourself."

There appeared to be an understanding between the girls. "Thank you," Emme said.

Landon picked up the cloth and opened it. He tilted it then nodded. "It's what she says."

"That's more than we usually charge for passage on our ship," Ontario said. "What's your motive?"

"My ship," the girl said with less patience. "I need to find my ship." She brought her hand to her locket and the dim light showed a glimpse of a scar on her pinky.

Finally the resemblance hit me. "You're the girl I met at the Sea Gala. You're not altering your appearance tonight though."

She grinned as if she'd been waiting for me to piece that together. "Very good, sailor. You're not hiding yours either. Last I saw you, you wore a stiff coat and pointed shoes." She eyed each of us. "Do we have a deal?"

"Yes," Ontario said. "Let's be off."

I had what I'd come for, I realized. Emme had a plan for healing, and she didn't need me. Yet I found myself tied to her, wanting to know more before I went away.

Landon cleared his throat. "This night will find trouble for us if we don't leave soon." That was all the prompting much of the crew needed, as they'd spent most of the time eyeing the castle and the ships on the sea. At Landon's beckoning, those who weren't already leaving turned toward town, where the lights were like diamonds and quiet music from the bagpipes filled the streets.

Emme stayed, and in her hesitation, the newcomer remained behind as well.

"This is perfect, right?" Arn asked Emme. "We accomplished the difficult part."

Her shoulders hung. "I won't survive the trip, and we both know it."

Arn tugged her hand to bring her close to him, where she lowered her gaze and rested her head against his chest. It was a tender posture, but also one of exhaustion. Arn breathed his words into her hair. "Tonight couldn't have gone better. We found Emric. And you are close to being healed."

"It's a month-long trip at least, and that's without complications. With us, there are always complications. Eventually, I have to accept that I'm going to die."

"We can help you," Arn argued.

She tilted her head up to see him and whispered as tears trickled down her cheeks, "We've run out of time."

Arn stepped back. "If you want to stay on the land, just say that. I can take the truth. But Emme, we can at least try to reach the island."

"I'm so weak. I . . . I can't even write anymore. I've known for a while that I won't survive, and I need to stop pretending that I can."

I stared at the girl who was my sister, trying to figure her out.

Mother had told me that Emme was a fierce pirate. I'd accepted that. But now, I found myself captivated by the woman before me who shook but kept her head high, who had tattoos on her skin yet a warmth in her smile that wasn't common on the seas.

For the first time since leaving the cursed island, I felt truly robbed at how wonderful of a thing the island stole from me.

Arn took Emme's hands. "We will heal you, and eventually have a beautiful life on your old sheep farm."

She pressed her lips tight. "Emric and I watched our mother promise our father millions of *eventuallys*. Eventually she'd leave the seas for him. Eventually she'd settle down. Eventually she'd be home for holidays. He never got that." She took a shaky breath. "I can't plan a future on eventually."

He was silent, while Raven and I feigned great interest in our boots. Arn's voice was low. "I'm not ready to leave the seas forever."

"I'm not asking you to," she said. "I have much less time

than that. But I see no good in dragging you all across the seas, just to die before reaching the island. Let me die here."

Every part of me wanted to ask her to fight. I wanted to make promises that I'd help her too if they told me what to do, but if even Arn's insistence wasn't enough to sway her resolve, mine would hold little value.

Emme turned to me. "Will you be certain Raven is granted passage on your ship? Without releasing the head? She needs it."

"Emme—" Arn began.

"Please?" She didn't take her eyes from me until I nodded.

"You're certain?" Raven asked.

"Very. Those children need the resources. I hope Sea King Valian grants you all three."

Raven grinned, then gave a small bow of her head. "Thank you."

"Please Emme," Arn pleaded. "I'm not ready to lose you."

She cupped a hand to his cheek. "Then stay with me for the next few months until I'm gone. We can pretend it's our forever."

His eyes clouded. "It'll be the grandest forever the world has ever known." He kissed her, and I looked away to Raven. Her hand touched her necklace, and her eyes faced the sea. She appeared just as she had when I'd first met her, scouring the view as if looking for someone, with a resolve in her blue eyes that said she would find what she was after. Her dress was dirty, nails coated in grit, and coat unraveling by the seams, but she was at ease.

"It was the king you searched for at the gala, wasn't it?" I asked.

She gave a sly smile. "It was. And now I have him. Or rather, your crew has him."

Arn pulled away from Emme. "Landon has him," Arn corrected, "and if we don't convince him to give it back now, he never will."

"You go ahead." Emme gestured toward the town. "I could use some time with my brother."

He kissed her cheek, then took off.

Emme reached for me and put weight on my arm to hold herself up. But she didn't move for the town. "Care for one last adventure with me?" Her eyes flashed with a light that Arabella's always had when she was up to something.

I raised a brow.

"Mother needs saving."

"Don't let her hear you say that," I said grimly

"I know." She looked back at the castle. The courtyard was lit, but the back half stayed shrouded in shadows, the trees planted on different levels to reach over the gate like claws to drag us into their cage. "For some reason, I can't leave her like this."

"I'll go wherever you lead," I said.

"I will not," Raven said. She handed over a vial. "But here is the last of the sleeping potion. Use it wisely."

Emme slipped it into her pockets. She looked at the other girl. "You never did tell me who you are."

Raven checked down the path, then drew Emme away to whisper in her ear. "Guard that secret," Raven ordered. Then she slipped away to blend with the shadows.

41
EMME

We wove through the frosted fields to the narrow gate, which led to a courtyard outside the cells. "She won't be here yet," Emric whispered as he breathed warmth into his hands.

"Neither will the guards," I said. Still, I clutched the purple bottle in my fingers. The two guards we'd put to sleep were still slumped on the floor. "Come on." I pulled on the gate until it opened just enough to slip through, flinching at the loud creak it made.

Emric kept a hand on his cutlass as he slipped through behind me.

We tiptoed into the courtyard to the two guards, and I placed a hand on their chests to feel for breathing. One twitched under my touch. "Just in case, we should give them more." I opened the cork with a pop and held the potion under their noses until a whisp of smoke drifted out, just like it had when Raven and I had used it to escape the prison earlier. It caught in the breeze before winding through their nostrils. Their breaths grew heavier.

I closed the bottle. It would put one more man to sleep. "With luck we won't need more than that," I said.

The hallway inside was just as dark as ever, with the tunnel feeling narrower and smelling more pungent than before. I trailed a hand along the wall to guide me further in.

"Is there only one exit?" Emric still readied a hand on his cutlass.

"We won't be long."

As we arrived at the cell door, a relentless chill licked its way down my spine. Gooseflesh covered my arms. Beside me, Emric shivered as well, and alarms went off in my head. I looked both ways down the hallway, where the black was as thick as wool and silence as deep as the ocean. As far as I could tell, it remained empty, yet as I reached for the door again, another shiver went down my back.

This was more than a chill. It was every ounce of my body warning me that something powerful was nearby. I'd never touched great power besides the healing nut, and the lure it gave off was miniscule compared to this. This was the stuff that Arabella told us about in her stories.

I drew my final blade from my belt.

Then the noise came. It was low at first, a rumble that grew with each passing moment until it formed into a defined sound. Something sharp scraped against the stone in the rhythm of steps, and it grew closer to us.

Emric pulled out his cutlass.

"There will be no need for that." The voice was cold enough that I might as well have been without a coat in the middle of a blizzard. It was impossible to tell whether it belonged to a woman or man, but either way, I stepped closer with my dagger out.

A small figure bled from the darkness. "You are a child," I breathed.

She reached to only my chest, and I wasn't very tall to begin with. She walked with a cane and a crooked back and hair of brilliant white, despite the flush in her cheeks and smooth copper skin. Her body was small, but those eyes were clouded with the knowledge of a thousand years.

Attached to her feet was a ball and chain that she dragged behind her.

The taste of power tinged the air around us, so strong that my mind buzzed with it. This child, this woman, this creature, the power was attached to her. And we were at her mercy.

"I am not young," she replied with a smile. "And no child could do what I can."

She tapped her cane against the ground once.

Twice.

A third time.

And with the echo of that final strike, reality shattered. The black of the stone walls cracked and fell away while a new illusion took their place—one of warmth made from the orange of a hundred lanterns, the shine of carved, golden settees coated in velvet cushions and the softness of luxury wools before a roaring fireplace.

"What is this place?" Emric asked. His cutlass lowered. It was like a throne room in size with a magnificent seat at the center of it, bedecked in jewelry of pearls and emeralds.

"My home," the child replied.

Power still buzzed in the air, but it didn't hit me with such a force now. It was more like a gentle song, drawing me in all directions at once and whispering small promises of what it could give me.

I'd had enough of promises.

"Let us go," I said. "We haven't time for this."

Her eyes flickered in amusement as if I'd said something unexpected. "But I have the time."

She moved, still dragging the chain behind her, to take a seat at the throne. Her bare feet didn't reach the floor, and the dirt between her toes showed. She was full of contradictions. Old but young. Dressed in rags but seated in such riches.

"What do you want from us?" Emric's tone was polite, but his eyes were wary.

"I believe that one wants to be healed. And I have the power to do so."

Emric and I exchanged glances. He sheathed his blade. "How?" The long waves of his dark hair fell across his face as he inspected the room. She let him look before shifting her gaze to me.

"I am the Caster."

My heart shuttered. I tucked my dagger in the loop at my side. "The one who gives new identity?"

She crossed one leg over the other. "The very one."

"But," I hesitated, "how does that help me?"

"I do more. You need time, and I can give that to you."

"You said you can heal her," Emric said.

She leaned back in the seat and plucked a coin from the armrest to twist between her slender fingers. "Depends on your meaning. I cannot take this disability away from you. But I can make it so you won't die from it. You'll be able to walk without needing your brother's arm. You'll be able to stand for more than a minute. You'll be able to write your own name again."

She seemed to know so much.

"I don't need to be healed." I let my coat fall from my shoulders as the sudden heat of the room circled me. Everything here was bright and golden and rich and so very warm. "I only want to live."

"I can give that."

"At what cost?"

"Simple." She flicked the coin from her fingers. It spun in the air a few times before clattering on a pile of gems near her throne. The Caster tilted forward. "You plan to leave a blade in the cells to save your mother? Don't. Walk away, and you'll be able to walk sturdily."

I exhaled. "No."

Again the expression crossed her face that I'd surprised her. "Arabella the Ruthless does not deserve to live."

"It is not for me to decide that." I searched for a crack in the surrounding gold that would lead me back to the black of my reality.

"Her death will not be on your hands," the Caster said. "If you do nothing, she will die in two days, and you will be innocent of it. All I ask is that you let this fate play out."

But my words were even more determined. "My answer is no. Please let us leave." Each moment risked those guards waking or new guards coming.

But the Caster had another magic trick to reveal. She stood and sighed. "Let me show you what you'd be missing."

She snapped her fingers, and strength I hadn't felt in months returned. My knees didn't wobble, and I didn't fear them giving out at any moment. My body didn't shake. And when I lifted my hand, I could hold it steady in front of my face. A tear slid down my cheeks.

"This is cruel," I whispered. Even my words came easier now, and I had no doubt that I could eat something without choking now. "This is cruel to remind me what I don't have."

"Yet, you can have it," she soothed.

Emric put his hands on my shoulders. "Emme, you deserve to be healed."

I squeezed my eyes shut. "Take it away. I will not let harm come to someone that can be saved."

Then I braced myself to lose my balance again, to be unable to control tremors, and to no longer speak with clarity.

When I opened my eyes, the Caster had retaken her seat on the throne and was stroking her chin. "What would you do with your life if you had it back?"

"It is cruel to make me hope," I told her.

"Humor me anyway, or you'll never be free."

I savored these last few moments of strength that she'd extended. "I'd sail with the girl I met in the cells and help the children she's rescued."

Emric startled. "Raven?"

I nodded.

The Caster lifted her cane and hit the ground again, just once this time, and the illusion around us melted away. The cold of the stone surrounded us again, along with the silence of the halls, and the reminder that we needed to be moving.

But one part of her illusion remained.

I swallowed. "Will you take it now?" I braced myself to lose my stability.

The Caster had already turned and was walking down the corridor with the ball dragging behind her. Its heavy sound echoed off the narrow walls. "No," she said.

I inhaled a deep breath. My chest remained coiled tight, yearning to know that this could be permanent.

She paused long enough to say, "Your kind heart has saved you. You will still be more unstable than others, but this illness will not kill you." And she was gone

For the second time that hour, tears rolled down my cheeks.

Emric put a hand on my shoulder. "Emme, we need to get back. Once we get to the town, we'll celebrate."

We were quick about leaving a dagger for mother and fleeing the castle. By the time we reached the courtyard again, I was more than ready. I buttoned my coat, tightened my boots, and for the first time in ages, I ran steadily.

I ran like I'd never run before—a little wobbly, but obsessed and elated with the feeling of freedom. One foot after the other, pounding into the ground, hair whipping in my face, my cheeks stinging with the wind.

The feeling was so grand that even when my lungs complained and my legs grew weary, I didn't stop. I might never stop. The sun was up by the time we reached the town, and with the new day I embraced that I had a new life.

Now I had something real to promise Arn. If he asked me to marry him again, I wouldn't say no.

42
CARN

Ontario and I waited around the corner of the tavern until Landon left. He'd hardly been gone long enough for a morning meal before coming back out. We watched him maneuver through the streets as the sun rose over the sloped roofs of the town.

I checked that my loaded pistol was in the holster. For the sake of the attention it would draw from any guards, I'd left my cutlass behind. We were all packed to leave as soon as we found what Landon was up to. "Time to see where he's going. I hope it's to the Caster."

"I need to stay with the crew," Ontario said. "But let me know what happens. And keep safe." He patted my shoulder without a trace of the animosity that had been between us. At least having Landon with us had been good for one thing.

Landon ducked under an oil lamp and around a bend with his cloak flapping at his ankles like a relentless wave. I parted ways with Ontario to follow. Landon was dressed like the night with his clothes in shades of dark blue and his shoes black, so he blended with the shadows. But then he crossed the streets that glistened with morning frost and stood out against the brilliant pink sky. I tucked my head to my chest to follow.

The streets of the large town weren't abandoned, but they

weren't filled with jolly merriment like last night. Instead, there was the slow bustle of musicians as they packed up their bagpipes and found somewhere for nourishment before going to wherever they were commissioned next. Townsfolk, who had been too soused or too tired to find their way to their beds, now littered on benches and under the warmth of windows to sleep. A few children were pickpocketing through those sleepers with stealthy feet like Tess's.

I was so busy watching them that I almost missed when Landon skirted off the main path to the rugged cut of land that led to the sea.

There would be less cover here. The buildings gave way to gray rocks and stubborn weeds, and a mist collected over everything. I pressed into the side of an old sea post to watch through its cracked boards as Landon made his way carefully down to the port.

Was he headed for the *Royal Rose*? He couldn't sail that alone.

Endless ships gathered along the berths, most bobbing quietly with an empty deck. But one had its sails raised and gangplank down, where a few sailors loaded barrels.

Landon turned before reaching them and disappeared inside the tax collector's booth.

I checked from every angle to spot him again, but the opening wasn't positioned right.

Ships wouldn't be coming in now. The collector had no reason to be there, so his booth would be empty. Landon had to be meeting someone, and curiosity overtook my better judgment. I slipped from behind the post and trailed after him along the back end until coming to the black lacquered planks of the back of the booth.

The sign creaked in the wind as it swayed, and the ocean played its rhythmic tune of waves against the rocks to the east, as occasional chatter came from the one ship that was awake in the berth. I heard all these sounds clearly, but I had to strain my ear to catch Landon's voice.

"He will never suspect a thing. That man is denser than a brick," Landon was saying.

Satisfaction coursed through me. I'd been worried this was an innocent meeting and I was being paranoid, but that one line confirmed that Landon would always be a slippery eel. I placed my hand on my pistol and crept around to the side where his voice came clearer.

"They are getting ready to sail now, so we can ambush them when they come to the shore. Just like last time. And again, they won't know what hit them."

The satisfaction gave way to fright, then boiling rage. He'd been lucky to board our ship after the stunt he pulled on the Island of Iilak, but to do such a thing twice was unbelievable— to have sailed with this crew, laughed and eaten and plotted with them, and then to turn around and shoot them in the back.

I'd led them to the Island of Iilak. I'd allowed Landon to live when we found him. I'd watched half my crew die.

Not again.

Landon had run out of forgiveness from me. I'd not mourn his death.

I drew my pistol. The rocks dug into the soles of my shoes as I navigated closer and held my pistol to my chest. The waves came faster from the seas as if in warning, either for me or for Landon. Either way, I ducked low and peeked into the booth.

Landon sat in a chair with his boots propped up on a crate and a fleck of straw in hand, plucking at the pieces. "Yes, sir. Everything will go perfectly. The *Royal Rose* will finally be mine." But he didn't look up as he spoke. And no one replied.

My blood ran cold.

"What do you say, Arn? As good of a plan as you've ever heard?"

In a heartbeat, he had his own pistol drawn and pointed at me.

I leveled mine at him while I made my voice as stern as possible. "Where is your companion?"

He gestured to the crate. "Right there."

I glanced around. The rest of the booth was empty. "No one is here."

His smile was more lethal than my voice could ever be. "Of course not. There is someone behind you though."

A blade pressed into my back. I didn't dare turn.

"Hello, Arn."

I'd been surprised a lot in my life, but perhaps never as much as hearing Tess's voice as the blade dug deeper. "What are you doing?"

"Avenging," she replied. The blade pressed deeper. I winced.

"Don't kill him," Landon said. He swung his feet to the ground. "I want to toss him into the seas. Let the thing he loves kill him. It's the only punishment for killing Ellie."

I frowned at the sharp pain in my back. Tess's blade only relented a little. It was almost ironic that while I'd been admiring how quiet those children in the town could move, Tess had been trailing even more quietly.

"I want to hurt him," Tess said in a broken voice. It wasn't cold like Landon's. It was pained. "I want to help avenge my sister's death."

"I don't know of whom you speak," I said. But as the words left my lips, I remembered when we were attacked on the Island of Iilak. A girl had charged after Emme with her eyes blazing violence and her cutlass drawn. I hadn't thought about it as I'd rushed to Emme's defense, and I hadn't thought about her more than once since. But as we'd fled, Landon had held the girl's body and wept.

We had seen him again shortly after, when we stole back the treasure, but he hadn't appeared to be in mourning. And Tess hadn't appeared to be there at all.

"Were you on the Island of Iilak?"

"No," Landon answered. "I found her later when I brought news of her sister's death."

Sister. Realization was sinking in.

"And your plotting began there?"

"It began there." Landon smiled. I was forced to step inside the booth as Tess pressed the blade harder between my shoulders. "You can take it easy, Tess," Landon said. She didn't let up.

Landon rested his elbows on his knees, his pistol still aimed at me. I didn't care to have a gun pointed my direction, but the only way to convince him to lower it was if I lowered mine, and I didn't care for that either.

Finally, Tess eased back. I turned to see her, and shock rippled through me. Her eyes were bloodshot and brimming with tears, and her lip quivered with both grief and anger.

She was only a child, twelve if Emme was right, and I'd wounded her beyond measure.

I reached a hand for her. "Tess, I am sorry. But your sister was going to kill Emme."

She swatted at my hand with her blade. "I don't need pity. Pity isn't good for anything but making you feel better about what you did. I do need the head though."

She looked to the ground, and for the first time I saw the bloodied sack sitting there. I swore silently. I had asked Landon for it last night and he said he gave it to Tess. She'd even shown me. I'd stupidly believed it was safe in her possession.

"That isn't yours. Emme needs it to break her oathbound and live. Or Raven needs it for saving some children."

"Emme plans to die anyway," Tess said. "And Raven isn't part of our crew. But the Sea King Valian can bring my sister back from the grave."

I choked on my breath. Landon examined the barrel of his

gun as if he didn't know perfectly well that it wasn't possible. "No, he can't. No one is that powerful."

Her hand trembled, shaking the blade with it. "Yes, he can," she insisted. "And he will." A tear spilled down her freckled cheek. "Ellie will live again."

I snapped my focus to Landon. "You know he can't. That isn't possible."

His expression was harder to read. Apathy? Denial? If he knew the Sea King Valian couldn't bring Ellie back to life, then he must have some other use for the dead king, and I almost didn't want to guess what that could be. He took a hand from his pistol long enough to pull parchment from his pocket. "Manty did an excellent job forging those invitations." He tossed the paper at my feet, and I bent to pick it up. "But this is his best work yet."

I gave Tess a sideways glance as I opened the letter.

My dearest Emme. I love you, but I'm not ready to leave the seas. I'm sorry. Yours forever, Arn.

It was written in my hand. More than that, it was snippets of my own words spoken to Emme. And the worst part was, if Emme found this, I had no doubt she'd believe every line. Nausea rolled through me. "You'll let her believe I abandoned her?"

"She wouldn't rest easy thinking you died," Landon said. He snatched the paper back. "And this pleases me more."

"Landon, I'm planning on staying here, on land, with her. I'm no threat to you."

"Until she dies and you come for my ship." He stood to full height, where cobwebs grabbed at his hair and shadows made his eyes appear as black as his heart.

"You won't take me from her." I held my gun higher.

Landon didn't flinch. "You aren't going to shoot me. Emme has made you soft."

I hated her name on his tongue. "I'm doing this for her."

His gaze flicked to Tess. "Shoot me and she stabs you."

"I thought you didn't think I would shoot you?"

"It's called insurance." He was close now, his gun near my own, and I could see the skin tighten beneath his eyes. Usually, when I looked at him, I could see hints of the man I used to know, but that person was gone now. Now, all I saw was his relentless string of betrayals and his anger.

I took a shaky breath before deciding I could kill my former best friend. The Fates would forgive me for this.

My finger tightened on the trigger, but before it could press, Tess groaned at my side. I turned just in time for her to collapse. Ontario stood behind her with the blunt hilt of his cutlass raised over her body.

My shoulders relaxed while Landon started forward. "You just hit a child!" His aim swung for Ontario instead.

"She's a malicious little thing," Ontario said plainly, wiping the end of his hilt.

I'd never been more grateful to see him.

My racing heart settled, and I stepped outside the booth while keeping my gun aimed at Landon in case he had another trick to pull. Over my shoulder, I spoke to Ontario. "You're timing is impeccable . . ." My voice died in the wind. Behind Ontario congregated twenty men, all clad in pistols, cutlasses, and thick, long-sleeved tunics bearing the crest of Admiral Bones. They stood in attention, their eyes all fixed on me while I scanned for their leader.

My heart sped again like a hammer in my chest. Bones's son had found me, and I couldn't easily escape now. Where was he, though? I turned my pistol in uncertainty.

Ontario's cold voice came from behind me. "Unfortunately, I'm not here to save you. I'm here to repay a debt."

So the line of betrayals continued, though this one was hardly a surprise. He'd disliked me for months and hadn't cared to hide it.

I pinched my brows together. "The debt to Admiral Bones?" Landon was backing into the booth to press on the walls in search of an alternate exit. This new twist put us on the same side, though as soon as we escaped these men, he'd be gunning for me again. At my feet, Tess breathed deeply, unaware of the number of men coming for us.

"Your debt will be paid through this as well," Ontario confirmed. "I'll accept it as payment. But no, this is Admiral Bones's debt to the king of Az Elo. Men?" He stepped aside, and the guards advanced.

The realization was a bitter one. Ontario was working with Admiral Bones's son. Anger surged through me. This betrayal was more vile than I'd thought.

In unison, Landon and I fired. But we aimed at the men coming for us instead of Ontario, who swung his cutlass upward to knock my pistol from my hand. Landon had two hands, and a better grip on his weapon, but each one of Bones's men had their own guns aimed it at him.

"Still care to fight?" Ontario asked. My mind worked to find meaning while also searching for a way to escape. I couldn't run past the men up the hill, and there was no other exit in this booth. The only other path was down the slope to the docks, and I remembered the one ship that had been preparing to set out. I could escape on it, if only I could reach it.

Ontario's focus wasn't on me at the moment. It was on Landon, waiting to see what the man would do.

"I'd rather fight than die," was Landon's response.

"Thought so." Ontario drew something from his pocket as Landon fired. He threw it at him—a purple shimmering mist enveloped Landon, and his eyes rolled up into their sockets. He fell at my feet. Still breathing, but no longer useful.

"I always hated when he used this on me," Ontario said as he eyed Landon. "But my father's sleeping potions always did work quite well."

"Take the men, leave the girl," Ontario ordered. Before I could run, he brought his cutlass slashing into the side of the hut, inches from my neck, to pin me there. The only other option was up the hill where the men were coming from, and within moments they were upon me, grabbing my arms with rough hands and cold fingertips to drag me out from the booth and toward the sea. The one ship that was being prepped a few minutes ago now appeared ready to sail with crates all brought aboard and a man behind the wheel.

A guard was speaking with someone on the pier next to the ship. The man handed the guard a hefty bag of coins, and the guard tipped his head, pocketed the money, and moved on. Two men lifted Landon onto their shoulders.

Ontario reached into his pocket. "I can use this," he said. He plucked out the forged note. "You know, this was the one part I couldn't figure out." He walked beside us as casual as any morning stroll while I thrashed against the men's hold. "I knew if you disappeared, Emme would do whatever it took to find you. She was determined to find Emric, even when we told her he drowned. Turns out she was right there. But imagine how hard she would have fought to find you? And now?" He glanced smugly at the letter. "That won't be a problem."

"Leave her alone," I ordered, thrashing against my captors. "She wants to stay here to live her final days. Don't hurt her."

"Wouldn't dream of it." He stopped on the pier as the men dragged me toward the gangplank. A flag snapped in the wind. It was Admiral Bones's flag.

I knew why Ontario wanted me off his ship. He wanted to captain and didn't want me there as a threat to that role. It was obvious Landon would one day try to steal the wheel from him too. But one piece was a mystery.

"Who is the son?" I shouted over my shoulder at Ontario before I could be pulled too far away. "And why are you working with him?"

He turned slowly. "Oh, Arn. Can't you figure it out?" His smile would haunt me forever. "I am the heir to the Bones Legacy." As soon as he said that, my mind fortified the moment in my memory, doomed to play it on repeat and wonder how I'd been so foolish.

It was never Ontario's idea to go to Admiral Bones in the first place. He let me drag him there against his wishes. He'd always wanted to be as far away from that man as possible. But Ontario hadn't wasted any time in taking over where his father left off.

The sudden wealth he had. It all made sense now.

"Consider the debt to my father paid," Ontario said maliciously. "And enjoy Az Elo. I hear it's a savage land."

I was shoved to the ground with my arms jerked behind me to draw a rope around my body, which anchored me to the main post. Landon was bound to the other side.

As Ontario walked back down the pier, whistling a tune, the ship set sail.

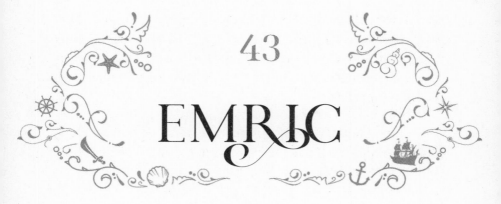

43

EMRIC

As Emme searched the tavern for Arn, I split away to go to the sea. The sun was well up, and a single ship sailed away from the land, while all the others rested in the docks. They'd be a flurry of activity as soon as news of the king's death came, but now was the calm before the chaos.

I stripped off my shoes to dip my feet into the freezing waters, waiting for her to sense me. Wondering what I'd say when she came.

Emme surprised me over and over. The strength inside her, even when her body was weak, made me want to know more. And why she offered herself up to save a woman who didn't care for her—I had to know where this came from.

I couldn't do that under the seas.

My chest was a tangle of nervous knots by the time Coral appeared, her head barely emerged from the water to scan the area.

"I haven't seen a guard in a while," I assured her.

She came up to the rocks. "Did you find your sister?"

I treaded to the shore's edge to sit beside her. "Emme is . . ." I searched for the word, "spectacular."

She smiled, but her expression was sad. She laced her fingers through mine. "But you've still no memory of her?"

"None. I kept thinking it would come back, but I don't think it will." I ran my thumb across her knuckles. "But I can always make more memories."

She smiled again, this time even sadder than the first. She was quiet for a while before lifting her eyes to mine. "I lost you, didn't I?"

"I'm right here," I said lightly, but the knots tangled themselves tighter inside, and Coral was stiff, like she felt them suffocating her too.

"You won't leave your people for me." The way she said it wasn't as a question.

I stared at our hands together. "Remember when we first met? How intoxicating that feeling was?" In just one look she'd enraptured me, and I lived for the moments when I could see her again. That was what got me through the death of my friends, and the hope of her was what got me through those nights trapped on the island with Arabella. She'd been my strength when I needed it, and she'd set my soul on fire in a way that I didn't think possible.

"I'll never forget it," she replied. "It was like finding a missing part of myself."

That made my next words harder. "I don't want to abandon Emme. I need to know more about her."

She took a deep breath and withdrew her hand. "I can give you back your memories."

"How?"

"An exchange." She closed her eyes to say the words. "Me for her."

I ran the option through my mind. "I give up all memory of you and regain my memories of Emme?"

"The island must have satisfaction. It was the only trade I could make." She licked her lips. "If you want it."

Her words were tremulous, almost begging me to choose her, but prepared for me to pick my sister. I clasped her hand in mine. "It only took looking at you to fall in love once. If we meet again, I'm certain I'll fall just as fast."

It was the same conversation we'd had on the island. Back when I swore I'd never lose her.

"So that is your answer then?"

I stole a look behind me, back to the town where Emme was. "I'd lose only a few moments with you," I said slowly to Coral. "I lost twenty years with her and clouded my entire life in a haze that I can't see through. I'm confident this relationship between us can return if you find me again."

She studied my eyes before nodding slowly. "Okay. I'll do it then. By the time your ship leaves the harbor, the island will accept the trade of memories."

My heart was in turmoil. Relief mixed with loss, but this time it was a price I was willing to pay. It wouldn't be something stripped of me without my knowledge, and that made the trade easier. And I believed Coral and I were meant to be together—nothing could truly divide us. I squeezed her hand.

"As soon as the memories trade, please find me. We will start our love story over again."

She pulled me to her. She looked at me for a moment, then kissed me.

I wrapped one hand around her neck and our kiss deepened. A love like this would be easy to reignite.

Then, just as suddenly as she'd kissed me, she let go and swam further out.

I stood up, water spilling from me onto the rocks. "Coral, I've been curious. I lost my memory of Emme, and I suspect Arabella lost what remained of her kindness. But what did the island take from you?"

Her mouth twisted. "I fear I lost you, my pirate boy. And I don't think I'll get you back."

44

EMME

I tore through the rooms in search of Arn. His room was nothing but an unmade bed, and his bags were gone. It was well past morning by the time Emric and I had reached the town, and much of the crew was packed to leave, but no matter how many rooms I searched through, I still hadn't found Arn when Emric returned.

"Did you go for a swim?" I asked him.

He looked down to where he was half soaked with sea water. "It's a long story. Arn?"

"Not here. Maybe he's already on the ship? His things aren't in his room." I hopped from the last step on the stairs to weave through the tables of the tavern. A few of our crewmates were there, finishing their meals, but most had already gone. Arn must have gone with them.

Raven sat with her feet close to the fire and a cup in her hands, watching the flames curl and crack. Each time I'd seen Raven, except the first where she'd pretended to be drunk, she had this air about her. Even locked in the cells or in the face of the king and queen, she had a stillness, like she was made of deep waters. It was there now. She sat as if certain that wherever she was in that exact moment was precisely where she was meant to be, and she was in no rush to get to the next moment. She wore her hood up, hair splayed over her shoulder.

I stopped beside her. "Have you seen Arn?"

She hardly glanced up. "I haven't seen him." She downed her drink and set it aside to stand. "But we should move out."

"He's probably at the ship already," Emric said, catching my arm to slow me down. The newfound energy I had was a ball inside me, crashing against my insides and prohibiting me from standing still. I needed to tell Arn I was healed as badly as I needed to breathe.

"You have other matters," Emric told me. His head inclined in Raven's direction.

She rolled up her sleeves and hoisted a bag over her shoulder. "What is it?"

I gulped. There were two things I needed to do now that I was healed, and one was more decidedly fun than the other—tell Arn I'm healed and ask a favor of Raven. I cleared my throat. "I need the, uh, king back."

Her eyes narrowed. "Why?"

"To be free."

Her gaze rolled over me. "What happened to you?"

I twisted in a circle for her, showing off how easily I moved now. Then I held up my hand so she could see how it didn't shake. There was still a slight tremor if you looked hard enough, and twice while running here I'd lost my balance and tumbled, but it was a life I could live again. And if I wanted to live, I needed to fulfill my oathbinding.

"I'm healed, but I'm still oathbound. If you let me fulfill my oathbinding, I promise we will do whatever we can to help you and your ship."

She let out a low whistle. "I'd counted you out for dead. Our original deal stands then, passage to find my ship, and you can live. I'll find another way to provide for my children." She headed for the door.

"Just like that?" Emric asked her.

"Is food more important than someone's life?" Raven repeated her mantra to him.

He looked at her like it was a trap. "No?"

"Then my choice is simple." Weight lifted from my chest, one that had been choking me for months. I'd be free from my oathbinding soon, and be truly free in this world. Raven went on with a knowing smile. "Plus, I suspect Emme will join my crew, so I'm still gaining something." She looked at me from over Emric's shoulder. "Am I right?"

I met her eye. Something had stirred in me when she spoke of the children she cared for, and now that I had the choice to do whatever I liked in this life, I was able to join her mission. I gave her a small nod. "You are."

She smiled. "Good. Then let's go." She left the tavern, leaving Emric watching her with an odd expression.

"Tell me about Raven's children," Emric looked out the window at the girl as she slipped the corner and headed for the sea.

"She finds lost ones and gives them a family," I told him. "She has a whole crew of children to return to."

He wore a faraway look. "That's quite noble of her. And do you plan to join her?"

"Yes," I said with confidence. "I've only known her for a short time, but I'd like to be a part of something like that." It was the first time in a long time that I felt purpose, and I was eager to chase after that. I looked at him curiously. "How about you? Will you go to be with your mermaid now?"

"I don't know." He swallowed. "A week ago I would have said yes. Now? I'd like to spend a little more time with you before I leave."

I couldn't have hoped things would settle better than they did, but Emric choosing to stay a while longer gave me the last wish I'd dreamed of. Before I could enfold him in a hug,

Ontario appeared at the door to corral the last of the crew to the ship. "Emric, are you coming?" he demanded.

"Me and my sister as well." Emric winked at me. "On the seas together, just like Arabella wanted."

At last, my heart wasn't unsettled when I thought of living on the seas. When I thought they'd taken Emric from me, I'd rebelled against them. I'd hated them with every part of myself. But my brother and my mother were returned to me, and having him back had healed the part of me that was uncertain. This time, when I thought of living on the seas, I felt hopeful.

I couldn't wait to tell Arn.

Emric went to join the crew, while Ontario shifted in the doorway.

Ontario stopped me before I could follow the rest out of town. "I thought you weren't coming. Arn told me you were staying here."

"I'm healed," I almost sang it. I loved how those words tasted on my lips—like redemption. "And I've found I like sailing more than I thought."

Ontario set his jaw. "I wish I'd known."

I paused. "Why?"

He withdrew something from his pocket. "Arn thought for sure you weren't returning to the sea with us. He couldn't stand the thought of being on the *Royal Rose* without you."

A sense of dread settled over me. My voice caught in the back of my throat. "What did he do?"

He passed the parchment to me. "He and Landon sailed away on the *Dancer* an hour ago."

It was as if his words brought my disease back full force. I collapsed to my knees. I had to take a minute as the words sank in deeper.

He and Landon sailed away.

He's gone.

Arn is gone.

My vision blackened. "He left? He said he was going to stay here with me." I was numb in disbelief as I struggled to open the letter.

"I'm sorry, Emme," Ontario's voice was filled with compassion. "But you are welcome to join me on the *Royal Rose*. We are still your family."

Family. The word left a dry taste in my tongue now. Family was supposed to be my mother, who had left me. Family was supposed to be Arn, who also left me. His words were there in my hand, with hardly an explanation as to why he was gone.

I crumpled it between my fingers.

Outside, I searched the paths through the town for a trace of his dark blue cloak or his golden tattoos, sure I'd catch him laughing with someone or plotting the next adventure. I'd find him giving orders to the crew to gather supplies—as if he were still captain—or rubbing the stub of his wrist like he did when he was deep in thought. But the streets held nothing of him.

"He's gone," I repeated in a whisper.

"Emme, we should go," Ontario urged me. "In a few hours, this town will be crawling with guards as news of the king's death reaches the people." He moved toward the docks. "Are you coming?"

I shoved the crumpled note into my pocked and forced myself to stand, though every movement ached with heaviness. I had always thought my father's broken heart sped up his death, and now I saw how such a thing could kill a person. It was a sharp, faceted stone in my chest, threatening to cut up everything. Still, I mumbled, "Yes."

The answer hurt to say. I'd eagerly expected to tell Arn we could have a life together on the seas, but now I'd have that life without him. The irony was bitter.

I followed Ontario in a daze to the docks where the knock of pullies hitting the deck rang through the air. Our sails were raised to snap in the wind before they got tied in place, and the deck was a busy stampede of crew organizing supplies and checking ropes. Raven stood at the prow with her gaze set on the sea where her ship was somewhere without her, almost oblivious to the commotion at her back. She held her spine straight with her hair loose in the wind and her fingers rubbing the sides of her locket.

"What's her story?" Ontario asked before we boarded.

"Just a girl trying to help others," I answered.

I trudged after Ontario, down the planks of the pier, and to the gangplank. I stopped, staring at my feet the moment I stood between the land and the water, wanting to remember it always.

The memory of Arn asking me to join his crew months ago burned fresh in my mind. I'd agreed, but only for a time. Since then, I'd gone from land to water many times, but this time was different.

This was the first time I stepped back on this beautiful ship without the intention of returning to land. Although I was certain I would touch land again, it wasn't my home anymore. The sea was. I was made of the water and the land, and the two pieces had always been fighting for a place in my heart. Now that I knew the seas hadn't stolen my family from me, both could share a part of my soul.

I took the step. A cool mist from the sea collected in droplets around my ankles, and it felt like a welcome.

Welcome to the seas. Welcome home.

On the *Royal Rose*, Ontario took his place at the helm. "Time to set sail, crew!" He appeared in a jolly mood, whistling to himself as he turned us westward.

I crossed to Emric's side. "Think we'll ever be back here?" I gazed over my homeland. It was where we'd grown up, where

I'd fallen in love with the sheep farm, and where we'd buried father. It was where I'd worked at the Banished Gentleman, where I'd met Arn, and where I'd faced the queen. It wouldn't be crazy to think this country had one last adventure for us, but it already felt like the chapter here had closed.

"Maybe, but I doubt I'll return," Emric said. "Besides, you and Arn will be too busy having the grandest adventures on the sea to come back here often."

I swallowed against the sudden lump in my throat. "Of course."

He gripped the rails, twisting his head to watch the shore as the *Royal Rose* left the berth. His breathing came shakily.

I put a hand over his. "Are you okay?"

Then his body froze, and his face went slack.

"Emric? Emric!" I was about to call for help when he looked at me, tears in his eyes.

"I'm okay," he said. "I'm okay." He surprised me with a strong embrace. "Just happy to be back with you." He held me for a while before finally letting go. When he did, he cupped my face in his hands. "I've missed you," he breathed.

I felt better about whatever had momentarily bothered him. "How long until you ask Ontario for the helm back?" I teased.

He laughed and dropped his hands. "I'm uncertain I will. Besides, the chap looks so happy that I don't want to spoil that for him. For now, I'm content on crew with you." He started to move away. "I want to know where we plan to go." As he stepped up to the helm, Ontario had a moment of panic cross his face. But Emric only stood politely at his side. It took a few moments for Ontario to relax, and gradually he began to converse freely with my brother.

I scanned the deck, knowing he wouldn't be here but hoping anyway. Bo and Jenner were up the masts, tending to the yardarms. Tess was in the crow's nest as always, her knees tucked into her. Ontario kept giving her glances, but she had her back to him.

Collins was in the cabin on deck, going through the logs. I had to tear my eyes away. That was always Arn's job.

I wanted to stay on the deck for hours, just to absorb all that the day had brought, but instead I found myself next to Raven.

She passed me a cup of something steaming. "The crew had cider made," she explained. "It's quite good."

I took slow sips. It felt so wrong to be here without Arn, and it took all my focus to think of something else. The *Royal Rose* slowly moved away from shore as crew from below rowed until we caught the wind, and the land drifted further away.

The sea mist was in my hair now, and it was a beautiful feeling. Though, I never thought I'd be here alone.

No. Don't think of him. "Where are we going?" I asked.

"I haven't been told," Raven replied with a look over her shoulder. "Is Arn below?"

If she hadn't said his name, maybe I would have gone without crying. But the tears rested so near to the surface that they spilled out and wouldn't stop. Eventually, I drew a hand across my cheeks and took the note from my pocket for her to read.

Her brows raised as she looked it over. Then she tenderly folded it up. "I'm so sorry." She passed it back. "He'll come back for you soon."

"He's going to think I died." I choked as I put the note in my pocket where my fingers brushed against the wolfsbane pin.

No, that wasn't right. I threw that away. I checked again by pulling whatever it was from my pocket. When I opened my fingers, the stolen ring that Arn had proposed with sat in my palm. I stared at it through blurry eyes. Then I shoved it away to the depths of my pocket to be dealt with another day when I had the courage. "Let's just worry about getting back to your ship to help those children."

Raven didn't ask any more questions. Her hand went to her locket again. "They will be lucky to have you."

"Not as lucky as I am to have them." I dried my eyes. That would be my focus every time I felt sad—those children on that ship and how I could help them. I would teach them to fight. I would teach them to read. I would teach them to be kind in a world that was cruel and self-serving. With luck, I'd find the family I searched for. "It's good to have purpose again."

"They'll be happy to have you. They think I'm too bossy, so you'll balance me well."

I was able to laugh at that. "If you say so." I was curious. "Do they know your real name on your ship?"

"They do." Her eyes twinkled. "It's the quickest way I had to build trust with them. On deck, you may call me by my real name as well."

"You aren't afraid they will tell someone?"

"No," she said. "They are good." She smiled at me. "They are like you."

Her true name was beautiful and suited her much better than Raven. I remembered thinking Raven was wrong for her when we met, because it was like the night while she was like the sun. Calypso fit her much better.

"Thank you." I dropped my head in a small bow. "Your Majesty."

45

ARABELLA

They picked the two largest men they could find to hold my arms—their grimy hands so tight I'd have bruises. Thirty guards bordered us to cross the barren courtyard, with a flank of men at the gate and another behind the crenels. They watched us move, hands at their pistols, looking jumpy enough that the next breeze rattling the trees would make them shoot.

The guard nearest my captor was hardly a grown man, and his skin paled with sweaty beads. He looked like a young sailor after his first night at sea.

I jumped at him the best that I could while being held. He yelped.

I laughed.

The grip tightened on my arms, but I didn't care. They led me to a dark hallway and threw me inside. "Laugh all you want," one guard said grimly. The younger guard looked embarrassed. "You'll be dead tomorrow."

"I wouldn't be laughing after my daughter let me die," the younger guard declared. So he did have a spine. "She must hate you."

They shut the door with an echoing bang.

The stones were cold on my bare feet as I circled the cell. They were wrong about Emme. That child couldn't hate anyone. As for me, I'd never been so proud of her than in that moment. She'd broken free and got away. She wasn't the helpless kitten I'd mistaken her for, and she didn't need her mother to clean up her mess. Had she picked herself, I'd only have to stay to free her. I much preferred saving myself.

I'd already searched through the dirt along the window earlier, so it was pointless to check again. Besides, it was best not to appear too desperate. Instead, I lay on one of the cots with my legs crossed at the ankles as if I hadn't a care in the world. But my mind spun.

Something dug into my back, and I navigated my fingers to find it.

A blade was there, hidden in the cot. One with a crimson hilt.

Well, well. Emme had saved more than herself. She'd saved me too.

My teeth grated together. I shouldn't need a child to look after me. Still, I'd take the chance.

I twisted the blade until it caught the light. It was sharp enough to go through a man's heart. The question now was when.

I stood from the bed. "You will feed me, right?"

After a while of silence, there was an answer. "Yes. We are not inhumane. You'll get one more meal."

"That's all I ask," I said. I tucked the blade away.

46

ARN

When I came to, it was with the mist of the ocean on my cheeks and a dull ache in my head. The ache grew as I opened my eyes to a harsh light. The ground moved beneath with bumps and creaks, and I bolted upward.

"What in the name of the dark seas?"

It was not the mist of the ocean on my skin, but the fog over mountains. I lay in a wagon next to Landon, who was still unconscious. We were being pulled by a horse up the steep mountainside. There was no rider, but the clatter of hooves told of other horses nearby.

Then there was a pang in my back when I sat that twitched with each uneven bump we hit.

I wore only a tunic and cotton pants yet was quite warm. We traveled south then. I searched my mind for mountain ranges I knew of in that direction, but beyond Kaffer Point, I knew little of that land. The warmth was welcome, as was the fresh scent in the air. But it was all ruined by the sense of dread in my stomach.

At my side, Landon stirred. I kicked him. He grunted, but his eyes opened. When he saw me, he groaned and rolled to his other side.

"I'm not your problem now, mate," I said. I kept my head

low enough in the wagon that the old boards hid me from anyone else's sight, not daring to risk alerting them that we were awake. The little that I saw was endless mountain peaks and dense clouds that shrouded everything in a veil of gray, along with air so thin that breathing was difficult.

Landon lifted his head. "You got your weapons?"

I didn't need to search. The familiar weight of my pistol was gone, and I'd left my cutlass behind at the town. Even the trusty dagger I kept in the loop at the back of my pants was gone. I shook my head.

He peeked over the edge. "Where are we?"

"Get your head down." I yanked his coat. "I have no idea. I was going to ask you."

He winced and pulled away. "How long has it been?"

"Days, for us to have traveled so far south that it's warmer. They must be repeatedly drugging us."

Landon frowned and raised his head over the edge again. I kicked him, but not soon enough. "That one's awake," a gruff voice came. A horse trotted up next to us, while another horse came from the other side. Before I had time to react, men dressed in forest green had dismounted and a cloth was pressed to my face.

Landon started to protest. His words were muffled by a hand over his mouth and men held his arms down. Soon, they held me too.

I struggled against the grip and the pungent smell. My strength waned quickly, and time drifted away.

I woke to silence and darkness and cold. I lay on my side atop hard ground that felt like ice, with my legs twisted and my back against a wall, with the barest wind coming from above. It wasn't the gentle sort of wind that soothed the neck on the hot summer nights. It was the harsh kind that found its way straight to the bone. I pulled my arms under me to ease upward. Had we traveled north again?

My eyes were taking their time to adjust, but pieces came to focus. The near-black walls around me were large enough to fit an entire ship, cold like ice but built of stone. I tilted my head back to the ceiling. There was none, only a wide-open arch that looked upon a stormy sky so close that it was almost touching it. I had no chains around my legs, but I wasn't free.

There was another figure against the jagged walls. We were in a mountain. In some kind of cell.

A horrible sound came of stone scraping against stone, and it echoed through the chasm. From across the vast room, I heard the figure groan.

"Landon?"

He muttered something, then said, "You tend to be present at all my worst experiences." I almost didn't hear him. The scratching came again, and we both went silent.

There was the sound of chains and iron and twisting of keys. Then the horrible scraping again, but this time it came with orange light. It burst from a sliver that turned into a wide doorway in the side of the cell, leading deeper into the heart of the mountain. Oil lamps lined a hallway with scorch marks, and banners hung between them at intervals, woven with gold thread through a black canvas in the design of a bear with sharp teeth and slender eyes.

I shivered. Az Elo.

The land where they sacrifice humans. The land where the king is mad and the mountains rich. The land where we were once tasked to deliver a princess to marry their prince, before Landon and I unintentionally brought about that princess's death. They say the prince of Az Elo died of heartbreak four days later, but they also say he had a gash in his chest whenever seaside towns found his body at night.

This land had no queen and nothing of beauty. It was of nothing but metal and rock and gold and cruelty.

One of the bear's eyes seemed to glitter in a wink. *Everything you've heard is true. Come further into the belly of my kingdom, and I'll show you.*

Eight guards came through, all built like mountains themselves. They took Landon and me and dragged us after them. Landon thrashed and got a hard knock to the lip for it, but I stayed still. Partly to hope my submission gained me my life. Partly to study this kingdom as we went through it.

There wasn't much to study. It was rocks and darkness and a growing pit in my stomach that worried I was being led to my death.

The tunnels in the rock brought us to a double doorway of wood—the first thing that wasn't stone. They swung inward to reveal a grand room, much like the cell in how it opened to the sky, but this had glass coating it and a wall open to a balcony before the raging sea. Wind hissed through the large opening to get lost in our hair and between our fingers.

I was wrong. There was beauty in how this castle was forged, but it was the fierce kind. The kind that could throw you from the cliffs. The kind that could demolish you with one storm.

A man stood at the edge of the balcony, his gray hair curling over a crown and a golden cloak billowing behind him. He stood still until we were a few paces behind him. His attire gave his identity away as King Isaac.

I looked halfway at him and halfway at the sea. It was beautiful in shades of gray like the storm preparing to rage above it. All hints of the ship that must have brought us in were gone.

The guards put us five paces behind the king then let go to step back. Landon and I exchanged a glance, and I could tell we both thought the same thing. We couldn't escape. We couldn't run through men of their size, and we couldn't fling ourselves from the balcony and hope to live.

We stood silently until the king saw fit to turn.

I prepared for the image of a tyrant, but when he at last faced us, his gray eyes seemed somewhat downcast, and his shoulders hunched. He'd turned away from the sea with difficulty, and even the way he stood revealed that it took all his strength not to turn back to the sea and stare at the water again.

"You are Arn Mangelo and Landon Brien?"

"We are," Landon answered.

I kept my mouth shut.

King Isaac rested a hand on the balustrade. "Good. You belong to me now."

That shook me, but Landon uttered a laugh. "I belong to no one, sire."

"No? You were sold to me. And I've zero intention of returning you alive if you do not obey my bidding. But that is your decision to make." His words were harsh, but his tone remained calm.

So this was how my debt would be paid—by paying off Admiral Bones's debt to this man. Sold out by Ontario. That betrayal cut deeper into my heart again with a fresh wound. Yet the king's presence was so magnetic that I couldn't think of Ontario right now. Instead, I found myself drawn to this quiet lion of a man who watched the seas as the skies released their rain. It thundered around us, finding its way inside to our feet and our cheeks, but the king didn't move.

"I'd take death over slavery," Landon said defiantly.

"Not too long ago, you sold me as a slave," I couldn't help but remind him.

His tone deepened to a growl. "That was more than 'not too long ago.' And this isn't the same. You earned your freedom."

"You'll earn yours here." The king's earlier sadness cracked with a hint of urgency. My curiosity grew. "You'll be my personal captains for ten years, then you'll have your freedom."

I tightened my jaw to keep it from falling open.

"Ten years?" Landon asked in disbelief.

Pieces of Arabella's story were summoned to remembrance. "Personal captains?" I said. "You mean mercenaries?"

"Among other things. I've less interest in your killing someone, but rather in your finding someone."

Landon crossed his arms over his chest. "Who?"

"First agree to the deal."

I looked at Landon. I didn't know what motivated him, but I knew what I wanted. I wanted to get back to Emme. She had only a few months left to live at most, and if I didn't return to her in time, then I'd never see her again. Refusing King Isaac meant certain death, but as the captain of one of his ships, I'd have chances to escape to Emme.

But agreeing also came with jobs that Emme might not forgive me for.

"You'll captain a ship together, crewed by a hundred men. You'll be fed and strengthened and released in ten years. Otherwise you die tonight."

Now I stared at the sea too. All I needed to know was how soon I could use them to find my way back to Emme.

"You don't give us a good choice," Landon observed.

"As I said, you belong to me. You're lucky you get a choice," the king replied.

"Fine. I concede. Arn?"

I waited. "Tell us who you search for."

"My daughter," King Isaac informed us. "The only heir to my throne. She disappeared years ago, and I need to find her before my strength wanes." He pulled out a parchment and unfolded it. The colors were worn from being held so many times, but the sketch was still good.

He wouldn't let go, but I saw all I needed to see. The

sharpness in those eyes and shade of hair couldn't be mistaken. Even in black ink, her hair appeared to shimmer like the moon. Landon was studying the image, and I could tell when he placed it. His mouth twitched.

"I will find her for you," I told the king. "We saw her recently. She has a scar on her finger, right?"

King Isaac startled. "You know her?"

"Your daughter does not go by the name Calypso anymore. But we can find her." I wouldn't give him the details of where we'd seen her for fear that he'd send others in our place. This was working out better than I could hope. He would be feeding and equipping me to sail straight to Emme. The king needn't know that Raven sailed from Julinbor when we'd left it. I'd take months to search the country, and find plenty of time to spare with Emme.

"I've sent hundreds of men to find her, and all failed me." King Isaac tenderly put the picture away. "I'm sweetening the deal to drive your motivation," he announced.

The rain died down enough to give his next words more emphasis. He pointed down the mountain to a large ship at its base. I caught my breath. It was the most glorious ship I would have sailed on yet.

"You will leave in the morning," the king said. "And whoever brings me back Calypso can marry her and be the next king of Az Elo. Just find my daughter."

Landon was quick to bend into a low bow. "Yes, sire," he said. His face when he straightened was one of triumphant victory. "You'll see your beloved daughter soon."

ABOUT THE AUTHOR

Victoria McCombs is the author of The Storyteller's Series and The Royal Rose Chronicles, with hopefully many more to come. She survives on hazelnut coffee, 20-minute naps, and a healthy fear of her deadlines, all while raising three wildlings with her husband in Omaha, Nebraska.

ACKNOWLEDGMENTS

I would like to thank duologies for existing, so authors can be freed from writing dreaded middle books like this one. There was a lot that went into getting this one done. Rewrites, scrapped outlines, cut scenes, and last-minute twists, along with some of my sanity lost. I owe a huge thank you to Jesus for patience. It helped get me through this story.

Having a family that supports me is invaluable. Thank you, Jonathan, for listening to all of my ideas and always being honest about them. Your steady support and your encouragement for my future is what I lean on through the day. I love our life together, and I can't wait for the rest of it. Also, to my kids, who are starting to reach the age where they understand that mommy writes stories and get excited about them, I hope to make you proud.

I have a huge community on Instagram that shows up to cheer me on, and you fuel my motivation every single day. Thank you so much. It's truly an honor to be a part of this community.

Once again, my cover designer has created a masterpiece, and I'm so grateful! Thank you, Emilie.

Thank you to the entire team at Enclave Publishing and Oasis Audio for all of your work. You truly support your authors, and I'm blessed to be one of them. Thank you to Trissina for always being there to answer questions and guide me through the social medias, thank you to my editors, Lisa, Megan, and Sarah, for the work you put into helping this second book be publish-worthy, and for Steve Laube for holding it all together. And everyone else who works behind the scenes to make this happen, I'm truly thankful for you.